Books by Jennifer Coburn

THE WIFE OF REILLY

REINVENTING MONA

TALES FROM THE CRIB

THE QUEEN GENE

THIS CHRISTMAS
(with Jane Green and Liz Ireland)


Published by Kensington Publishing Corporation

# The Queen Gene

## JENNIFER COBURN

KENSINGTON BOOKS
http://www.kensingtonbooks.com

KENSINGTON BOOKS are published by

Kensington Publishing Corp.
850 Third Avenue
New York, NY 10022

All Kensington titles, imprints and distributed lines are available at special quantity discounts for bulk purchases for sales promotion, premiums, fund raising, educational or institutional use.

Special book excerpts or customized printings can also be created to fit specific needs. For details, write or phone the office of the Kensington Special Sales Manager: Kensington Publishing Corp., 850 Third Avenue, New York, NY 10022. Attn. Special Sales Department. Phone: 1-800-221-2647.

Kensington and the K logo Reg. U.S. Pat. & TM Off.

ISBN-13: 978-0-7582-0984-9
ISBN-10: 0-7582-0984-3

First Kensington Trade Paperback Printing: February 2007
10   9   8   7   6   5   4   3   2   1

Printed in the United States of America

*For my queen gene, Carol Coburn.*
*With gratitude for her terrific sense of humor.*

# Acknowledgments

My gratitude to John Scognamiglio and everyone at Kensington Books for giving me the opportunity to spend my days doing what I love. And to my wonderful agent, Christopher Schelling, for not shimmying out the vent too often.

I am always grateful to my friends who are willing to read my manuscripts and provide feedback. Thanks to Rachel Biermann, Toni Cacciatore, Phil Lauder, Audrey Jacols and Marg Stark. For always helping with parties and my endless technical difficulties, I'm lucky to have friends in Evelyn Waldman, Vince Hall, Rob Mackey, Jim McElroy, Cynthia Thornton, Catherine Hill, Barb Brainard, Milo Shapiro, Greg Tate, Laura Jane Wilcock, Maxime Dumesnil, Jacquie Lowell, Julie and Kellie Quinn, Joan and Steve Isaacson, Belen and Mike Poltorak, Hilary and Tom Stall, and Cheryl and Bob Slavik. And for its wonderful support of my efforts—the Del Cerro community.

My family is a great source of inspiration and joy (and material) and I love them deeply. The late Aunt Rita and Uncle Arnold were my early model for a happy marriage. Aunt Bernice continues to be my model for a happy life.

My mother never stopped listening to my jokes and has *the* best laugh ever. My father, Shelly, whom I miss dearly, taught me how to tell a good story by doing it so well himself. He and his sister, Rita, lived by the motto: make it funny; accuracy be damned. My cousins (add the inflection, guys) will get some of the jokes that are just for the Coslow-Ellenson-Krickett kids. This is meaningful to me far beyond the scope of this book.

Most important, William and Katie, the two loves of my life, don't just make everything possible. They make it wonderful. William, thanks for being my best friend (and for having a normal job). Katie, I hope to be like you when I grow up.

# Chapter 1

I can usually count on a phone call every day from my mother's dog, and today was no different. Paz is my mother's new toy Chihuahua that she totes everywhere she goes. When he sits in Mother's purse, his little paws often hit the redial button on her cell phone which means I'm in for at least ten minutes of unwilling eavesdropping on Anjoli's life until she finally hears me shouting, begging her to hang up the phone. My mother discovered a phone with a personality that matches hers. It doesn't allow me simply to hang up. She has to be the one who decides to disengage. I can hang up on her, but when I pick up the phone a few minutes later to make a call of my own, she's still there. This is the story of my life.

With most women her age you might think I'd hear her attending lectures at elder hostels, playing bridge, or consulting a podiatrist. After a lifetime with Anjoli as a mother, I've come to expect nothing less than the shocking, ridiculous, and thoroughly appalling. Hearing the details of her life firsthand (rather than the somewhat sanitized version she tells me) is a bit much, though. Just last week I heard her mantra consultant telling my mother that if she wasn't willing to chew her food until it was fully liquefied, the chanting couldn't possibly heal her lower back pain. I also heard Anjoli telling one of her customers at the Drama Queen bookshop that he had tweezed his eyebrows too thin. She then proceeded to give him tips on creating a dramatic, but not overdone, arch. And truly disturbing, I heard Anjoli having sex with her Pilates instructor. I hung up immediately, but moments later when I picked up the phone to make another call, Mother had still not disconnected. Literally. Some of my friends complain that their parents are overly involved in their lives and thought I should be grateful my mother has such a full schedule. But Anjoli's myriad interests and activities does not preclude her from her favorite activity—"helping" me with my two-year-old son, and visiting Jack and me at our new home in the Berkshire Mountains.

We closed escrow on an old, four-bedroom home last winter and have been making improvements to the main house and three guest cottages with the intention of opening them to visiting artists next month.

Don't get me wrong. I love my mother dearly. But as Jack has noticed, she's like a vapor. When she enters a room, she occupies every bit of space. Corners we hadn't even discovered are suddenly filled with the presence of my mother. Still, she's my mother, so like most daughters I have feelings about her that range from complete adoration to total frustration. And if I'm being entirely honest, there's a tablespoon of jealousy added into the mix.

Not only is Anjoli the darling of New York's theatre district, with friends—and enemies—around the globe, she's also a drop-dead gorgeous, blond version of Sophia Loren with a ballerina body that has stayed firm well into her sixties.

Anyway, Paz is the newest addition to our family. Anjoli called me a few weeks ago to thank me for hosting Thanksgiving dinner. As she put it, "Having family around the dinner table activated my issues, darling. It reminded me of how very important our connections to others are. You know what a nurturing soul I am so this shouldn't surprise you too much." Without pause, she continued, "I've adopted a puppy and I'm calling him Paz."

This would have been the end of it for most people. They might put a photo in their wallet, mention the new puppy at work, or maybe even buy a few silly dog toys. My mother sent a formal announcement on white textured silk cards which invited guests to *the* puppy blessing of the winter season. After Paz was lightly doused with warm water, my mother's friends raised their champagne glasses to toast the puppy of honor. She served organic hors d'oeuvres shaped like mini dog bones.

"Isn't he the most adorable little pound puppy, darling?" Anjoli said when she brought Paz to visit for Christmas.

Despite my mother's delusions that she was a great nurturer, I was surprised when she first announced the adoption. "I didn't know you liked dogs," I said.

"I don't," she returned quickly. "But Paz isn't like other dogs, darling. He's the sweetest little teacup Chihuahua. He fits in my purse and doesn't even bark. He has a tiny little yelp that you can hardly even hear, and when you do, it isn't the least bit disturbing. Oh darling, I adore this little peanut!"

"You're going to carry a dog around in your purse?" I asked incredulously, wondering if my mother knew this was a long-term commitment, not a new accessory. "Who are you, Paris Hilton?"

"Who?"

I tried again. "Who are you, Zsa Zsa Gabor?"

"Would I ever slap a police officer, darling?"

"That's true, you'd probably have sex with him."

Anjoli laughed. "That's something your father would say."

They divorced early enough in the marriage that they remained quite civil. Whenever my father had come to pick me up on Sundays, it had been very amicable. Without everything else that comes with a marriage, my parents got along astonishingly well.

"So you're calling this dog *Paws*?" I asked when she first told me about the adoption.

"Not *Paws*, darling. Paz, Paz. It means 'peace' in Spanish. Paz is Latino."

"I'm just a little surprised. I never saw you as the type to own a dog."

"It was love at first sight, darling. As soon as I saw him, I knew he was my baby."

The more I thought about my mother saving this Chihuahua puppy from the dog pound, the more I thought it was a sweet idea. So what if she dressed him up in little outfits and paraded him around Manhattan in a Louis Vuitton satchel? The fact of the matter was that my mother was connecting with her nurturing side. And Paz didn't exactly get a raw deal. This Chihuahua would have the best of everything, which is a hell of a lot better than the life he would have known at the dog pound, or even if he'd been adopted by a normal person.

When I first told Jack about Anjoli adopting a dog, he was surprised to say the least. "Does she realize how much work a dog is? Does she understand she needs to take the dog out of her purse every couple hours to take a crap?"

"I'm sure she's aware of a dog's biological functions," I defended. I think it's a commonly shared sentiment that the only person allowed to be critical of parents is their own children. Since I had no siblings, I cornered the market on Anjoli-bashing.

Jack continued, "You think she'll remember to feed a

dog every day? You told me she forgot to feed you most nights."

That's not exactly what I said. During that starry-eyed time when a couple is first getting to know each other—comparing their childhoods, their families, and their hopes for the future—I mentioned that my mother didn't prepare meals the way most did. Her usual dinner preparation was what I came to know as "ten on the table," which meant Anjoli left ten dollars on the dining room table so I could buy myself the meal of my choosing. Back in the seventies and early eighties, this was a windfall for a kid. There were dozens of restaurants from sushi bars to hot dog stands all within a short walk of our brownstone on West Eleventh Street. There was Balducci's Italian market, Joe Jr.'s diner, and Ray's Pizza, among others. There was Chinese, Indian, and Cambodian. Nearly every nation was represented by its cuisine.

As a child, I loved the freedom, nonetheless Jack had a point. I giggled at the image of an undersized Chihuahua in a Burberry's Nova check pattern beret and poncho bopping down Sixth Avenue clutching a ten dollar bill in his teeth. Poor thing couldn't even reach the counter to place his order.

"Jack, I'm sure Anjoli will be wonderful to the dog," I assured him. "Let's give her the benefit of the doubt. The New Year is all about people changing for the better. Neither of us is perfect, but we're getting better every year," I said, winking.

Jack pulled me in toward him with one arm and hugged me. "That's what I love about you, Luce. You always see the best in people."

"I really think she's going to surprise us both," I said. "This dog could be just what she needs to tap into her maternal instincts."

Anjoli had changed over the past year. When she visits

the house, she always generously volunteers to supervise the handymen so I can take Adam to the park for a few hours. She recently announced that she was willing to change urine-only diapers. Anjoli even broke down and bought a cell phone last summer so we could talk more often, despite the fact she believed they cause ear cancer. When she first started using the phone, Anjoli kept sterilized cotton in her ears to protect herself from the radiation, but found that this also made it difficult to hear. Then she discovered that her phone had a speaker, and now keeps it on so she doesn't have to bring the receiver to her ear. Admittedly, this is less than considerate to the people who have to listen to both ends of her phone conversations, but New Yorkers have seen—and heard—everything. What's another designer-clad grandmother carrying on a semipornographic conversation with a lover who's unaware that his voice is being blasted through Astor place?

Adding to the list of Anjoli's changes was that she not only agreed to take Adam to the Central Park Zoo last summer, *she* was the one who suggested it. When I was a child, she said the zoo was dull. "The animals don't even *do* anything, darling," she explained. "I'll get tickets for you and your father to go to the circus this Sunday. The lions will do tricks instead of simply standing around and growling. *That's* entertainment?!" Thirty years later, she realized that children love to see animals, and the entertainment for the adults was witnessing the look of delight and discovery in a child's eyes.

When Anjoli and Adam returned from one of their days at the zoo last summer, my mother was a bit miffed because a goat ate a *Playbill* that was sticking out from her purse. "What in my consciousness attracted *that* interaction?!" she asked Jack and I, who were waiting at my mother's apartment.

"What?" Jack asked, not because he didn't hear her,

but because he wanted to clarify what she meant. And truth be told, I'm sure he understood exactly what she meant, but delighted in having her repeat it. He said that getting to hear all of Anjoli's New Age musings added to the benefits package of this marriage. Meaning, he enjoyed laughing at my mother's frivolity. It was just one of the many things we shared in common.

She repeated, "What in my consciousness attracted that animal?"

"Mother, it's a goat. You had paper hanging out of your purse. Goats eat paper," I said, nudging Jack with my elbow.

"Darlings, several people had paper in their possession!" she explained.

Jack rested back in the couch, hoping this conversation would continue. "How close were you to the gate?"

"Who knows?" Anjoli said, shooing with her hand. "Who pays attention to that sort of thing? I don't know, a foot, three feet? Ten feet? Somewhere around there."

"Anjoli," Jack said, laughing. "If a goat ate from your purse, you must have been pretty close to its enclosure."

I added, "What were you doing when the goat took the *Playbill*, Mother?"

"I don't know. Alfie called and said there was some sort of problem with the credit card machine at the store. I guess I was near the goat cage."

Mocking Perry Mason, Jack added. "Was your bag zipped, Anjoli?"

"Zipped?" she said as if she'd never heard of the concept.

He continued, "Or was it wide open like it is now?" He rushed over to her purse and held it up as if he were presenting Exhibit A to the ladies and gentlemen of the jury. "Look at this bag. There are two take-out menus, a day planner, five sheets of loose paper, and a pack of tissues. You've got a regular goat feedbag here." By this time, Anjoli was laughing her silent inhale of a laugh. Jack continued, "I must argue that it was not, in fact, your consciousness that attracted said goat, but rather the paper, paper, paper tempting, taunting, dare I say *inviting* any normal red-blooded goat to help himself to the contents of your purse!" Anjoli laughed and declared herself guilty of being a flake.

Jack was such fun these days. It's hard to imagine that just three years earlier we almost divorced. My cousin Richard always says that everyone has two marriages, but the lucky ones get to have them both with the same person. Jack's and my marriage was far from seamless, but it was definitely experiencing a renaissance. Appropriately enough he's a painter. And my body is pale and doughy.

As I thought back to the day last summer when Anjoli's *Playbill* was snatched from her purse by the goat at the zoo, I hoped that she'd be more careful now that Paz was her cargo.

Of course, at the core, Anjoli was the same goddess of her own universe. She still dabbled in every New Age healing workshop New York offered. When Jack and I first moved in to our new place, Anjoli offered her "space-clearing" services to us as a housewarming gift. She'd just completed a six-week ghost-busting class and danced around the house burning sage incense and ringing Ting-sha bells in every corner. For Christmas, she gave us a refresher cleansing, using the techniques she recently learned at an advanced space-clearing class in Los Angeles. She chanted and blew high-pitch notes through a thin bamboo flutelike instrument. Jack and I learned long ago just to roll our eyes and thank her. There was no use fighting Anjoli and her magical thinking. She was convinced that all old homes were potential apparition hotels, and insisted she save us from some crotchety dead colonial dude with an ax to grind. Jack and I just shrugged and let her chant away while our neighbors sang "Silent Night" at the doorstep. She is odd for sure, but she's my mother. Plus, what harm could she do?

# Chapter 2

So anyway, I digress just a bit, which I must confess is quite typical. Back to Paz and his phone call to me.

"Just relax and breathe deeply," I heard an unfamiliar Chinese man's voice say in the background. I knew my mother must be at one of her alternative healers and that Paz must have hit the redial button before being removed from her purse. Anjoli had a troubling and persistent ailment called perfect health that she was determined to overcome. It's hard to keep up with all of her recovery programs, but she's done the gamut. She's spun her chakras, had her eyeballs and tongue analyzed, and even flown to New Mexico to have protective white light woven around her aura. She always manages to do a little shopping wherever she is as well.

Once when I was in the fifth grade, I returned home to find my mother and eight bare-breasted women chanting, "I am in the center of light, I am here to express delight." Mother was so filled with spiritual delight that she got laryngitis. A guest got a nasty mosquito bite near her nipple.

One of Anjoli's tenants called to say that their expression of delight was causing his expression of anger.

"Relax and breathe," the Chinese man repeated.

"I'm not sure he understands," I heard my mother's voice through the phone.

"Mother!" I shouted. "Mother, I'm on the phone! Can you hear me? Hang up the phone!" Where was she? And why was the person she was with so zoned out that he couldn't understand the Chinese man's simple instruction to relax and breathe?"

Anjoli continued, "Doctor, will the needles hurt him?"

"He won't feel a thing," the doctor assured.

*Who won't feel a thing? Needles?* This sounded more serious than eyeball analysis. "Mother! It's Lucy. Your dog's calling me again. What's going on?"

"Lucy, is that you, darling?" I heard her voice in the distance.

I shouted, "Pick up the phone."

"Doctor, do you have any sterilized cotton?" she asked. A few moments passed before I heard her voice again. "Lucy, darling," she whispered, undoubtedly clutching the phone to her ear. "It's such a relief to hear from you. I'm in *crisis,*" she said with her usual accent on the word crisis. She meant to sound French, but it actually only sounded plural.

"It sounds like it. What's going on?" I wondered which of her boyfriends she'd put into such a state of shock that they needed an injection to return him to the world of the living.

"It's Paz, darling. He's ill."

"The dog is sick," I said, sadly.

"Yes, darling," she sniffed. "Little Paz is not well, but we're with Dr. Hwang right now."

"Dr. Hwang your acupuncturist?" I asked.

"Yes, I'm a bit worried that the needles will hurt him. I know the needles are thin, but Paz is so tiny," Anjoli sniffed again.

"Back up, Mother. What's wrong with Paz and why is he at your acupuncturist?"

At that point, Dr. Hwang repeated that Mother's toy Chihuahua should relax and breathe deeply. "This will not hurt you, *Pars.*"

"It's *Paz,*" Anjoli corrected him.

"Mother, what's wrong with Paz?"

Anjoli sighed, "Oh darling, Paz has trichillomania."

"He has what?" I asked, hearing the dog squeak as the first needle went into his fur. The poor thing sounded like he was dying, and the last thing he did before going under the needle was call me. I was touched. Then again, so was everyone in my family.

Dr. Hwang was as kind as one could be while puncturing a dog. "Relax, *Pars.* Your chi will flow like a river, and you will feel all better soon. Breathe deeply."

*Again with the "breathe deeply." It's a dog, Dr. Hwang. They have one breathing mode and it's panting. Perhaps this is why puppy yoga never caught on.*

"Oh God, this is awful to watch," Anjoli told me. "He's looking at me as though I've betrayed him, darling."

"Yes, well, I really feel for you, Mother. What is trichillomania?"

"It's a hair-pulling disorder, darling," Anjoli said as though I were a dolt for being unfamiliar with the obsessive-compulsive disorder.

"The dog pulls his hair?" I queried.

"Poor darling is biting the fur from his paws. You should see him, Lucy. You can see his skin. It's just awful to look at."

"And you think acupuncture is going to help?" I asked.

"It has to! I'd do anything to help my little Paz," Anjoli said. "He's my baby. I coated his feet with nail polish remover so it would taste bad when he chewed, but nothing would keep him away. It's like he's possessed."

"You should take him to an exorcist, not an acupuncturist," I joked.

"Hmmm," Anjoli said, considering it. "Kiki's pet therapist—the one who diagnosed Paz—said we should consider antidepressants if it doesn't get better pretty soon, but you know how I feel about western medicine."

With that, Paz yelped again. Dr. Hwang became frustrated that the little dog was not breathing deeply. Do his other patients cooperate? Has he ever treated a dog before?

"Was he like this when you got him?" I asked.

"Please, darling. Do you really think I would have picked a mentally ill pet?"

"Mother!" I scolded. "He has a problem, that's all. I'd think you'd be happy to help this puppy on his journey back to health."

"I suppose you're right, darling," Anjoli began. "This is pushing my buttons, though. I feel so powerless to help my little Paz. It's activating my issues. I don't like feeling useless, Lucy. I have no experience with mental illness."

*I wouldn't go quite that far,* I didn't say aloud.

After a few moments of silence, I asked Anjoli if everything was okay. "I don't hear Paz anymore."

"Oh, Lucy, I think this is going very well," she said with a tone of awe at what she was witnessing.

"What's going on?!" I asked, reminding her that I couldn't see through the telephone.

Gleefully, Anjoli answered. "Paz is totally relaxed right now. He's not moving a bit, which is a relief because he was quivering a few seconds ago. He's standing completely still, staring into the distance. God, I wish I had that kind of focus when I meditated."

"Is he okay?" I asked, wondering if perhaps he'd died.

"He's in another place, darling. Paz is in a completely altered state right now."

Poor dog was probably melancholy about his days on the euthanasia waiting list.

"*Pars,*" said Dr. Hwang, "I'm going to take out the needles now."

Did this man have any concept of what a dog even was? Did he expect Paz to give him a knowing nod then lift a paw to help the doctor gain easier access to the needles?

"*Pars* should be all better now," said Dr. Hwang.

"Dr. Hwang, look!" my mother's voice cried with alarm.

"What?!" I shouted. "What's going on?"

My mother remembered I was on the phone and replied, "Oh, Lucy, he's chewing his paws again. His chi is still blocked," she said with defeat.

"It takes several hours for chi to flow fully again. *Pars* will be better by dinnertime," Dr. Hwang assured.

*Say evening!* I wanted to shout to Dr. Hwang. *My mother doesn't eat. She doesn't understand this dinnertime of which you speak!*

After she left the office, Anjoli confided that she thought Paz's acupuncture was a complete waste of time. "I hate to resort to western medicine, though," Anjoli said. "I'm going to have to do some more research on canine nervous disorders and see what other options I have."

At that point, I heard Jack return home with Adam after having spent the afternoon at a birthday party at a kiddie theme-restaurant. I remember when I was thirteen, I spent every Saturday at a different friend's Bar or Bat Mitzvah. Adam was in the toddler version of this circuit—the weekly birthday parties. After we both attended three of these parties, we both agreed that they were like "Fear Factor" personal challenges for us. First, you have to eat a piece of pita bread with ketchup and melted American cheese served by an overgrown rodent character who's telling you it's pizza. Then you have to force a smile as you watch your child climb through tunnels of rotavirus-infected plastic tubes only to land in a pile of colored plastic balls glazed with toddler snot. For the final challenge—and the grand prize of getting to leave—parents have to watch a two year old attempt to unwrap his presents and "ohhh" and "ahhh" convincingly. All the while parents must suppress the urge to blurt, "Just for the record, if any of you ever give my child a toy that makes animal noises like the one little Cayenne has just opened, I will put a Mafia hit on you." Anyway, after three of these parties, Jack and I agreed to take turns bringing Adam to these festivals of parental torture. Yes, I know I might sound a little like Anjoli with her aversion to zoos. The difference is that Jack and I actually make sure Adam goes to the parties. We hate it, but we take him anyway.

"How was the party?" I asked Jack, giving the "I didn't have to go" smug smile we each sport when it was the other's turn.

"Hell on earth," Jack returned, with the "you're on deck" smile we'd each perfected. He walked across the living room carrying Adam, and leaned over to give me a kiss. "Get a lot of writing done this afternoon?"

"Some," I said. "Not as much as I'd hoped. Paz called again. Apparently he's got some sort of nervous disorder and is pulling his fur out of his paws."

Jack moved toward the kitchen and filled Adam's sippy cup with orange juice. As he was screwing the top on, our little boy grabbed the cup and said, "My do it!"

"It's all yours, little man," Jack said, forfeiting the cup. "Luce, want some OJ?"

"Okay, thanks."

"So tell me about the dog. Come sit," Jack said, patting the kitchen chair beside him.

We had recently finished remodeling the kitchen to maintain the rustic look of the rest of the house while modernizing it. The cabinets were cherry wood with handles that looked like pewter Rorschach splotches. Every appliance bore a stainless steel face. Brightening things up were oatmeal-colored limestone countertops and floors that were similar except for a few brown glass tiles inserted into the pattern. We had knocked down almost an entire wall in the kitchen to make way for a sliding glass door leading out to a deck that Jack built with the help of our neighbor, Tom. The two were so thrilled with the outdoor-indoor effect of our new kitchen that they later installed a large skylight, then moved on to our family room to do another there. Jack painted twelve ceramic tiles representing each month, and hung them around the periphery of our kitchen. He is going through his abstract expressionist phase so our kitchen has a Jackson Pollock meets Swiss Family Robinson feel.

I sat next to my husband and couldn't help notice how well his thick gray sweatshirt expanded across his chest. Smoothing his snow-dampened brown hair with his fingers, he urged me to continue, "So the dog's got a nervous disorder?"

"He pulls out his own hair," I said, shrugging.

"Trichillomania?" Jack asked.

"You've heard of it?" I was amazed.

"One of my old clients had it. Put the hairs on the canvas, if you can believe it." Before Jack started—rather, got back into—painting, he was an art dealer and owned a fabulous little gallery in SoHo. He continued reminiscing about the artist. "Sold well, though. Who'd've thought people wanted hairy art, but he was one of my best-sellers."

"Well, Paz has got this trick, trick—what do you call it?"

"Trichillomania," Jack offered.

"Paz has got this trichillomania thing and is pulling his

paw hairs out. Anjoli took him to her acupuncturist today, and the poor thing went into a taxidermic freeze."

"You were there?" Jack asked.

"No, Paz called me right before he was taken out of Mother's purse, I guess."

Jack sipped his orange juice and went to get Adam the cookie he was pointing at. "Luce, have you ever considered that Paz is calling you for help?"

"Very funny," I said scrunching my mouth to one side. "Seriously, I feel sorry for little Paz. Can you imagine being so wound up that you'd want to pull your hair out?"

Jack pondered that for a moment. "After living with your mother for a couple months? Yes."

"Jack!" I swatted him but couldn't help laughing. "It's a chemical imbalance. Anjoli's not responsible."

"I don't know, Luce. That whole nature versus nurture debate has never been settled. All I know is that a couple months ago your mother adopted a perfectly healthy puppy who is now in need of psychiatric care," Jack said. "It explains a lot, though."

"What do you mean?"

"Well, she raised you, didn't she?"

"You are just a riot," I said, sipping orange juice into my straw then blowing it into his face. When Jack got up, I knew it was time to run. He caught me at the couch and tackled me down onto it and started tickling me, the ultimate torture.

"Stop!" I shrieked, laughing uncontrollably.

From the kitchen, we heard Adam squeal with delight in his high chair. "Mommy, Daddy silly!" he shouted.

"Daddy is bad!" I shouted, still laughing.

"Mommy, crazy!" Jack corrected.

"I come play now!" he demanded. "Mommy come get now!"

I whispered, "I've got to get him, but *this*, my good

man, is not over. You have been very bad today. Tonight, I shall exact my revenge." I winked suggestively.

"Counting the minutes, my dear. Counting the minutes," he said. Then raising his volume, "Who's ready for a snowball fight?!"

# Chapter 3

The next week, Jack reminded me that we only had another twenty days before our first visiting artist and his wife arrived for their six-month stay with us. The other two would follow shortly thereafter. "Let's get away for a few days before everyone starts arriving," he suggested. Eventually, Jack and I would leave the guests on their own, but we agreed that for our first season, we'd stay put and make sure everything ran smoothly. "Let's visit your Aunt Bernice in Florida," he suggested. "I'm freezing my ass off."

"Daddy freezing my ass," Adam said, giggling. I was amazed at how he'd gone from chubby-cheeked infant to little boy in just the past six months. Like his dad, Adam had thick brown hair, a broad face, and mint green eyes.

"Watch your mouth in front of the baby," I scolded. "He repeats everything we say."

"Daddy's freezing *his* ass off, not yours, little man," Jack corrected. "Think about it, Luce. Bern's always asking us to come to visit her. It'll be warm in Hollywood. We can take some time off from house repairs and just hang. You're always saying you miss Bern since she moved to Florida and we moved here. Let's go."

"Maybe," I considered. "We've got so much to do,

though. Oh! By the way, thanks for rewiring my office. I can finally turn on my space heater and computer at the same time."

"Look, I said I'd get to it," Jack defended himself against what he thought was my sarcasm.

"No, I really appreciate your fixing the wiring in my office because—"

Jack interrupted. "I didn't rewire your office. It's on my list, but I haven't done it yet."

"That's impossible, Jack. You told me the computer and heater couldn't run at the same time unless the area was rewired. I had both on yesterday, so it had to have been rewired."

"Not by me," he rebutted. "Maybe Tom stopped by while we were out. I mentioned it to him."

"Honey, Tom and Robin are in Jamaica this week."

"See how smart they are escaping this cold? Come on, baby. Let's make like the neighbors and fly south for the winter. One week. We'll be ready for Maxime and Jacquie. Besides, they're staying here for free. They're not expecting the Four Seasons."

The house wasn't in perfect shape yet, but the guest cottage Maxime and his wife Jacquie would stay in was comfortable. Jack and I had been hard at work for a full year, and yet it felt like we'd only made a dent in our list of repairs. We fixed the heating and plumbing in all of the guest cottages. As I mentioned, we fully remodeled the kitchen and built a deck. We insulated, plastered walls, reroofed, upgraded windows, and refinished 3,000 square feet of hardwood floors. Still, the place needed a lot more work and the landscaping was in dire need of tender loving care. Nonetheless, Jack and I were living our dream. When Maxime and Jacquie arrived in February, the dream would become reality. In early March, Chantrell the cellist would arrive, and by the end of that month, when his cottage was ready, Randy the glass sculptor would come to join us.

The plan was to open our home to the community over Labor Day weekend for an art show where people could look at (and hopefully buy) Jack's paintings, Maxime's ink pen sketches, Chantrell's recordings, and Randy's sculptures.

Jack and I were amazed at how many applications we received after we posted our advertisement on the Internet last summer. Most were dabblers simply looking for free room and board, but more than a hundred were serious artists, all worthy of our support. I loved Maxime's work in which he used a pinpoint to dot his ink onto the page. When you take a step back, his work looked like a black and white photograph, but upon careful examination you could tell that it was a composition of hundreds of thousands of tiny dots. Shades of black and gray were created by altering the density of the ink points. I fell in love with the concept of art that could dramatically change its appearance by repositioning the viewer. It was beyond a mere transformation in look. Maxime's work took on the qualities of an entirely different medium when the viewer moved just a few feet. This seemed to drive home the basic principle that perspective and distance affect perception. Maxime was my choice. I must admit I also liked the fact that his wife was my age and seemed to have an easygoing manner about her. Perhaps it was because Maxime's portraits of her conveyed a certain sense of etherealness. Maybe it was the photograph of the two of them hiking that Maxime submitted with his application. Whatever it was, I felt I would enjoy having Jacquie around the house for the season.

I also liked Chantrell, but she was really Jack's pick. He said he wanted to be sure that all of our guests were not visual artists, but I think it was her long flowing red hair that Jack really liked. I wasn't jealous. I knew that Jack appreciated how hard we'd worked to get our marriage back on track and would never screw that up by straying.

The fact that he noticed beautiful women was not the threat it would have been a few years ago.

Chantrell said she had been part of a research project that investigated the claim that cello music made plant life grow better. It sounded like the flaky sort of assertion my mother would make. In fact, Anjoli once brought a harp player to her apartment while I was visiting to see if he could cure my insomnia. Chantrell, however, had well-documented evidence that suggested plants grew up to thirty percent faster when they heard cello music for three or more hours a day for twenty-one consecutive days. We were really going to need to hire a gardener before she arrived. Chantrell asked if she could plant two vegetable gardens on our property after she had settled in. One would be right outside her studio, giving it exposure to her music; the other would be out of earshot of her cello. Research had never been done on vegetable-bearing plants, only flowering and fruit-bearing trees. We figured, what the heck? Chantrell is exactly the type of person we weren't meeting when we lived in New Jersey. Jack and I figured if we were going to start an arts colony in the mountains, we may as well open the doors to people and ideas we considered a little far-fetched. And who knew, she could be right.

Of course, there were artists who were just a bit too bizarre for our taste. Some guy sent in a photograph of his painting titled "Various Stages of Orgasm." He dipped his fingers in different colored paints as his intensity level rose. It began with periwinkle smatterings with his finger-tips, which then became more curved and fluid. Then, the up-and-cumming artist moved into more dramatic, straight diagonal scratchlines in yellow and green. Finally, it appears he grabbed fistfuls of red paint and threw them onto the canvas as he climaxed. "We gotta try this sometime," Jack teased when we saw the photos. I don't have a problem with art that is sexually provocative. I just couldn't get past the horror when I thought about what our cottage would look like on the mornings after he painted. Jack and I once watched an episode of "Real Sex" on HBO where couples had sex using dozens of different types of food from chocolate and butterscotch ice cream to self-adhering rainbow-colored sugar bullets called Dickin' Dots. Instead of being titillated by the kinky exhibitionists frolicking around their white sheets, I watched in horror, thinking *that's gonna stain*.

Then there was the guy who painted a Freddy Krueger mask on Mona Lisa, and made Rodin's Thinker hunch over to snort a line of cocaine. His letter said it was a pulling together of classic art with modern issues. We thought it was just plain trite.

We almost accepted a woman who melted plastic toys until they were flat as pancakes. She called it "Hot Toys" and said it was a commentary on selling trends to youth, but I just thought the colors looked cool. As a parent, I suppose there was some sick satisfaction I derived from seeing Baby Bop fried like an omelet. Jack said the toys were probably melted in a microwave oven, but we still couldn't run the risk of inviting a potential pyromaniac to our treehouse in the woods.

Jack and I mutually agreed on Randy the glass sculptor from Napa Valley. He found a way to use blown glass in concert with stained glass to create windows that were sculptures. At the sight of just one of his square-foot window inserts, we were sold. The glass pieces were cut into tiny geometric shapes to create a pink sunset over the 3-D mountains. He claimed to have never been east of Michigan, but somehow managed to capture the exact view from Jack's and my bedroom, which is exactly where we placed Randy's piece. We had to cut out a piece of our window and have a wooden frame built around the sculpture to make it work, but it was worth it. No one sees our bedroom without commenting on our unique window.

Jack's voice returned me to the present where he was still lobbying for a getaway to Florida. "Here's the deal," I began. Jack looked at me in eager anticipation. "I'll call Aunt Bernice and ask if she's up for a visit, but you have to strap on Adam's carrier and take a hike with me right now. Five miles. And at the end you must say, 'Thank you for making me appreciate the glorious winter'."

"I have to say 'glorious'?"

"Did I tell you Bern's condo just put in a new Jacuzzi down at the pool?"

"Grab Adam's backpack and let's go, glorious wife."

I realize we've only lived in the Berkshires for a year, but I know I'll always be awestruck by its beauty. A crisp layer of pure white snow carpeted the woods around our property. I loved the sound of how it crunched beneath our feet as we walked. It reminded me of chewing cereal. Bare hickory and ash trees stood stoically, lining our path. Oak tree branches and pine needles were dusted with white powder from the season. Though it was a little over forty degrees, the sky was bright blue without a trace of cloud and the sun was shining as if for only Jack, Adam, and me. On these hikes, it was the unwritten rule that we said as little as possible. During the spring, I had been prattling on about an article I was working on when Jack hushed me. "Listen," he said. We heard the ravens rustling about, rebuilding their nests. We enjoyed the squishing of damp earth beneath our feet and the breeze rustling the maple leaves. At that moment, I learned not to pollute the forest with my chatter. Even Adam abides by this rule and only speaks up to alert us to something truly amazing, like he's seen a deer or made a poop.

I watched my breath escape and tried to make rings like people do with cigarettes. It never works, but I always try anyway. Glancing to my left, I smiled at the sight of Jack in his thick flannel jacket and wool hat carrying bundled Adam in his hiking backpack. As if he were reading my mind, Jack glanced at me and winked. "This is nice," he said. "You look pretty."

I turned to thank him and tripped on a large rock hidden beneath the snow. My ankle rolled inward and I heard a snap. "Are you okay, Luce?" Jack bent to the ground where I had fallen. He untied my boot and examined my ankle, asking if it hurt when he moved it from one side to the other. "Does this hurt? How 'bout this? What about up and down like this?"

"It all hurts, Jack!" I said, trying not to cry for fear of frightening Adam. Jack filled his hat with snow and made an ice pack for my ankle.

"Do you want me to carry you?" he asked. Jack's offer to carry Adam on his back and me in his arms was a generous one, but I said I could make it the quarter-mile back to the house. Jack found a large tree branch for me to use as a cane, and I hobbled back home. I looked like my Aunt Rita, who walked with a limp and a cane until she died suddenly at a Red Lobster in Florida last year.

# Chapter 4

We returned home from our hike to the sound of the phone ringing. It was Anjoli calling to tell us that Paz had not responded to his new hypnotherapist. "I may have to take him to Brazil, darling!" she cried. My mother periodically visits a healing center in the Amazon jungle where the longitudinal and latitudinal position on the map makes it the ideal place for recovery. Recovery from anything. That's the way things work in my mother's world of magical thinking. According to Anjoli, the healing center was very exclusive and only accepted a handful of applicants. To qualify, one had to place his or her hand on a sheet of paper, hold it still for an hour, then send the paper to the center for analysis. They would only tell you whether or not a person has been accepted to the program. They never give their handprint diagnosis because they don't want clients to "put their energy into disease." Mother has gone twice now and says they are gifted healers. Nothing was bothering her, but Anjoli just knows the week in Brazil prevented something terrible that was on the horizon.

"Hold on, Mother," I said. "Jack, can you change Adam's diaper, please? I think it's poopy." He shot me a look as if to say, *Gee, thanks,* I returned with one that let him know I owed him.

"That reminds me," Anjoli continued. "I had Paz's stool analyzed to see if the trichillomania might be related to diet."

"And?" I urged her to continue.

"Well, naturally I'm feeding him exactly what his nutritionist suggested, darling, but there's hair in his stool. Isn't that horrid?"

"He's *swallowing* the fur he pulled from his paws?"

"He's a very disturbed little dog," Anjoli said. "Thank the divine spirit he found me. Perhaps we're together for a reason. You know what the woman said when I had my past life regression done years ago, right?"

"I know, I know, I saved you from a fire during the French Revolution and now we're together so you can repay your karmic debt." Where would I be without my mother's constant salvation?

Anjoli switched gears. "When are you coming to the city? I miss my baby!"

"I'm sorry, Mother. Jack and I just agreed that we're probably going to see Aunt Bernice in Florida next week. If she says it's okay, that is."

"When has Bernice *not* said something was okay, darling?" Anjoli reminded me. "Drive in to New York, spend a few days with me, then take off from Kennedy or La-Guardia. We'll go ice skating, do a little shopping, go to the theatre."

Anjoli's suggestion reminded me that strolling and skating were not in my immediate future. "I sprained my ankle today."

"When I first joined the Joffrey, one of the dancers sprained her ankle and she was out for six months," Anjoli reported. I waited to hear her suggestions for alternative physical therapy, but none were forthcoming. "I was thrilled when Miss Dorothy suggested that I dance in her stead. Well, of course by the time she healed, everyone agreed that I was a far better Giselle than Natasha Frank had ever been. That's how I got my first lead dance role, darling," she sighed.

"What a lovely story, Mother," I returned. "Anyway, yes I *am* putting ice on it and keeping it elevated, and as far as I can tell there are no other writers waiting in the wings to replace me."

"Good thing it wasn't your hands, darling."

"Yes, thank goodness for that."

As Anjoli predicted, Bernice was more than happy to have Jack, Adam, and me visit her in Florida. This was no surprise coming from a woman who hosted hurricane parties at her condo. There simply was no curveball life could throw her that would knock the smile from her face. As Jack predicted, Anjoli would insist on squeezing in a visit with us before we left for Florida. This was no surprise coming from a woman who hosts parties for herself on my birthday. ("Was it *not* I who did all the work that day darling? Am I entitled to *no* recognition in this life?") At least she offered to come to us.

"Hello, my gorgeous darlings!" Anjoli said, bursting through our front door. Anjoli's entrances were a familiar extravaganza, but now upstaging her was Paz. Despite the fact that my mother wore a full-length fur coat dyed candy apple red and wrapped a black wool turban around her head so that all one could see were Anjoli's enormous black sunglasses covering her flawless ivory skin, Paz now stole the show. He wore a red fur vest that matched Anjoli's coat and what looked like a rhinestone-studded cone around his neck. She explained that it was a protective cover to prevent Paz from chewing his paws.

"How many channels come in on that thing?" Jack

asked, leaning in to give my mother a kiss. "Hey, little buddy," he said bending down to pat Paz. "How are the bitches treating you?"

"Hello, Mother," I said, bringing Adam to her. I was always amazed at how I unexpectedly filled with warmth when I saw Anjoli. We kissed on both cheeks, then she reached out for Adam. I long since learned that this gesture did not actually mean that she wanted me to hand her the baby. It was just her way of greeting him. He did not feel slighted in the least, though this time he did seem quite eager to pet her coat, and was equally fascinated by the tiny dog whose head looked like it was an undersized scoop of coffee ice cream lost at the bottom of a rhinestone-studded cone.

"My Honky here!" Adam shouted.

Honky was what Adam called Anjoli. When he was thirteen months and started speaking his first words, Anjoli announced that she did not feel old enough to be a grandmother and would prefer it if Adam called her by her first name. She rejected the titles Grammy, Mum-Mum, Nanna, Mom-Mom, and even Grantastic, and insisted that Adam should simply refer to her as Anjoli. I think my child is as bright as the next, but asking a toddler to pronounce Anjoli was setting the bar too high. Despite her coaching, all he could manage was "Honky."

I adore watching the expressions on African-American people's faces when they hear my baby referring to his ashen-face companion as "Honky."

After Anjoli got settled in her room she insisted on taking us all out for dinner at her favorite restaurant in the area. "I have some very important family news, darlings."

"What is it?" I asked. Jack was too smart to take the bait.

"I'll tell you at dinner while we're all sitting down," she said. Jack rolled his eyes. "Then when we come home, I'll Reiki your ankle, Lucy." I smiled. Mother swears she has healing hands, but I just enjoy her focusing attention on me. I knew my ankle would feel no better from Anjoli's "energy work," but it would be a nice chance for us to catch up.

"So what's the big news?" Jack asked. I wondered what people would think of our little table for five, Adam and Paz in their high chairs, Mother in her turban.

"Adam, don't feed the dog the crayon!" I yelped.

Our waiter looked amused when Anjoli ordered rare filet mignon for Paz and promised him a special treat if he didn't nibble on his paws when his cone was removed.

After we placed our order, Anjoli posed her hands flat on the table and paused for dramatic effect. "Someone in our family is going to have a baby," she said.

"You're pregnant?" Jack joked. Then turning to me, he added, "Didn't you talk to her about birth control?"

Anjoli smirked. "I must say, darling, ever since your recovery from the car accident, you're much funnier than you used to be."

"Yeah, nearly lose your life and suddenly you realize how much humor there is in the world," he smiled.

Anjoli continued, "Yes, well anyway, as I was saying, there's going to be a new addition to the family. Guess who's having a baby?"

"I don't know," I said.

"Guess!" Anjoli implored as Adam knocked the cup of crayons to the floor.

"Just tell us," I demanded.

"One little guess."

Jack, who was picking up Adam's spill, offered, "Paz?"

"Paz is a boy," Anjoli reminded us. "Now you guess, darling."

"I don't know."

"I'll give you a hint. She's the last person in the family you'd expect to be having a baby right now."

I pondered for a moment. "Um, me?"

"Everyone's a goddamned comedian in this family!"

"Who is it, Mother? Who's pregnant?"

Now fully in the game, Anjoli perked up. "Did I say *pregnant* or having a baby?"

"Alfie and George are adopting?" I asked.

"Nope. Are you ready to give up?" Anjoli asked. Jack shot me a side glance, trying to contain his smile.

"Yes, Mother. I give up," I conceded.

"Kimmy!" she announced as if she were opening the envelope to announce the Oscar winner for Best Picture.

Kimmy is my cousin who jilted her fiancé at the altar of St. Patrick's Cathedral then months later decided to marry herself in a ceremony at Anjoli's apartment. She wore a gown that my friend Zoe made from small mirrors used on disco balls and bounced around to Billy Idol's *Dancing With Myself* to kick off the reception. Anyone else would've been laughed out of town. Since Kimmy is a former model who bears a remarkable resemblance to Cameron Diaz, she was applauded for her ingenious expression of self-love and unconditional acceptance. *Glamour* magazine ran a two-page spread on it in its January issue.

In August, Kimmy annulled the marriage. It was not because the relationship fizzled, but rather Anjoli's astrologer said that if Kimmy was already married, the universe would consider her unavailable. Her love channel would be blocked and a relationship with a man would never materialize. I never challenged this idea, but was always tempted to ask why Anjoli's married boyfriends' channels weren't blocked to her.

"Kimmy of Kimmy and Kimmy?" Jack asked.

"You know that's over, darling," Anjoli said.

"Is she seeing someone?" I asked.

"No," Anjoli said, begging us to inquire further.

"Turkey baster?" I asked.

"No," Anjoli said. "We looked into sperm banks, but the ones who offered what we're looking for in a baby had so many silly little rules. I said to her, 'Kimmy, darling, you're a gorgeous young thing. Who needs these self-satisfied, smug shitheads in lab coats? Take the train up to New Haven when you're ovulating, find yourself an adorable little Yalie, screw his brains out and be done with it.'"

I glanced at Adam as he mauled a piece of bread. One day he would learn that all of this wasn't normal. He smiled and waved. "My Honky," he said.

"Honky loves her little babies," Anjoli blew kisses at Adam and Paz. Our black waiter's body jolted as he heard the proclamation.

"Oh, darling," Anjoli said, using her disappointed voice. "I asked for Paz's steak to be cooked rare," she said, gesturing to the dog. "This is medium. I hate to be a pain, but he has," she dropped her voice to a whisper, "a medical condition."

"You're sending back the dog's steak?" I asked.

"He doesn't mind, do you, darling?" she asked the waiter.

"Not at all," he said, smiling, though I could hear him silently finishing the sentence, "Honky."

I gave the waiter the "I'm sorry" face, hoping he wouldn't hate us.

"No problem, ma'am," he said. "We aim to please every customer. Even the dogs."

Before we left for Florida, we asked our friend Tom to check out the heating in the house. We had a bizarre pattern of cold patches in our home, which became even worse when Anjoli visited. Despite the fact that the heat was on full blast, there were spots where a full-on cold breeze blew through the house. I can't even say it blew through the house. It was select locations, like a chair or a patch of carpet that felt about forty degrees cooler than the rest of the room. If anyone could fix this, it was Tom, our local jack-of-all-trades.

# Chapter 5

On the plane ride to Florida, Jack turned to me. "You're not going to chicken out again, are you?"

"No," I assured him as I glanced at Adam, who had drifted off for his afternoon nap. "This is the perfect place for it. No one will know me in Florida. There's no chance anyone will recognize either of us. You're sure no one's going to be pissed off that I'm there?"

"Nah," Jack said. "It'll be fine. They'll be very welcoming, I promise."

"You're sure?"

"I'm positive," he said.

"God, I'm nervous just thinking about it."

"That's because it's the unknown. Five minutes there, you'll be fine. I promise. Have I ever led you astray?"

"Jack," I laughed. "You asked me for a divorce on the same day I told you I was pregnant. I'd have to answer yes to that question."

"I wouldn't have if I'd known. You know that was bad timing, baby," he said, patting my knee. "Plus, it all worked out in the end, didn't it?"

I giggled. "Three years later, look where we are."

"On a plane?" Jack asked, knowing that was not what I was referring to.

I scrunched my face as if to say, very *funny.*

"Going to Bernice's place?" he asked again.

I gave him the same look. "You know very well what I'm talking about."

"Seriously, Luce. If you don't want to do this, it's okay. This was *your* idea, remember?"

"I know," I said.

"Any time you don't want to go through with it, you just say the word, okay?"

"No, no, I want to do it. It's just new, so I'm a little nervous, that's all."

"That's fine, Luce," Jack said. "Don't start chewing on your paws, okay?"

Aunt Bernice lived in a high-rise condo on South Ocean Drive in Hollywood, a strip identical to most in south Florida. It was lined with white dormitories of senior citizens who spent their days playing cards and bridge and swimming in the sparkling blue pool. Of course, there was the elderly version of a road trip which was the five-mile van ride to jai alai, greyhound races, or the "broadwalk." Not the *board*walk; the broadwalk where every Monday evening a different band would cover anything from country western to pop. Along the broadwalk, vendors offered food and drink, seashell necklaces, and sunglasses until everyone turned in at nine.

As our taxi pulled into the curved pebble driveway, we saw Bernice waiting in front of the building, sitting on a wrought-iron bench of mermaids and dolphins. She lifted her right arm to wave and smiled brightly. Aunt Bernice didn't look like she was eighty-four years old, though her skin was tan and loose, her hair white. There was an energy about her that made her seem youthful despite the physical attributes of a senior. Her hips were wide enough to support what looked like the roast turkey Bernice carried around in her brassiere. Her arms were fleshy and soft; her hands a thin layer of brown tissue paper covering thick blue veins. Her vitality made her beautiful, though. Bernice and her sister Rita were constantly dieting together. Then again, they did everything together. In fact, the two widows purchased the condo as a joint purchase, but on the very night the deal was inked, Rita had a fatal heart attack at Red Lobster.

Every time I visited Bernice's apartment, I was struck by how modern and hip it is. The eye was immediately drawn to a glass patio door which offered a view of the intracoastal waterway. Bernice's apartment had funky art including wire sculptures, hand-beaded couch pillows, and a World War Two-era quilt sewn by her grandmother. My grandmother and grandfather were compulsive gamblers and lost quite a few family heirlooms in poker games. My grandmother lost her mother's quilt in a ladies' card game, and Aunt Rita reclaimed it twenty years later at a temple rummage sale in Brooklyn. The temple was about a mile from the home where they grew up, before Rita and Bernice both moved to Long Island.

"I'm so happy yaw here!" Bernice said in her thick New York accent. "Sit, sit, let me get you something to drink. You've had such a lawng trip, you must be exhawsted."

"I can grab some drinks," Jack offered. "You've got a great view here, Bern." I forgot that this was his first visit to her new place. I went into her bathroom and saw an enlarged black and white (really brown and white) photograph of Bernice when she was Adam's age. She was in a light-colored wool peacoat and matching hat, clutching on to a rag bunny. Her cheeks were full and chubby, but the piercing brown eyes and thick brows were recognizably Bernice. It was the 1920s, before the quilt was sewn and lost. Before the Holocaust that my family lived in fear of. Before the two miscarriages that preceded my father's birth. Before her sister Rita was diagnosed with polio at six weeks old. Next to the large photograph was a framed parchment with calligraphy writing. It was titled "A Woman of Valor." On the floor was a pair of satin Chinese slippers with dragons embroidered on the tops.

Adam walked around the living room, pointing out which areas needed to be baby-proofed. As much as Aunt Bernice wanted to believe that we could simply tell him not to touch her porcelain teacups, the reality was that the kid was a typical two year old. "Come here, *mamaleh*," Bernice said to Adam. Amazingly, he complied. He climbed onto her ample lap and let his head sink into her breast. "Yaw mothah used to love when I tickled her arm," she said as she began to run her perfectly manicured nails up and down the length of Adam's arm. She was right. I did love that. It put me in such a dreamlike state, it was easy to fall asleep. Both Bernice and Rita offered arm-tickling services, but truth be told, Bern's was far superior. At about age ten, I figured out that their technique revealed a lot about their personalities. Bernice's was a slow and sensual stroke which caused me to relax. Rita's was more of a frenetic scratching, one that often left white trail marks where her nails had clawed. "Is there anything special you two want to do while yaw here?" I knew not to glance at Jack for fear that we would blush. "There are some wondahful shows down here. Nothing like that all that jazz on Broadway, but some lovely musicals. We can go to the dawg races this weekend if you'd like."

"Let's play it by ear," Jack suggested.

"The condo shows movies in the community room, you know?" Bernice continued. "It's Meg Ryan week. Tonight it's the movie where she's Einstein's dawtah but she really loves Tim Robinson who also turns out to be very smart. Tomorrow is *You Have Email* and Friday they're showing *Sleeping in Seattle*. Right after that it's *Harry and Sally*." I've never heard my aunt get the title or details of a movie correct, even when she was younger. When I was nine years old, it was Bernice who took me to see my first R-rated movie immediately after defying my mother's directive *not* to let me get my ears pierced. She had hers done right after me at Neuman's Jeweler on Merrick Boulevard, then the two of us went to the Sunrise Mall to see *That Barbra Streisand Was Born to Sing*, otherwise known as the remake of *A Star Is Born*. I remember watching the screen agape at the sight of half-naked Barbra Streisand and Kris Kristofferson engaged in heavy foreplay. Bernice seemed unbothered by the whole thing, casually dipping her hand in the popcorn tub. "He is so sexy, don't you think?"

Still stroking a zoned-out Adam, Bernice agreed. "Okay, you do whatever makes you happy. This is yaw vacation. Whatever you want to do, we'll do. You want to sit by the pool and relax, we'll sit by the pool and relax. You want to wark on the beach, you'll take yaw wark on the beach. You want to go down to South Beach and people-watch, you'll go down to South Beach and people-watch. You want to go shopping, we have beautiful shopping. I made up your room so you'll be comfortable, so whatever you want to do, you'll do."

"Okay," I said, smiling. The fact that Bernice and Anjoli were not blood relatives was plainly apparent sometimes.

"You want to get yaw nails polished, there's a beauty parlor downstayahs," Bernice continued. "You want to exercise yaw bodies, we have a state-of-the-arts gymnasium downstayahs. You want to get a suntan, you'll sit by the pool and get yaw suntan."

"Okay," Jack said.

"Whatever you want," Bernice concluded. At least we thought she'd concluded.

"It's yaw time to do whatevah makes you happy." With

that the phone rang. Bernice answered. "Oh hello, Anjoli," she said before pausing. "Yes, they just arrived safe and sound." Another pause. "He most certainly is." She listened. "Yes, *the* most gawgeous baby. I couldn't agree maw." She nodded. "I don't know yet. I think they want to go to the dawg races." A moment later, she continued, "Greyhounds." She stopped to listen again. "Oh no, I'm shuwah they treat them very well." After another moment, "No they didn't tell me about yaw dawg. Well, I'm shuwah they were going to. They just warked in the dooah." This time Bernice paused for a full minute, nodding her head attentively. "Oh my Gawd, that's awful. How harrable that must be. Uch, bleeding? Listen, if you think he's suffering so much, why don't you have him put to rest?" Silence. "Yes, she's right here. I'll get her for you. Good tawking to you. I hope it awl works out for yaw Pez." She made a kissing noise.

On the way to dinner, Jack asked Aunt Bernice if she'd be willing to babysit for Adam while he and I went out for a drink.

"Of cawse!" she said, delighted. "He's no bothah at awl! We'll have so much fun, won't we, *mamaleh*?" She pulled a five dollar bill from her purse, offering to buy Jack's and my first round of drinks.

"Oh, no!" I immediately protested. The guilt was too much. "Please, we'll be fine."

"It'll be my treat," Bernice said. "You'll go to the Diplomat Hotel acraws the street. They have a bawr by the pool with beautiful drinks."

In the few hours we had been in Hollywood, Jack and I already heard an earful about the Diplomat Hotel. "You have to see the Diplomat," a ninety-year-old woman with a wig and gravelly voice told us as she looked up from her bridge game. In fact, everyone in the card room stopped their respective games to recommend the bar at the Diplo-

mat Hotel. As we were leaving for the restaurant down-
stairs, our group passed a sea-foam green room where
four women were parked at a card table. Two of them
were in wheelchairs. It went something like this:

**Bernice:** *Ladies, I don't want to interrupt yaw game,
but I want to introduce you to my niece and
her family. This is Lucy, my brothah's dawtah, her husband Jack and their little boy,
Adam. This is Ina, Ezra, Fanny, and Sylvia.*

**Ina:** *Oy, so beautiful! And look at that baby.
What's his name?*

**Sylvia** *(shouting): It's Adam.*

**Ina:** *Eh?*

**Ezra** *(shouting louder): It's Adam!*

**Sylvia:** *Where are you visiting from?*

**Bernice:** *New Yawk. They just got in today.*

**Lucy:** *Actually, we moved to the Berkshires a year
ago.*

**Bernice:** *Just say New Yawk. What do they know
from the Berkshires?*

**Ezra:** *I know the Berkshires. We spent every summer there. It's lovely.*

**Jack** *(Inhales to speak, but is unable to begin.)*

**Ina:** *Not now. It's not so gorgeous with all that
snow and the like. They can keep their
Berkshires with all that cold.*

**Ezra:** *What's the matter with your ankle?*

**Me:** *I sprained it hiking.*

**Ina:** *Uch, these kids and their hiking. They can
keep their mountain-climbing. It causes
nothing but broken bones.*

**Bernice:** *After dinnah, they're going out for cocktails
while I play with the baby.
(Collective gasp)*

Ina: You're going to the Diplomat, of course!

Sylvia: *Of course, they're going to the Diplomat, where else would they go? It's across the street and they have such a beautiful bar by the pool.*

Ina: *Whenever my grandchildren come to visit, they stay at the Diplomat.*

Ezra: *It's a lovely hotel. They re-did it.*
(Collective head nodding)

Sylvia: *Come back tomorrow and tell us all about it. Oh do I love that Diplomat!*
(Jack and I smile.)

Bernice: *Come on, you two. Stop yapping and let the ladies get back to theyah game.*

As Jack and I headed out the door that evening, my heart raced with fear. Bernice told us not to worry about Adam, but the truth was I was scared that I might faint from nerves. "Just wark across the street."

"Um, we might not go to the Diplomat," I said.

Jack shot me a look as if to ask why I had said a word.

"Not go to the Diplomat?!" Bernice asked incredulously. "Why wouldn't you go to the Diplomat? It's lovely. There's a bar right by the pool."

"I know, it's just—"

Jack saved me from the inevitable stammering that would have followed. "We might want to try something different. Someplace less touristy."

"Less tawristy? What makes you say the Diplomat is tawristy?" Bernice asked.

"I don't know," Jack began. "The fact that it's a hotel."

"It's a beautiful hotel," Bernice said, now pursing her lips with disapproval. "They re-did it."

"We've heard," Jack said. "Listen, we may end up there yet. Who knows?"

"Who knows?" Bernice muttered. "They could go to a bar right next to a pool at the Diplomat, but that's not good enough for these two big shots."

Rita's absence was felt when no one added, "Imbeciles."

# Chapter 6

The next morning, as Jack, Bernice, Adam, and I were waiting for a table at the International House of Pancakes, my aunt asked us if we had a good night out. Jack nodded, still tired from our adventure outside our normal lives. "Where did you wind up? The Diplomat?" Bernice asked Jack.

"Um, no," he returned. He was groggy from getting to bed late, then listening to Bernice's leaky faucet all night.

"Where did you go?" she pressed.

"A local bar," Jack answered.

"What was it cawled, this local bar of yaws?" Bernice asked.

Sheepishly, Jack answered, "I don't remember."

"You don't remembah the name?" Then turning to me, she asked if I remembered the name. I nodded that I did. "Well, what was it cawled?"

"I'll tell you later," I said, glancing at the assortment of Floridian chubsters in the waiting area. I felt positively svelte here. Last night I felt like a Teletubby.

"Why laytah?" Bernice demanded. "Why can't you tell me now?"

"Uh, I gotta go to the bathroom," Jack said, walking away.

"I'll tell you later," I said, shooting glances at Adam.

"Why can't you tell me in front of the baby?" Bernice asked. "Where in God's name did you people go last night?!" I shushed her and promised I'd tell her later. "Tell me now!" she demanded.

I mouthed the words *a strip joint.*

"You went to a steak joint?" Bernice asked loudly.

I placed my finger over my lips and tried to contain my laughter. "A *strip* joint," I whispered.

Her eyes popped open and her mouth dropped. "A strippah club?" she whispered. "Why would you do something like that?"

"I'll tell you later," I assured her. I never saw a person eat pancakes faster.

An hour later, we stood in the shallow end of the condo swimming pool as Jack and Adam splashed in the kids' wading pool. "What made you go to a strippah club?" Aunt Bernice wore a black lycra one piece swimsuit with a skirt that came to her midthigh and a white swim cap with large pink daisies on it.

"I don't know," I said, watching the sun dance, casting a mosaic of light on Bernice's turkey neck. "I've always been curious about what goes on in strip clubs. It's like this secret world women aren't supposed to enter, where none of the rules of the outside world apply. There's something erotic about that."

"Do you think you're part lesbian?" she asked.

I laughed. "Nah. You'd be surprised how many other female customers were there."

"Really?" she asked.

"Really."

"What kind of women would go to a place like that?" Bernice asked.

"I don't know. Women who are curious. Women on

dates. Women who were checking it out as a place to work."

"Oy, women on dates!" she said. "If your Uncle Irv evah took me to a strippah club, there would be no marriage."

"Really?" I asked. "You've never been even a little curious about what goes on there?"

"Nevah!" she said. "I do have one question, though."

"Shoot."

"String panties or totally nude?"

"Totally nude," I answered.

"And what about the pubic hayahs?" she asked. At that point, Sylvia's thick pearlescent toenails approached the poolside. She came by to ask how we enjoyed the Diplomat last night. "They didn't go to the Diplomat," Bernice answered, rushing off her friend.

"They didn't go to the Diplomat?" she said as though I wasn't right there.

Hurried, Bernice nodded. "They went to a local place. We'll see you laytah, Sylvia."

"Oh that reminds me, Bernice," Sylvia said. "Sally Schimpkin can't make it to bridge next Tuesday because she has to take Fred to get his dialysis shunt put in. Can you give me a ride, please?"

"Of cawse, dawling. Now if you'll excuse us, my niece was catching me up on family mattahs."

Sylvia was offended. "Oh, I see. Fine. I'll let you get back to your family matters."

Bernice turned her head back to face me so quickly, I swore I heard a *swoosh* sound. "Anyway, what about the pubic hayahs?" she asked.

"What about them?" I returned.

"Do they shave them awl awf or do they do those pubic hayah stripes?" Bernice asked.

"Some of each," I said.

"That must help keep theyah vaginers cool in the summah," Bernice offered. "It gets very humid in Florida and if you have a lot of hayah, it can get very muggy down theyah." I nodded, not sure of how to respond. "What type of girl would be a strippah?"

"I don't know," I said, shrugging. "Women who like to dance, women who like money, women who don't mind being naked around a lot of guys. Money-loving, dancing exhibitionists, I guess."

Bernice made a face as if I was crazy. "I mean what kind of goil would lowah huhself like that?"

"Oh, don't say that," I said, feeling oddly protective of the dancers we met the night before. "It's only if you buy into the whole idea that nudity and sexuality are somehow bad and dirty that you consider a stripper as *lowering* herself."

"You don't think it's lowering her moral standards?" Bernice asked. I shook my head. "Then it's raising them?"

"Bernice!" I said. "It's neither lowering nor raising them. It is what it is and that's all that it is."

My aunt exhaled in frustration. "What about their breasts?"

I contained my smirk. "What about them?"

"Awl celluloid?"

"Some," I answered, playfully keeping it brief. "Listen, I know you have no curiosity about the whole thing, so I'm going to go join Adam and Jack in the kiddie pool."

"Okay, but answer one more question for me," Bernice asked. "Do they sit on yaw lap?"

"Only if you pay extra," I said. "Okay, I'll be go—"

"I'll bet it's hard to walk in those Ho Chi Minh shoes," she said.

"Ho Chi Minh shoes?" I knit my brows.

"Those glass slippahs that make you look like a Ho Chi Minh."

"Do you mean *Hoochie Mama*?" I asked.

"Hoochie Mama, Ho Chi Minh, what's the difference?"

I shrugged. "Look, walking in anything with heels is hard for me with this ankle," I reminded her.

"What kind of men go to strippah clubs?" she continued.

"Guys with dicks," I quipped. "Straight guys with dicks."

"Were there any fights?" Bernice asked.

"Fights?"

"I can imagine those mowtahcycle hoodlums with earrings and tattoos fighting ovah the girls," Bernice said.

"Aunt Bernice, you make it sound like an X-rated version of the Pirates of the Caribbean ride at Disney. There were *no* fights. Let me explain something to you," I began, now an authority in strip clubs. "Guys go there, and they don't say much. They are completely and solely focused on watching naked women. If they chat with their friends, or start fighting with other guys, it takes attention away from what they're there to do."

"Look at naked goils!" Aunt Bernice finished with the excitement of a child who just answered a tough question correctly.

"Exactly."

"Do you think yaw Uncle Irv evah went to one of these places?" she asked.

"Aunt Bernice, I couldn't know."

"Then guess."

"Okay, if I had to guess I'd say yes."

"Really?"

"Yes," I said. "But I'm sure he hated every minute of it."

"What about my son?" she asked.

*Oy.*

And on and on the list went. Bernice asked me about every male member of our family—including uncles I hadn't seen in more than a decade. She then moved on asking about the men in the condo from the security guards to

Mark Abramowitz who was sunning his global belly by the pool as we spoke.

"Aunt Bernice," I said, after about a half hour of this game. "You sound like you're very curious. Do you want to go and see for yourself?"

She gasped at the proposition. "Me? At a strippah club?! I am not curious about it, I simply want to know. So, do the goils tawk to you, or do you just watch them dancing around?"

Jack came over with Adam and reapplied his sunscreen. "What are you two in conference about over here?"

"Oh, you don't want to know," I said, saving him the embarrassment of having to know that my aunt knew about our night at Scarlett's.

"Sure I do," he said, smiling innocently.

"Trust me, honey, you don't."

We packed our towels and headed inside. A sign on the door read: "Guests must be fully dressed when entering the lobby. That means shoes too!" We slipped on our flip-flops which slid against the marble floor of the foyer and rounded toward the elevators. Aunt Bernice turned to her left and gasped in horror. "*Gavalt,* it's happening again."

"What's happening, Bern?" Jack asked. "Do you feel okay?"

"It seemed like such a good idear at the time, but now I regret what I did," she said.

"What did you do?" I asked.

Bernice continued, "If I'd known it would come back to hawnt me like this—"

"What happened?" Jack asked.

"Wha happen?" added a concerned Adam.

"Look at them," she said, pointing to young men leaving the condo maintenance room.

"Those guys?" I asked. "What did they do?"

"They're the building maintenance men. Do you notice anything familyah about theyah clothing?" Bernice asked.

"Um," Jack began. "They're not wearing uniforms?"

Bernice sighed. "When I moved here last yeyah, I brought awl of Irv's clothing and hung it in the closet even though he'd been dead for yeyahs." This made sense coming from Bernice. She also told guests at her sister's memorial service that she was going to pretend Rita was still alive so she could carry on daily conversations with her. "Then one day I said, 'Bernice, enough is enough. Irv is gawn and he's not coming back. He does *not* need his slacks any maw.' Besides, I needed the closet space. So, I rang Javier downstayahs and told him to bring awl the maintenance men up to the apawtment and take whatevah they wanted. Well, Irv was a very dappah dressah so an awah laytah, everything was gawn. His clothes, his shoes, his ties—awl gawn in an awah. I thought I was doing a *mitzvah*. They work so hard, why shouldn't they enjoy some beautiful new clothes? Well, new to them anyway. But now every night at foive when they get awf duty, an army of young men dressed in Irv's clothes come out of the maintenance room. It's really very spooky to tell you the truth. I saw a guy last weekend at the bowling alley in Irv's favorite short-sleeve."

"You still bowl?" Jack asked, amazed.

"Not like I used to," she shrugged.

"Do you want to ask the guys to give the clothes back?" I suggested, already knowing it was an absurd idea.

"I can't do that," she said. "Let's go upstayahs and forget about it. Maybe I'll have a cocktail."

"Aunt Bernice! You never drink," I reminded her.

"One won't kill me, will it?" she dismissed.

By seven-thirty, Aunt Bernice was completely drunk. She had one large glass of red wine and was laughing hysterically at everything Jack, Adam, or I said. She had another glass of wine with her dessert, then asked if she could speak with me in private.

"Sure," I said. "What's up?"

We stood in the bathroom with the photo of her as a two year old. She leaned in to whisper in my ear. "I want to go," she said. I panicked. Last year Bernice announced that she wanted to jump off her balcony on her ninetieth birthday. She said she didn't want to be like Rita and have death catch her off guard. Bernice asked me to fly down to Florida to help her climb over the rail and plunge into the intracoastal when the time came. I thought she'd given up her suicidal tendencies. She seemed so happy until she saw the maintenance men. Come to think of it, though, she was quite chipper when discussing killing herself, so it was tough to tell when Bernice was actually troubled.

"Aunt Bernice, is there someone you could talk to about this?"

"I'm tawking to you about it," she answered.

"I mean, like a professional."

"So you go to a strippah club and yaw some sort of liberated woman, but I want to go and I need a psychiatrist? I think yaw attitude is very ageist!"

"You want to go to Scarlett's?" I asked in amazement.

"Just to see," Bernice said.

As I helped my eighty-four-year-old aunt out of her midnight blue Lincoln Continental and ushered her into the club, the bouncer gave us a look as if to ask if we were aware of where we were. Bernice turned every head as she sat down. A perky platinum blonde approached our table. "Hey girls, howya doin' tonight?" she asked. Bern ordered two glasses of red wine for us and sat back in her seat to watch the dancer on stage. *Celluloid,* she mouthed. "They-ah too full," she whispered. I remembered seeing her get out of the shower that morning and thinking that she must roll up her breasts to get them into her brassiere. They were flat and hung down to her belly. It reminded me of the banners the king's horsemen carried to announce the royal arrival. They'd blow a horn, then drop a banner with the royal crest. Those were Auntie's boobs.

After a half hour, she owned the place. It was still early, plus the dancers were enjoying the novelty of having an elderly female patron. Four dancers were huddled around her, telling her they wished they had a grandmother as cool as her. "My own mother won't even speak to me," said Candy.

"Very smawl-minded," Bernice dismissed, sipping her wine through a straw. "It's only people who believe sexuality and nudity aw bad who would have a problem with what you goils aw doing. I think it's beautiful. Believe me, if I had a gorgeous body like yaws, I'd be dancing around awl ovah the place too."

"You are so sweet!" squealed Daphne.

"I love her!" said Larice.

Finally, Aunt Bernice got up the nerve to ask the question that had been on her mind all night. "Do you mind if I ask something a little personal, goils?"

"Oh my God. She is so cute!" shouted Candy.

"Whatever you want, Auntie Bernice," said Larice.

"I notice that some of you girls shave awf yaw pubic hayahs," she began. They nodded. "I suppose it's so the men can see yaw vaginers bettah?" They nodded again, wondering where this was going. "Do you find that it helps keep things coolah? It can get so muggy down theyah."

# Chapter 7

I woke up the next morning to the sound of my aunt beckoning me into the bathroom. "Lucy!" she whispered. "Lucy, get in heyah." I figured she had a hangover and was crouched over the toilet. Perhaps she was rifling through her medicine cabinet to see what would help relieve her splitting headache. When I arrived in the bathroom, I was stunned at the sight before me. Fresh from the shower, Bernice lifted her stomach so I had a plain view of something no one should ever have to see—an eighty-four-year-old bald snatch.

"It's not cute like the goils had last night, is it?" she asked. I'm sure Miss Manners has never addressed the appropriate answer to this question. "Maw like a big knish." She shrugged. "But it's going to be a lot coolah, I know it."

Awkwardly avoiding the topic, I asked if she planned to get her shower faucet fixed. "Doesn't the dripping drive you nuts?"

"I don't even notice it anymaw," Bernice replied. "So, aw you going to shave yaws too?"

I shifted uncomfortably. "You're probably wasting a lot of water."

\*   \*   \*

The next few days were far less exciting. Our days were spent building sand castles along the Atlantic shoreline and watching Adam muster up the gumption to put his face in the swimming pool water. Our only reminders of our first nights at Scarlett's were when Aunt Bernice would point out men and ask, "Do you think *he's* evah been?" I answered affirmatively to all of the condo staff and residents, waiters, gas attendants, and a shoe salesman. "What about *him*?" she asked at Friday night Shabbat services.

"The *rabbi*?" I whispered.

Then there was the Daily Snatch Report. Three days after she took the razor to the knish, she beckoned me into the bathroom. Lifting up her belly again, she showed me her stubble. "It's growing back!"

"Auntie, it's hair. It'll do that," I said.

"It's like velcro!"

"Wanna toss a tennis ball at it and see if it sticks?" I suggested.

"Yaw a regulah comedienne," she said.

"Or you can squat down and pick up socks from the floor," I said.

"Lucy, what should I do?!" she asked, genuinely panicked.

"Shave it again or let it grow out."

"Let it grow out?! Do you have any idear how much coolah my vaginer is without awl that pubic hayah nonsense?"

"You make it sound better than central air-conditioning," I said, nearly tempted to grab her Lady Bic and mow my own lawn right there and then.

The phone rang. It was my mother calling to tell us that she was scheduling a rebirthing for Paz the following day. "Darling, I think I might know what's wrong with Paz," she began. "It's very likely that he experienced a trauma at birth, but the good news is that Kimmy knows someone who does dog rebirthing."

Anjoli is a strong proponent of rebirthing. We once had a rebirther stay at our house for months. Finding my way to my bedroom was like walking through a minefield of human bodies on the floor. I once accidentally stepped on a guy's pinky finger and the whole group was disrupted by his wail.

"Sounds like you've got a plan," I said to my mother.

"Not only are we going to rebirth Paz, my numerologist says he needs a new name. Once he's rebirthed and renamed, he'll release all of the toxic anxiety causing him to chew off his fur. Isn't that wonderful, darling?"

"Splendid!" I said.

"We're having a good time, by the way," I told her. "There's a woman in the building whose grandson is about Adam's age and the two of them have been inseparable at the pool. They even look alike so everyone keeps mistaking them for brothers."

"Oh, that reminds me. For the rebirthing, I'm adopting four puppies to simulate the litter of pups little Paz was born to."

"You're adopting *four* more puppies?" I asked, incredulous.

"Not permanently, darling," she said. "Just for the rebirthing."

"You're renting puppies?"

"Not renting them per se," Anjoli explained. "I'll adopt them in the morning and return them later."

"Return them?!" I was shocked. "To whom will you return them?"

"To the pound, of course, darling."

"Mother, that's horrible! You can't lead these dogs to believe they've been adopted then return them to the ASPCA. Don't you have any compassion for these animals?"

"They were there to begin with!" Anjoli justified. "It's not as if I'm taking them from good homes and bringing them to the pound. That's where they live. I'm taking them for an outing. Why can't you look at it as a positive thing, like a field trip?"

"I'd hope you would have a bit more sympathy for these dogs. After all, Paz was once a pound puppy. Where's your heart, Mother?"

"Paz was never a pound puppy," Anjoli exclaimed. *That* is the charge she defended.

"Mother, when you adopted Paz, you said he was a pound puppy," I reminded her.

"I meant he weighed a pound, darling. I got Paz from a breeder. Do you honestly think I could ever find a little gem like Paz at the pound?"

I refrained from chewing the flesh from my wrists. "So you're just going to bring these puppies back to the ASPCA at the end of the day?"

"Uh-huh," she affirmed.

"And what do you intend to say to them when you walk in with four puppies that you adopted just that morning?"

"I'll say 'here,'" Anjoli said.

"*Here?!* You're going to say '*here*'?"

"I don't need a receipt, darling," Anjoli informed me.

"You're one of a kind, Mother."

"Thank you." Anjoli moved on. "I wonder what Paz's new name will be. Now, Lucy, it will be very important for you to call Paz by his new name after the rebirthing. Any reminder of his old life could trigger a relapse."

"Mother, I go through that every time we talk," I said. "Maybe I should get a new name. From now on, please call me Jennifer."

"Blah!" she said.

"Mother I need to go," I said. "Aunt Bernice is taking us to the broadwalk tonight, and it's getting dark."

Jack, Bernice, Adam, and I made it to the ocean in time to watch brushstrokes of periwinkle settle into night. The broadwalk offered a Latin Jazz band reminiscent of Tito Puente. How my aunt had the energy to dance every number while carrying Adam in her arms was beyond me. "Care to dance, miss?" Jack asked me.

"Uh, I don't know," I said shyly, pretending we just met. "I'm not sure it would be a good idea."

"It's a very bad one, I assure you," Jack said, winking. "Dance with me until we're old enough to live down here."

"Then what?" I asked, batting my eyes coquettishly.

Jack grabbed my hand and yanked me on to the dance floor. "Have I mentioned how beautiful you look on this trip?"

*Mentioned how beautiful I look on this trip? Or on this trip has he mentioned how beautiful I am—always?*

Upon our return to Bernice's apartment, there were two messages. Each was from Paz. I'm sure because I could hear my mother chattering away in the background.

Early the next morning, Paz hit redial yet again. He must have known of his pending fate. I picked up the phone.

"Bernice's house," I answered. Pause. "Hello?" Silence. "Hello?"

*Yap yap yap.*

"Paz, is that you?"

I heard my mother and Alfie in the background. They were talking about the price of real estate in Greenwich Village while also discussing "what a shame" something was.

"Mother!" I shouted. "Hang up the phone!" No response. "It's Lucy. Your dog is calling me again. Please hang up!!!"

"Darling, it's not like she was a young woman," Anjoli said in the distance.

"Hello! Hang up the phone!" I shouted.

I heard Alfie's voice return, "Well, call me the bleeding-heart queen, but I hate to see anyone kick the bucket."

*Oh my God, who died?!*

"Hello! Pick up the phone, please. Who died?!" I shouted louder than before.

Aunt Bernice rushed into the room. "Lucy, stop tawking like that. You'll frighten the whole building. It's bad luck to tawk about dying in the condo."

*It is?*

I heard Anjoli again. "She bought the place before I did, so I know she's not carrying a mortgage. Four apartments. If I could buy it below market, it would be an incredible investment, darling. And think about how easy the property management would be with me right across the street! Maybe I could convert it into co-ops!"

Alfie interrupted my mother's real estate fantasy. "And why, pray tell, do you think her kids would sell you the place below market?" Pause. "Oh Jesus, they're taking the body."

"Why would they put her into an ambulance like that, darling?" Anjoli asked.

"Like what?" Alfie inquired.

"Like *dead*, darling."

"I'm going to miss Mrs. MacIntosh," Alfie said. "She was like an institution on your block."

"Me too," was Anjoli's empty return.

So, Mrs. MacIntosh from across the street had died. When Anjoli bought her place, Mrs. MacIntosh was the first one to come by and give us an old-fashioned welcome to the neighborhood. She was the only one on the block who consistently provided chocolate for trick-or-treaters. She was the one I'd go to for the spare key when Anjoli accidentally locked me out.

My mother was appraising the property before her

dead body had been removed from her home. "Four apartments," my mother said dreamily.

"*That,* my darling Alfie, is why I think I'll get the place below market," Anjoli replied.

*What was why? What was why?! I hated only being able to hear. Who had just entered stage left?*

"Lord have mercy, look at those bangs!" Alfie said.

*Whose bangs? They couldn't mean Mrs. MacIntosh, could they? Were they really saying a dead woman was having a bad hair day?*

Alfie continued, "Oh God, I hate it when they cry like that. Honey, get a grip. Throwing yourself on the body is not going to bring mumsy back to life."

*They're making fun of a woman who just lost her mother?*

"Those bangs really are atrocious," Anjoli added.

*I cannot believe what I'm hearing!*

"Tell me about it, she looks like Xena the Warrior Princess got married and moved to the suburbs," Alfie added.

"Xena is a lesbian," Anjoli corrected.

I stood in Aunt Bernice's guest bedroom, unable to speak. Paz was silent too, presumably as appalled as I was.

"Oh, sorry, love," Alfie snapped. "How ludicrous of me to suggest that Xena might get married and move to the suburbs. Not like the other oh-so-realistic elements of that show. Bangs on a warrior, puh-lease! She'd have to get the damned things trimmed every six weeks. Have you ever seen a salon on the show?"

"Hello!" I shouted. They continued.

"So why do you think Xanax the Suburban Warrior is going to sell you the place below market?" Alfie asked.

"Anyone with hair like that won't have a clue what the place is worth, darling," my mother said with satisfaction. "She's the type of dullard who thinks experimental theatre is Cathy Rigby crossing gender lines to play Peter Pan. Do you think it would be in poor taste to go over there now?"

"To make an offer?" Alfie asked.

"Uh-huh," Anjoli returned.

"Very. Why don't you go over and extend your sympathy or something?" Alfie suggested.

"Fabulous!" Anjoli exclaimed. "Lay the groundwork. Alfie, run to Jefferson Market and pick up a pie for me, won't you, darling?"

"I'm already there," he said. Then he gasped. "Oh Jesus! Look at what's under those bangs! Curse the breeze that revealed *that* to my fragile eyes!" *What the?* Alfie's next comment filled me in. "Has she *not* heard of Botox? I could compose music on that forehead."

"It is unfortunate, isn't it?" Anjoli said.

"Tragic," Alfie agreed. "Okay, I'm off to pick up pie. You go do your thing."

# Chapter 8

When Jack, Adam, and I returned home, we were delighted to see that Tom had repaired the front stairs to our house. Before we left, one step looked as if it would break off the next time someone set his weight on it. I hoped he had had similar success with removing the cold spots from the house.

Later that afternoon, we drove past Tom and Robin's. We saw Tom unloading groceries from his car and slowed down to chat.

"Thanks for all your work around the house, Tommy boy," Jack said, catching his attention. "Make sure you're keeping track of your hours, okay?"

"Yeah, I gotta tell ya', bro, something weird's going on at that place of yours," Tom said, skipping the niceties of exchanging details of our respective vacations. "Robin and I stopped by on Wednesday to see how much tile I needed to pick up to finish the bathroom. Thursday I come back with all the stuff, and it's done."

"What do you mean done?" I asked from the passenger seat of our Volvo wagon.

"I mean the job is finished. Done. Someone finished the bathroom tiling between Wednesday night and Thursday morning."

"Impossible," Jack scoffed. "No one else has the key to the house."

"That's not all," Tom continued. "When we're there on Wednesday night, Robin tripped on your front steps and broke her ankle."

I glanced at Robin who was now standing in the doorway, waving. Her ankle was in a cast.

"Sorry 'bout that," Jack said. "We'll be happy to pay the medical bills."

"I'm not worried about that, bro. We got insurance. But what freaks the fuck out of me," Tom paused, glanced at Adam and apologized. "What freaks me out is that when we went back the next day, first thing we noticed—before we even make it inside to see the bathroom tile—is that the steps are brand-spanking new."

"You didn't fix them?" Jack asked.

"I wish I could take credit. I'd love to charge you for it, bro, but I didn't do a thing."

Jack and I spoke in unison. "Then who did?"

"No idea," Tom said.

Robin slowly made her way out to say hello. "How was Florida?" She brushed her blond hair away from her full face.

"Fun," I said. "I'm so sorry about your ankle."

She waved a hand dismissively and said she's always been a klutz. "I've been due for an injury for months."

"So is your husband just being uncharacteristically modest or did he really not do all of that work on our house?" I asked.

"No, he really didn't do it," she said. "What can I say? You must have elves."

We all gave a collective shrug, though Jack and I were concerned. When we returned home, we checked to see if any of our valuable items were missing. Everything was exactly where we had left it. It appeared that we had an intruder who stole nothing and did home repairs.

* * *

"I have some news, darling," Anjoli said the next day when she called. "Spot is doing worlds better."

"Who?" I asked.

"Spot," Anjoli said. "It's Paz's new name. I know it's très passé, but the numerologist says it's his true name and if we address him as such, he'll feel at ease and stop chewing his fur."

"Really?!" I was amazed. "And you say it's working?"

"He hasn't chewed once today. Oh, no! Stop it, Paz! I mean, Spot. Lucy, darling I'll have to call you back. He's at it again!"

"Who was that?" Jack asked.

"Who do you think?" I asked.

"The dog?"

"No, it was her. Paz was rebirthed last night. She's calling him Spot now," I updated Jack.

"Rebirthed?"

"It's a breathing exercise that's supposed to help you overcome the trauma of birth," I said.

"Oh, of course," Jack laughed. "How silly of me. Why is she calling him Spot?"

"It's his *true* name according to her numerologist," I explained.

We both rolled our eyes. Jack said he wanted to take Adam to see Clifford the Big Red Dog who was visiting a local bookshop. He asked if I wanted to join them. "I'm going to pass if it's all the same to you," I said. "Maybe I'll call Robin and see if she wants to swim laps at the gym since we're now both members of the bad ankle club."

Jack kissed my forehead and went into the kitchen where Adam was playing with a See 'n Say toy. "Suit yourself," he said. "You couldn't keep me away from an overgrown red dog that's free of nervous disorders. Hey, maybe that should be your next book, Luce—pets who undergo New Age healing therapy. I can see it now, Clifford's first séance. Whaddya think?"

"I think you're adorable," I laughed.

"Or Minnie Mouse's cousin from California who wants to know who moved her cheese?" Jack continued.

"Or maybe she goes to an acupuncturist because someone moved her chi?" I added.

Jack pouted playfully. "I hate it when you one-up me."

"Go!" I said. "Let me get some work done. Say hi to Clifford for me."

A week had passed since we returned from Florida, which meant we had only four days until Maxime and Jacquie arrived from France. Although Jack and I had been corresponding with them for months, they were still strangers, and the prospect of having them come live with us until after Labor Day was a terrifying one. They seemed like an easygoing couple, but Jack and I were still nervous about how our first guests would react to our artist colony. It seemed like a lifetime ago that Jack and I sat at Steve's Lunch in Ann Arbor, eating Bi Bim Bops, sketching our dream on their plain paper napkins. In many ways, it was another lifetime. We were just dating then, and hadn't been through four miscarriages and a tough pregnancy. We hadn't nearly divorced, then found our way back to each other.

After her cast was removed, Robin and I swam laps together twice, but neither of us saw any progress. My doctor said that sprains could take several months to heal completely and gave me a list of exercises to do at home. Admittedly, I had done none of them, but I blame Robin for my lack of motivation. After her first attempt at self-administered physical therapy, she reported that her ankle actually felt worse. I decided that the most therapeutic route to take was to do nothing.

As I was shopping for bedding for Maxime and Jacquie, my cell phone rang. The caller ID indicated it was either my mother—or her dog. "You are not going to *believe* what is happening to me, darling!" Anjoli shot.

"Hello, Mother," I said. "How are you?"

She failed to get my point. "How am I? I am in *crisis*, darling, that's how I am. Can you not detect a tone of horror in my voice?!"

"What is the crisis du jour, Mother?"

"I'm sure you remember that I put an offer in on the brownstone across the street, darling," she began.

"Oh yes, Mrs. MacIntosh's place," I said, sadly. "The block won't be the same without her. I'm sorry we couldn't make the funeral. How was it?"

"How was it?" Anjoli snapped. "It was a funeral, what do you want, a review? We drove out to Queens, listened to an hour of prayers and speeches, then stood outside in twenty-degree weather and watched them drop a casket into the ground. People cried, survivors wore black," she rushed. "Anyway, I specifically told her daughter to talk to me before she listed the property with a realtor."

"You told her this at the funeral?" I asked.

"Don't be ludicrous, darling," Anjoli said. "I waited until the reception."

"The reception?"

"You know, darling. The reception. It's where we all cram in to someone's house, and they put out a crumb cake, some cheese, and coffee," Anjoli said.

"So you approached her about real estate at her mother's funeral?" I asked.

"I said it was at the reception!" Anjoli defended. "Anyway, she promised she would call me, and the next thing I know, I hear that Mrs. MacIntosh bequeathed the damned place to NYU."

"Wow, what inspired that?" I asked.

"I don't know," Anjoli sighed. "Apparently Mrs. MacIntosh is an alum there and wanted to 'give something back' to the university."

"That's incredible," I said, astounded. "That place has four apartments. It's worth a fortune."

"You're telling *me*!" Anjoli said. "Are you ready for the worst?"

"I always am, Mother."

"Sit down for this one, darling," she said.

"I'm sitting," I lied, as I browsed the selection of sheets and duvets, wondering if an artist would find floral prints appealing or pedestrian.

"The leases run out this summer, and they're turning the place into student housing—for *girls!* It's going to be a goddamned sorority!"

Even I felt for Anjoli this time. Here was a woman who made unthinkable sacrifices to maintain her youthful appearance. She drank ten glasses of purified water and four ounces of wheat grass juice every day. Anjoli ate organic vegetables and legumes, avoided all meat, wheat, sugar, honey, gluten, and dairy. She did yoga, tai chi, and spinning class religiously. Vampires had more contact with the sun than Anjoli. She had hats with brims that could double as umbrellas. The idea of her opening her window every morning and seeing bouncy co-eds bopping down the stairs of the old MacIntosh house was Anjoli's version of Dante's Hell.

"Oh, Mother, that is hard," I said, careful not to address the real issue. "I know how noisy students can be. What will you do?"

"What will I do? I'll do as I have always done, darling. I will go on. I will survive. I shall overcome." It's tough to manage sounding like Scarlett O'Hara, Gloria Gaynor, and a one-woman civil rights movement all at the same time, but Anjoli pulled it off with aplomb.

"You're a true inspiration, Mother," I said.

"You think *I'm* something? You should see your cousin Kimmy. She got herself all dolled up and took the train up to New Haven this afternoon. She could pass for a twenty-five-year-old," Anjoli said with admiration. "She obviously paid attention to all of those makeup artists from her modeling days because she looked smashing. Anyway, she packed a small purse with nothing but lipstick and a change of panties. She said she wasn't returning to the city without an Ivy League zygote. How's *that* for determination?"

"Wow, she's really going through with this whole baby thing?" I asked.

"Uh-huh," Anjoli replied. "She said we've inspired her, darling. Isn't that touching?"

"How did we inspire her?" I asked.

"You with little Adam, and me with Paz, I mean, Spot," Anjoli said. "Between us, Lucy, I detest this new name. Who would name their dog Spot?"

"Dick and Jane?" I suggested.

"Precisely," she said. "Do I strike you as a Jane?" she asked. Without pause she continued, "Do I even know a Dick?"

"So change it back to Paz," I suggested. "How is he anyway? Has he stopped chewing his fur?"

"No, his front legs look like raw chicken," she said. "It kills me to see him chewing, chewing, chewing the way he does. Kiki thinks I should give him a colonic."

"Mother, do not give that dog an enema!" I shouted, noticing shoppers staring at me. I suppose this is not the sort of thing they're used to hearing while selecting pillowcases and towels. I lowered my voice. "If you do that, I'm going to report you to animal cruelty. Seriously, Mother, no dog should have to live this way."

"What way? Spot is spoiled rotten. Do you know what he had for supper last night, darling? I fed him steak tartar!"

"Then let the dog enjoy his steak tartar without fear of it being sucked out of his ass the next day," I said.

"It was just a thought," she said sheepishly. "What do you think I should do? You know I can't stand to witness suffering."

"Well, Mother, you might try taking him out of your purse every now and then and letting him burn some of his energy doing normal dog things."

"Such as?" she inquired.

"I don't know, chasing sticks, burying things. Maybe you could take him to Washington Square Park and toss around a Frisbee."

"He couldn't get his little mouth around a Frisbee, darling!"

"Then one of your old diaphragms, Mother. The point is that he needs to burn some energy."

She sighed. "I don't know. Let me give it some thought."

"Our guests are coming in four days," I told Anjoli.

"Guests?"

"The artist and his wife, remember? I'm buying sheets for the guesthouse. It feels so real all of a sudden," I said.

"It must," she returned. "I spoke with your Aunt Bernice yesterday."

"Oh?" I said, wondering how much she revealed.

"I think the woman's losing her mind," Anjoli said. "She was carrying on, telling me I had to shave off my pubic hair. Can you imagine? She says you told her it would keep her vagina cooler. Anyway, she's convinced all of the women in her condo to try it, and apparently it's the rage among seniors in south Florida right now. I'm very concerned about her stability, darling."

"Well, it seems harmless enough and—"

"Hang on a sec, would you, darling? I've got a call waiting." After two full minutes, she returned. "I'll call you back, Lucy. It's Kimmy. She's lost in New Haven."

# Chapter 9

I had just put Adam to bed for the night when Jack's car pulled in to the driveway with Maxime and Jacquie. It was a snowy Valentine's Day, which I thought was an appropriate, however coincidental, time to bring French artists into our lives to fulfill a dream concocted on Jack's and my first date. My heart raced with anticipation.

When a cold rush of air burst in the front door and I saw them, I knew everything would be fine. Maxime had a wide, weather-beaten face with black razor stubble that matched his shoulder-length wavy hair. He had high cheek bones, icy blue eyes, and a dimple in his chin. When he smiled, one side of his mouth opened a bit wider than the other. Jacquie's eggplant-color leather coat was the first thing I noticed about her. That, and her brightly colored Kandinsky-patterned silk scarf. Her hair was long and wavy, mostly pepper, but some salt too. It was twisted and pinned up in the back. The couple seemed utterly unafraid of appearing their age, which I knew from their application to be early forties. They placed their one suitcase in the foyer and immediately made their way over to me for kisses and hugs. I was unprepared for such warmth from strangers.

After both cheeks were double stamped by each of our

new guests, Jacquie informed me that she and Maxime brought a bottle of wine from near the town where they live. Or used to live. They gave up their apartment in Lyon and planned to travel through the United States when they left our place after Labor Day.

"Your accent," I said, without thinking. "You sound American, Jacquie."

"This is what I tell her," Maxime said, laughing. "That is perfect when she speaks English, but not so good when she speaks French," he said with the *zeeses* and *zats* of a man's whose native tongue is French.

"I was raised in the United States until I was twelve," said Jacquie, seemingly not offended by Maxime's comment. She then turned to him and snapped something in French. I hoped the two wouldn't have their private asides in French. I hated when people did that.

Before I could fret about our relationship dynamic, Jack offered to show our guests to their house. "You have a beautiful home," Jacquie said. "Rustic and yet modern." I knew I liked her. Those were the exact words I told the decorator when he asked about the look we wanted for our home.

Fifteen minutes later, I had poured four glasses of wine and started a fire. Funny how Jacquie saying that we'd achieved a modern rustic ambience made me want to create more of it. Suddenly I was setting logs in the fireplace and breaking out the Frank Lloyd Wright coasters.

Jacquie settled into Maxime's arms as they sat on the couch. "We made it, *cheri*," he said, brushing his wife's long hair with his fingers. She had let it down while the two got settled in the guesthouse.

"Rough trip?" Jack asked.

"You can say that again," affirmed Jacquie.

"The past five years has been a rough trip," Maxime said. No one followed up, lest Jack and I seem like nosy

Americans. By midnight they filled us in on how they met seven years ago when Jacquie went to see her then-boyfriend playing soccer one weekend. "I saw her standing on the sidelines and I thought to myself, who is this beautiful girl cheering for the wrong team?" Jacquie giggled.

"Maxime was amazing," she recalled. "You couldn't help but notice him on the field. I was stunned when he came over at the end of the game and asked me if I understood how it pained him to see his future wife rooting against him," she said. "I thought he was just being, well, French. He told me that all his life he had a vision of the woman he would marry and I was her. I laughed, but he said that I should at least give him a chance, and insisted that I come to watch his match the next week. He said, 'You will zee, *cheri*, next week, you weel come and watch for me and I will score zees time. You weel zee.' I thought the man was crazy, but charming."

"Correct and correct," Maxime said. "Tell them what happened the next week."

Jacquie smiled. "I came to the match."

"And?" Maxime became animated.

"And he was brilliant."

"Three goals," he said. "I have never played so hard in my life. She was my good luck charm."

Somehow, I expected them to have met in front of the Mona Lisa or at Monet's gardens. I suppose it was a cliché fantasy, but I liked it.

Maxime continued, "Then the next week, I went to her apartment to pick her up for dinner, but I was early so I stopped into an art shop, and I see this man putting tiny pinpricks of ink onto paper. I had been painting all my life, but never even considered ink drawings before—and never with the pinpricks. I brought her back to the shop with me, and she told me to give it a try. I said no, but the next week after we went to see a film, she gave me a bottle of black ink and a needle pen. I figure, what have I got to lose? I can invite this beautiful girl to my studio and convince her to take off her clothes perhaps?"

Jacquie burst into laughter and swatted him with our couch pillow. "You were trying to seduce me?! You are such a rat!"

"Trying, nothing. I think if you will recall—" he started.

"Maxime!" she scolded.

He bowed his head in playful deference to his wife. "So you see my wife has brought me nothing but good luck since the day I met her."

"It's been a hard few years, though," Jacquie told us with a serious tone.

"It has, but it was Jacquie who found this beautiful guesthouse for us to live," Maxime said buoyantly. "Life will give us troubles, but as long as I have you, I know it will turn out for the better."

I glanced at Jack whose eyes had beat me to the gaze. We contained our smiles. It was always comforting to be with other couples who've been through hard times, but were still optimistic about their future together.

In bed that night I told him I thought we made the right choice with them. He agreed. "Are you that in love with me, Jack?"

"*Mais oui, cheri,*" Jack said rolling closer to me. "Life, eet will hand me zee troubles, but wis you by my sides, eet weel all be for zee better." With that, he nuzzled his face into my breasts and muttered something in bastardized French. I knew he was speaking French gibberish, but it sounded pretty authentic as his lips moved down my stomach. Either his "bleus" and "rues" were convincing, or my ability to discern had gone completely out the window.

During Maxime and Jacquie's first few days with us, they spent most of their time getting settled. They made a short list of repairs that needed to be done—things that no one would notice until trying to live in the guesthouse. Tom and Robin were eager to meet our guests so we arranged a lunch on one of the days that Tom was sealing their windows.

"Do you have anything special you're planning on working on here?" Robin asked solicitously as she sipped her wine.

"No," Maxime said charmingly. "We will see."

How a French accent could make anything sound sexy was beyond comprehension. I'll be honest. If Jack said, "No, we will see," I would tell him to get his lazy ass into gear and make a plan. Yet we excused the Frenchman as artistic and fluid.

"Both your and Robin's ankles are broken?" Maxime asked.

Robin jumped in too quickly. "Mine is broken. Lucy's is just a sprain."

*Oh yeah, well I once had a ruptured disc,* I refrained from saying.

Jacquie smiled, utterly unperturbed by the fact that Robin was obviously smitten with her husband. "Would you like Maxime to draw a picture on your cast?"

"Would I ever?" Robin jumped.

"He does hilarious caricatures," Jacquie said. "Maybe he could do one of you and put it on your foot so you can always be reminded of the funny way he sees you."

*Meow!*

Tom pronounced the artist's name, Maxim, like the men's magazine, not as a dig, but as an honest mistake. "You say on your list there's a crack in the bathroom mirror, but I was in there this morning, and no crack, Maxim."

"I know, it is crazy!" Maxime said with his usual flamboyance. "I apologize for my mistake. It looked cracked to me, but it is fine."

"Don't sweat it, bro," Tom said. "You just saved these guys a couple bucks. Probably just a hair or something made it look like a crack at the time."

"No, it was a crack," Jacquie said. "I saw it." She paused awkwardly. "I mean, who cares about these little cosmetic things? We are so grateful to be living on this beautiful property with you generous patrons." She lifted her glass to toast us.

As I drove Adam to preschool the next morning, my cell phone rang. Anjoli charged forward without introduction. "We're waiting for Kimmy's pregnancy test results," my mother announced. "It takes a few minutes so we're doing a little chanting while we wait. I need you to join in. What is that noise in the background?"

"Raffi," I said flatly, knowing she'd be unfamiliar with the children's folk singer or his mega-hit, "Baby Beluga." Surely, she'd think it was a song about caviar.

"Well, tell him to be quiet. I need you chanting with us, darling. Can this Raffi person join us in a simple chant for fertility?"

"It's a CD, Mother," I informed. "It's Honky," I told Adam.

"Honky!" he shouted. "I say hi to Honky!"

"Mother, Adam wants to say hello," I said, handing the phone to him in the back seat of the minivan.

"Honky, Adam go to school with Max," he told her. He stopped to listen. "Okay, Adam try." Then he began speaking unrecognizable sounds. I glanced at him through the rearview mirror. "Mash mash boo boo," he struggled.

"Give Mommy the phone, honey," I said reaching my arm back. "Are you asking him to chant for Kimmy's positive pregnancy test results?" I asked.

"What could be more powerful than a baby beckoning another baby?" Anjoli asked. "Was he closing his eyes, darling?"

"I don't know."

Anjoli sighed with disappointment. "His eyes needed to be closed so he can block out any distractions. Okay, you close your eyes and repeat after me—"

"Mother, I'm driving," I said. "Can I call you back after I drop Adam at preschool?"

"The test will be done by then, darling. Can you pull over? Do they really care if he's a few minutes late?"

I couldn't believe it, but I was searching for a turnout in the road. As much as I loathe to admit it, there's a small part of me that holds hope that maybe some of Anjoli's hocus-pocus really could work. After all, what was the harm? If my cousin had her heart set on conceiving a child with an anonymous Ivy League grad student with good teeth and an ear for music, I would support her in that. Isn't that what family was all about?

I silenced Raffi, taught my two year old a chant, and spent the next thirty seconds feeling equally ridiculous and hopeful.

"Shit!" I heard Kimmy cry in the background.

I opened my eyes. "Negative?" I asked.

"Strike one, darling," Anjoli said cheerfully. "Not to worry, it simply means that was not the baby for us."

A half hour later, Spot called from my mother's purse. I knew it was him because neither Kimmy nor Anjoli had any idea that I was listening.

"I wanted a Libra baby!" Kimmy sobbed.

"There, there, darling," my mother consoled her. "Trust that there's a plan wiser than ours. Look at the long and arduous journey Lucy had to motherhood. It seemed so difficult at the time, but now we know that Adam was the perfect baby for Jack and Lucy, and he arrived at the perfect time in their lives." My eyes welled. Who was this kind and sensitive woman? "Now, darling, wipe away your tears and put your chin up. We'll go to SoHo for lunch and afterward we'll buy a knockout outfit for your next trip to New Haven. You'll find someone even better this time. Someone even better-looking who's not shooting blanks."

# Chapter 10

By March, only one thing had changed remarkably. Rather, I should say, one person had undergone a complete transformation of character. She had gone from charming guest to wicked witch in two weeks. In her constant fights with Maxime, she threw plates at him (ours!), overturned furniture (ours again!), and broke a window with her horrific operatic shrill (you already know whose window it is). I'm not entirely convinced that it was her screaming that broke the glass, but the timing was perfect, so I like to think it was her horrendous pitch that shattered the glass. Jack's and my dream was slowly becoming a nightmare.

There were still a few inches of snow on the ground and a chill in the air around our home. My love for the new place hadn't waned, though I had grown tired of limping on my slow-healing ankle. I tried to stay focused on what was positive. Adam was enjoying his new preschool. Jack and I were sustaining our marital renaissance. Kimmy was still religiously trolling around Ivy League campuses desperately seeking sperm. Well, that wasn't necessarily positive, but she wasn't breaking anything other than a few preppie hearts.

My family remained as crazy as ever. Aunt Bernice called with her now weekly Snatch Report, praising with an evangelical zeal the benefits of a hair-free crotch. And Anjoli held steadfast to her motto: "I'm fabulous. Why tamper with perfection, darling?" (Of course, this was incongruous with her lifelong pursuit of healing, but I learned at age eight not to correct my mother.)

Oddly, the house was still in a state of auto-repair.

Jack and I were slightly concerned about Maxime, who seemed frustrated by his lack of creative inspiration. He was pleasant about it, but we could sense he was growing impatient with his inability to complete a single drawing since arriving at our arts community. The person who had undergone a truly dramatic transformation was his wife, Jacquie. She showed a bitchy side of herself at our luncheon with Robin and Tom, but it was done in a somewhat playful manner. It was also easy to dismiss because Robin was clearly flirting with Maxime. She was simply establishing her role as alpha female in her husband's life, which wasn't terribly out of line, I thought. But for the last two weeks, she was like a different person than the life-loving, wine-drinking woman who showed up telling stories of how she and her husband first met.

"That mall you sent me to was a joke!" Jacquie snapped as she came in from an afternoon of shopping. All she seemed interested in pursuing during her stay in the United States was consumption. It was a close tie between shopping and complaining, and it was tough to tell which was in the lead since she often did both simultaneously.

During her first week with us, I accepted Jacquie's invitation to go shopping, thinking it would be a nice chance for us to get acquainted. I shot self-conscious and apologetic looks at salespeople as Jacquie pulled at blouse seams and spat that the stitching and fabric were low-quality. She insulted the designers' choices of color and pattern, then tried to bargain with the saleswomen. "This is more shopworn than something I would find in a thrift store," Jacquie barked at the owner of an upscale boutique next to the café where we ate lunch. "I'll give you eighty. Not a penny more."

The owner of the store smiled politely and explained that the items on the sale rack were already marked down, and that none of her prices were negotiable. With a white bouffant hairdo and a long string of pearls that hung down to her burgundy silk blouse, the shop owner looked like the matriarch of a soap opera. I would have been far too intimidated by her regal presence to dare haggling.

"You want me to pay one hundred-twenty dollars for a secondhand sweater?" Jacquie snapped as I tried to bury myself under a nearby jewelry counter.

The woman seemed undeterred. "I don't want you to make any purchases you're not entirely comfortable with, dear," though it was clear from her tone that she found Jacquie anything but dear.

Jacquie raised an eyebrow. "Because all sales are final, right?"

The woman paused, patiently, but was clearly annoyed by the exchange. "My dear, I've lived in this community and run this business for forty years now. My hope is that customers leave fully satisfied with their purchases because having to return to the shop for a refund is a dreadful waste of time."

"That advice is the best thing in this wretched little store," Jacquie shot as she tossed the top over a lavender velvet chair. "Let's get out of here, Lucy."

This reminded me of shopping with Aunt Rita.

I bought a pair of chandelier earrings I only somewhat liked just so I could show the shop owner that *I* was not a pain-in-the-ass like Jacquie.

I hadn't been shopping with her since that day, but when she returned from her trip to the mall, Jacquie had obviously not changed her ways. In fact, every day when she returned from her shopping excursions, it was with a long list of complaints about everything she bought.

"An absolute joke!" she said, punctuating her disdainful comment by dropping four oversized shopping bags. "Crowded with Americans and their pitiful American clothes."

*Wearing our pitiful American clothes or selling them in the stores?* I wondered, before I realized it didn't matter.

"If anyone every wonders why Americans are so fat, all they have to do is look at one of your wretched food courts."

"Jacquie, don't you think you're being a little harsh?" I asked.

"You've obviously never been to Paris," she sniffed.

"Actually, I have," I said. "I adored the people we met there. It's really quite a gift you have, perpetuating stereotypes about the French while simultaneously ridiculing Americans. Any other entire nations of people you'd like to characterize with sweeping generalizations? Anyway, aren't you American?" I asked.

"Spending a few years in the United States does not automatically convert me to Americanism."

I laughed. "This is true, but spending an entire two weeks shopping very well might."

She breezed through the living room, making me wonder why she was in my house and not her own. Jacquie waltzed toward my pantry and grabbed a twelve-pack of toilet paper. "Perhaps you can make it through the spring with one roll, but we need more!" She about-faced and huffed out the front door, asking if I knew where to find Maxime.

"Probably in your home," I said.

"You mean in my *shanty*!" she said, the door slamming behind her. I watched her storm down the dirt path to the guesthouses, wobbling in her absurdly high heels.

I longed to hear a voice of comparative sanity. I dialed Anjoli's cell phone.

"Lucy, darling!" she greeted me brightly.

"How are you, Mother?"

"F-a-b-u-l-o-u-s," she whispered. "I tried your idea. You remember when you suggested walking Spot in the park every day?"

"Oh yes!" I replied. "Is the exercise helping his trichillomania?"

"No, he's still chewing at every last hair he's got on those little paws, but I must tell you, he's quite a little magnet," she said, beaming. "I found the most adorable little collar and matching leash for him, and he is the hit of Washington Square Park. There isn't a day that goes by when I don't get stopped by at least one attractive man who wants to quote, unquote, chat about dogs. I wish I had come up with this years ago."

"So he still has his nervous disorder?"

"I took him in for chakra-spinning, and the doctor said he was simply going through a phase," she said. "Hello!" she brightly greeted someone in the park. "He's a toy Chihuahua." She paused while I heard a man speak. "I know, isn't he a sweetheart? He's the most sensitive little soul." Another pause. "Really?! Well, I certainly would be interested in that!"

"Mother!" I shouted into the phone. "I'm still here."

"Excuse me," she said. "Lucy, let me call you back, darling. This gentleman says he knows another dog who was cured of trichillomania by a pet therapist on the Upper West Side who specializes in canine nervous disorders." She paused again as I heard the man add something. "That's nice, but my little Spot isn't anorexic." She signed off.

I walked down to Maxime and Jacquie's place. Before I reached the door, I heard them shouting at each other. Maxime accused her of becoming a complete lunatic since their arrival. I couldn't agree more. Then he began sobbing that he was a failure as an artist. "I have nothing! I sit here all day and look at the paper and nothing. I do not even have the ideas anymore!" Oh my. I knocked lightly and immediately regretted it. The door flew open and Jacquie stood at the entrance with her hand on her hip.

"What?!" she snapped.

"I'm going in to town to get Adam from preschool and wanted to see if there's anything you need," I offered. "Maybe some toilet paper?"

"My husband has lost his art!" Jacquie barked. "Unless you can buy that at your American supermarket, then no."

"Jacquie!" Maxime scolded. "Do not be rude to our hostess. She has done nothing to you." He addressed me, "Please, please forgive my wife. When she is tired, she gets very angry."

"Do not apologize for me!" Jacquie yelled. "I am not a child!"

"You are acting like one, Jacquie!" Maxime said. "Please, Lucy, we need nothing from the town. Thank you for asking." He then turned to his wife and began speaking harsh words in French. She replied in kind.

I returned to the house and was surprised to see that Jack had come back early from running his errands. He unloaded new tubes of acrylic paint, canvases, and brush cleaner. "Getting ready to do a new painting?" I asked.

"Painting Adam," he said, as I followed him into his studio. I couldn't help imagining our toddler covered in royal blue. "I'm thinking kind of a cubist thing where each section has him breaking out and doing a different thing."

"Ah, the fractured life of a toddler?" I suggested.

"Yeah, fragmented but all coming together," he said.

"Sounds interesting. I heard a poem once written by a mother that was just single words strung together that were elements of her baby's life. They were obviously all independent words and ideas, but she put them together in such a way that they still made sense, but not really. It was confusing, cluttered, and bordering on nonsensical at times. Still it had a fun, lyrical quality about it."

"Like kids," Jack added.

"Like kids. Hey, I'm about to head over to the school to pick up Adam. Wanna join me and maybe we could all do something together? Adam has been saying he wants to go see that new movie about those clay sea creatures."

"How does he know about movies?" Jack asked.

"Preschool," I replied. "Ever since he started spending time with other kids, he knows everything there is to know about kid world. Last week he asked me to take him bowling."

"Bowling? He couldn't even pick up the ball."

"Nor do they make bowling shoes in his size, but he doesn't know that. Tyler McGreggor swears he goes bowling with his older brother and father, so now Adam wants to go too."

"Does he even know what it means?"

"Please," I said with an eye-rolling tone. "He's a little boy. What about throwing a ball down an alley with the goal of knocking over ten pins does *not* sound appealing?"

Jack laughed as he unloaded the last of his supplies. "Okay," he said. "Let's do it."

"Good," I said, smiling. "It's been awhile since we got out as a family. Plus, I want to get away from the house for awhile."

"How come?" Jack asked.

As I pointed out the window, gesturing to the guesthouse, I caught a glance of Randy's glass sculpture inset into our bedroom window. I hoped our next guests would turn out to be more pleasant than Maxime and Jacquie. Maxime was nice enough, but there's something incredibly depressing about an artist who is going through a creative dry spell. And Jacquie, well, let's just say, I was being careful not to put my face too close to hers for fear she might bite.

# Chapter 11

Chantrell the cellist moved into her cottage in mid-March. Randy the glass sculptor called and said that his arrival would be delayed two weeks because he had the opportunity to show his work at an arts festival in Aspen. I was more disappointed than Jack because we had worked so hard to finish the guesthouse by his expected arrival date. Jack was too engrossed in his new painting of Adam to care. When he got the call, Jack just shrugged, wished him luck, and told Randy that he was welcome to come in April.

Maxime still had yet to produce a single drawing, and was tortured by his lack of productivity. From my bedroom window I watched him pace outside, shaking his head and muttering. His stubble had grown into a beard over the last month, and he always looked tired. I knew he wasn't simply slacking off. He was clearly tormented by his creative dry spell. And we were all tormented by Jacquie, who had stumbled out of bed drunk one night and injured her knee. No one knew exactly what she'd done to it, but she walked with a distinct limp and used a cane. Still, this didn't keep her from daily excursions to the mall. All she needed was a New York accent, and people might actually mistake her for my Aunt Rita.

It was a rainy Wednesday morning when I decided to write an article for a *Healthy Living* magazine. I'd done a few pieces for them in the past, and the editor said if I ever wanted to pitch an idea for his magazine's lifestyle section, he'd be very eager to hear it. When I told him that Jack and I had just bought a place that we were converting into an arts community, Earl was particularly interested in a "living the dream" type of piece. I snuggled into the chaise by my bedroom window and watched the rain fall through the trees, melting the snow and exposing the wet ground beneath. I could hear Chantrell's intoxicating cello music come to an abrupt halt when Jacquie slammed the door of her house behind her and hobbled outside. Maxime chased her outside in his undershirt and boxer shorts, shouting at her in French. She replied shaking her fists, and I could see the curtain at Chantrell's being pulled back a smidge so she could peek at what was going on. Jacquie stormed off as quickly as she could and Maxime returned inside quietly. I sat and watched as if I were seeing a European film without the benefit of subtitles.

Moments later I saw Chantrell walk to Maxime and Jacquie's cottage and knock on the door. She had wrapped a scarf over her head to protect herself from the rain, yet she wore no shoes. Maxime shook his head, presumably telling Chantrell that everything was okay. She nodded back and took a step back to leave before Maxime said something to her. They both glanced around self-consciously. Chantrell stepped inside.

What kind of an article could I possibly write for *Healthy Living*? My dream community had become a cultural dead zone for a once-brilliant artist. It had turned his wife into a maniac. And now it looked as though it was going to become a breeding ground for an extramarital affair. I'd have to pitch this one to *Dysfunctional Digest*.

"Robin?" I said into the phone receiver. "When Tom

comes over today to work on the house, do you want to go to the gym for a swim?"

"Sure," she replied. "Is Maxime around?"

"He is, but he's, um, working right now. Hey, how's your ankle doing?"

"Not so good," Robin replied. "My doctor says he's never seen such a slow-healing bone before."

"My doctor said the same thing about my sprain."

"Who do you go to?" Robin asked.

"Mazzarella."

"Me, too!" Robin said, though she soon thought better of her excitement. "Hey, how could both of our ankles be the slowest healing ones he's ever seen?"

"Yours is broken," I said. "Mine's a sprain."

"Still," Robin said. "I don't know. It strikes me as a bit disingenuous. How could we both be the slowest he's ever seen?"

"Maybe he just sucks as a doctor. None of his patients are healing, and we're all the slowest cases. Sounds like he's the problem."

She laughed. "Okay, Tom was planning on coming back at around two. Will that work for you?"

"Perfect. Wendy's coming by at one to watch Adam, so I'm all clear. I was going to pitch an article, but on second thought, the idea probably isn't going to work."

"When's your book coming out?" Robin asked.

"November," I said.

"Why so long?" she inquired, like everyone else when I told them my publication date.

"I don't know," I dismissed. "It just takes a long time."

When I found out I was pregnant with Adam, Jack asked me for a divorce. Well, that's not why he wanted to split up. It was just a case of bad timing. I had his favorite meal on the table and was getting ready to tell him that I was pregnant when Jack sprang the news that he wanted to dissolve our relationship. Anyway, we decided to live together as friends and raise Adam as co-parents. That situation had its ups and downs, to say the least, but ultimately we found our way back to the happy marriage we started. Truth be told, it's actually better this time around. We spent Adam's first Thanksgiving at Anjoli's apartment where I met her friend, Chris, a literary agent. When she heard about how Jack and I had emotionally divorced, then come together again, she asked if I'd ever considered writing a book about it. I gave it a shot and was amazed how easily it flowed. I had such fun writing *Tales from the Crib* that I finished it in six months, which was incredibly fast considering I had spent years prior struggling with a few meager chapters of a horrid little story about a woman named Desdemona who died from pneumonia after being caught in a rainstorm. This November, I would see my book in stores, a thought that was simultaneously electrifying and terrifying.

As Robin and I returned from the gym, we joked about how much we looked forward to wearing high heel shoes again. "I'm buying six-inch strappy shoes when this thing heals," she said.

"I'm getting total Hoochie Mama shoes," I added, remembering my Aunt Bernice and her Ho Chi Minh models.

The next morning, Anjoli called. "What do you think of entering Spot in a dog show?" she asked.

"Good morning, Mother."

"You have no idea how many people stop me to tell me that Spot is simply the most gorgeous dog they've ever seen. Frankly, I couldn't agree more. I'm walking him home right now, and two people have stopped to tell me how cute he is. Why shouldn't he have a few blue ribbons? I remember how proud you used to be with your horse show ribbons."

"I take it this means Spot has stopped chewing his

paws?" I asked, making my way to the window to watch the soap opera in my backyard. I knew Maxime and Jacquie were inside their home because I could see them through their windows. I saw that Chantrell had lit a fire because smoke was coming from her chimney, but for the first time since her arrival, there was no music coming from her home.

"No, darling, he's still chewing like crazy," Anjoli sighed. "I don't know what to do. I've tried absolutely everything to help him. Last night I gave him an aromatherapy bath. Would you believe he cried?!"

"You didn't by chance use lemon oil, did you?" I asked.

"I did!" she said with a tone of concern. "Is there something wrong with lemon oil?"

"It irritates the skin," I said, remembering Jack's and my fiasco with a lemon oil bath.

"The woman at the health food store said—"

"I know, I know," I interrupted. "They say it's calming, but if you read the bottle, it says that it irritates skin."

"Mommy is so sorry, Spot!" Anjoli cried. "I had no idea, darling." Anjoli began interacting with the dog before I reminded her I was still on the line. "Do you think I could get him a pair of cashmere sleeves to cover his paws?"

"Isn't it getting warmer in New York yet?" I asked.

"Not for warmth, silly," Anjoli said. "For the dog show. Alfie is a whiz with knits. He could make something kicky to cover Spot's paws, and the judges will never see where he chewed."

"Mother, I think you should focus on curing your dog's anxiety disorder before entering him in any dog shows."

"You don't think they'd discriminate against him because he has a psychological disorder, do you, darling?"

I laughed. "No, I think you'd sue them under ADA if they even mentioned Spot's problem. Maybe you should focus on figuring out what's wrong with him before you get involved with the whole dog show circuit. How's his therapy going?" I couldn't believe what I was asking.

"Slow," she sighed. "Dr. Ken says Spot has abandonment issues."

I didn't know what I found more laughable—Dr. Ken or a dog having issues of any sort. Nonetheless I was drawn in to my mother's bizarre world. "I thought you said you got Spot from a breeder. Why would he feel abandoned?"

"Dr. Ken says that Spot's siblings were probably adopted before he was. Poor thing had to watch his family sold off to different homes. Can you imagine the feelings of rejection he must've experienced, darling?"

"Mother, most dogs are separated from their litter. They don't need psychotherapy to get over it. Maybe the dog just hates the mundane name you've given him."

"Nonsense! The numerologist said Spot was his true name," Anjoli said.

"Please. How could Spot be the name of a Mexican breed?! Spot belongs to Dick and Jane, not Paco and Maria. At least translate the damn name to Spanish."

"Oh my God!" my mother cried. "Do you think that's it?"

"No, Mother, I was kidding," I replied.

"How do you say Spot in Spanish, darling?"

"I'm not sure." I thought about it for a moment and remembered my high school Spanish teacher saying that she spilled lunch on her blouse. "Um, I think it's 'mancha' but it may mean stain, not spot."

"Mancha!" Anjoli shouted gleefully. "As in *Man from La Mancha*? How could I have been so insensitive, darling? Of course, your name is Mancha." I realized she was talking to the dog. She returned to me. "Lucy, you are a lifesaver. I don't know if I'll ever forgive myself for denying Mancha his Latino roots."

*Oh, somehow I'm sure you will, Mother.*

"Mancha, of course you are Mancha!"

Finally, I saw Jacquie emerge. I ducked down so she wouldn't see me watching her as she quietly left. No drama. No yelling. She quietly exited and headed for the main road.

"I hate the artist's wife," I told my mother.

"Is she still shopping nonstop?" Anjoli asked.

"The only breaks she takes are to complain or to fight with her husband," I returned.

"So kick her out," Anjoli suggested.

"I can't do that," I said. "She'd be homeless."

"Well, she should start acting like someone who's on the brink of homelessness."

"And how is that, Mother?"

"Grateful, darling. Only people with money should complain. We've earned it." She paused. "Oh good God! I cannot believe what I'm seeing."

"What?! What's going on?"

"I'm dying right now. Dying, darling! Call an ambulance because I am really and truly dropping dead."

# Chapter 12

Later that evening, Mancha called me and I could hear that my mother was not only alive and well, but regaling dinner guests with tales of her crisis du jour. "Stop laughing!" Anjoli said playfully. "This is not one bit funny."

"Shouldn't that be one *iota,* love?" Alfie shot. The group laughed. I didn't get it.

As it turns out, NYU will have its first Kappa Alpha Theta sorority house right across the street from Anjoli's home. What she saw that afternoon was a sign being posted on Mrs. MacIntosh's old place, the brownstone facing Mother's. Everyone in her dining room was looking at brushed silver letters reading "KAT House."

"Like a whorehouse?" asked my mother's friend, Kiki.

"Sounds like it, doesn't it?" Anjoli lamented.

"Imagine how that's going to affect business here!" Alfie shot.

"You ought to take your show on the road, Alfie," Anjoli quipped. "And I mean now, darling." A crowd of about five or six people laughed and applauded my mother's advance in the battle of the wits. "It's Kappa Alpha Theta, and I hear they're all goddamned adorable. Sixteen of them are moving in this summer. I will simply die from the noise. Mancha, put that down."

"Mancha?" a man asked, "Is that what we're calling him this week?"

"I realized I needed to acknowledge his heritage," Anjoli said. "Stop biting!"

"Here baby, come sit with me," Kimmy said. "Have you tried doggie massage, Auntie Anjoli? I'm taking a baby massage class."

Kimmy had been to Princeton twice this month, which was unusual since she typically only made these road trips while she was ovulating. According to my mother, Kimmy was no longer having sex with random students. She met an anthropology professor she was actually dating. Still, Kimmy held to the notion that she would be pregnant soon. I wondered if she was the only student in baby massage who not only didn't have a baby, but hadn't even conceived yet.

Anjoli was not at all happy with Kimmy's choice of mate. She hadn't yet met Nick, but she already knew she didn't like him. Anjoli griped about his job. "What does one do with a PhD in anthropology?!" Anjoli asked Kimmy and the dinner guests.

Alfie answered, "He's an anthropology professor, love! At an Ivy League school. He's hardly a slacker."

"I hate those academic types," Anjoli said. "So snooty. They think they're better than everyone else who has to live in the real world."

Alfie quipped, "Since when do you live in the real world, love?" Thunderous applause and laughter followed his retort. By now, I would usually be shouting into the phone, demanding to be recognized, but I found myself as entertained by the exchange as if I were an invited guest.

Kiki chimed in: "Why don't you just admit what's really bothering you?"

"And what's really bothering me, darling?"

Kiki cleared her throat. "What state is Princeton in?"

In unison, Anjoli's guests answered, "Jersey." It's a

commonly known fact that my mother detests the entire state of New Jersey, Princeton University included. She grew up in Newark and never quite got over being disqualified from a beauty pageant for a piece of performance art that was deemed obscene by the Catholic Youth Association. I've heard it a thousand times: "Yoko Ono did the same thing twenty years later, and everyone said she was a genius."

My mother let out a shriek that sounded as though she may have spilled hot water on herself. All of her guests were laughing, which meant Anjoli was fine. Or she had the sickest group of friends in Manhattan. "It's true!" Anjoli screamed dramatically. "Kimmy, you mustn't do this to me, darling. I beg of you. I had to visit Lucy in that godforsaken state for four years before she had the good sense to move to the Berkshires. I can see the handwriting on the wall. You're going to marry this guy and live with him in, in—Jesus, God give me strength—*New Jersey*." She cackled as her friends laughed. "I'm going to have to come visit you and this baby of yours in *New Jersey*." I imagined Anjoli with her hand on her forehead dancing across the dining room for dramatic effect. As she swayed back and forth, I imagined little Mancha squealing under her stiletto heel.

"You must have some past life issues to resolve that can only be addressed in New Jersey," Kiki offered. I waited for the laughter, but no one so much as chuckled. Was this woman serious?

"Darling, you think I have bad New Jersey karma?" Anjoli said with terror.

"Not karma, per se, but perhaps this is the universe's way of pulling you toward a spiritual polar point for your healing," Kiki said.

It can never just be that some people choose to live in New Jersey because they like the suburbs. With my mother and her friends, there's always some sort of crazy

theory that focuses around them and their spiritual healing. The fact that a Princeton professor lived in New Jersey had absolutely nothing to do with him and his housing
needs. It was all about my mother and her unresolved issues from a past life.

"You know what I'd love to see?" Alfie asked the
group. "I hope this professor's home is right across the
street from the Kappa Kappa Cutie house, so everywhere
Anjoli goes it'll be Girlstown!"

"Bitch!" Anjoli said, laughing. "I simply don't want to
be bothered by their vile giggling at all hours of the morning."

On April Fool's Day, two wonderful events happened at
the house. First, Jack finished his painting of Adam. It was
magnificently colorful with thick swirls of yellow and red
and orange defining his face. The painting wasn't the cubist piece that Jack had originally intended, but it was
even better than what he'd envisioned. There was a bright,
modern quality about the texture and color that captured
the spirit of our two year old. "You're not going to sell it,
are you?" I asked. "I want to hang it in the living room."

"I'm glad you like it," Jack said. "I'm going to do another and use that scattered concept we talked about." He
seemed so happy when he was painting. I wish I knew
what Maxime was like when he was creating, but no one
had seen that side of him yet.

The second joy of the first day of April was the arrival
of Randy, the glass sculptor. Maybe it was the fact that the
clouds literally parted and the sun began shining within an
hour of his arrival, but I seriously thought Randy was a
gift from heaven. He was about thirty with a body chiseled
from stone. He had short dirty-blond hair and squinty
brown eyes. There was no other word but yummy to describe Randy. Maxime was indeed handsome, but these

days he looked like a castaway. Randy looked like the rescue boat.

Robin thought so, too. When she and Tom stopped by the house, she whispered into my ear that she may have actually had an orgasm through her eyeballs. We felt guilty watching our husbands help Randy unload his duffel bag and boxes of supplies as we silently envied the glass he touched.

Chantrell tried to act disinterested, but there was no looking past this man. She tried to sneak a glimpse at Randy and stepped on a gardening hoe. I found this more than a tad ironic considering she'd been carrying on with Maxime for weeks. Meanwhile Jacquie terrorized store owners up and down the east coast. She disappeared for days at a time, returning with shopping bags from as far as New York and Boston. This was fine with Maxime and Chantrell who seemingly gave up their respective arts for a career in screwing each other.

"Ouch!" Chantrell shouted as she hopped around holding her bare foot. "It's bleeding! My foot is bleeding!"

Randy dropped his bag and ran to her aid. Robin and I looked at each other in disbelief. If we'd known all it would take is slicing our feet open with gardening tools, we'd have done it first. "Did he *not* see my ankle?!" pouted Robin.

"I'm limping around like Quasimodo with mine," I added. "You think I'd get a little first aid?"

The next week, I saw Chantrell try to plant her vegetable garden and begin playing cello to her zucchini. She did not visit Maxime for three days. I kept an eagle eye on Randy's place and, thankfully, Chantrell hadn't ventured there either.

"Jack, take Adam to preschool with me this morning," I requested.

"Do we need to talk to his teacher?" Jack asked.

"Nope."

"What then?" he asked.

"I just want to hang out with you a bit," I said, hiding my real agenda.

After we dropped Adam at school, I drove to an area I'd scoped out a few days earlier. As I slowed the car near a grove of trees, Jack looked at me knowingly. "You either brought me here to kill me, or to—" his voice trailed off, but his eyebrows raised hopefully.

"When was the last time we fooled around outside of the bedroom?" I asked.

"Or at eight-thirty in the morning?" he added.

As our bodies met, Jack's elbow sounded the horn. We laughed and continued kissing like teens on prom night. "Let's go in the back," Jack said.

My heart raced. "Okay." I may have actually giggled.

Minutes later our clothing was strewn across the mini-van, and Jack was lowering himself into me. His head turned quickly as his face changed from lustful to terrified within a second as he looked out the back window.

"Luce, get dressed, quick!" Jack said hurriedly as he jumped back into the driver's seat. I looked up to see a police car with its lights flashing driving toward our car.

"Shit!" I said as a layer of sweat covered my naked body.

"We've got to move," Jack said, starting the car.

"Jack, I'm naked!"

"So am I, Luce!" he said as the car engine started. "Grab my pants. They're right there by your side." The car began moving quickly, and the police car began to follow. I reached into the backseat and started grabbing our clothing and putting on whatever I could find. "You're dressing yourself?! I can't believe you're dressing yourself! Grab my pants over there!"

"Give me a sec!"

"You're buttoning your blouse?! Just throw the thing on and get my pants. We're on the main road in about thirty seconds and my dick is hanging out."

"Well, technically it's not hanging *out* because there's nothing for it to be hanging from," I said.

"Luce, I've got a cop behind me and I'm fucking naked! Grab my pants!"

I held Jack's pants out for him so he could slip into them. As soon as he was covered, Jack stepped on the gas and began to outrun the police car. The officer turned on his siren and demanded that we pull over. "I can take him," Jack said.

"Stop the car!" I shouted. "Jack, you're talking crazy. We're not getting into a police car chase over this. Pull over."

"Pull over?!" he said incredulously. "Pull over and say what?"

"Don't say anything. Zip up your pants and let me do the talking."

"Luce, you've got no pants on!" he reminded me.

"Pull over, and hand me my underwear. They're right down there next to the gas pedal."

"I can take this guy, Luce!"

"Jack!" I shouted. "Snap out of it. We are not Butch Cassidy and the Sundance Kid. We are never going to outrun this guy. He can see our license plate. Even if you can outrun him, he'll be at our house in twenty minutes. Now pull over and hand me my panties!"

Thankfully, Jack knew to reverse the order of my demand. As I was pulling the elastic waist band over my hips, the officer looked in our driver's side window and gestured for Jack to roll down his window.

"Don't say a word, Jack. Let me handle this." The window rolled down. The officer looked at my bare legs and blouse unevenly buttoned, then glanced at shirtless Jack.

"Is there a problem, officer?" I said sheepishly.

"I expected you to be kids," he said.

"Nope, just a boring old married couple trying to re ignite some passion into our relationship," I said, giggling nervously. "I was going to tell you a whole big story about losing my contact lens, but frankly you seem like the kind of guy who would understand our predicament. I mean, not that you seem like a guy whose marriage is boring or anything, but well, you know. Are you married?" I asked, glancing at his left hand.

"Thirty years," he said, flatly.

"Wow, congratulations! That's amazing. You and your wife must really have something special." He said nothing. "This was my idea, officer. I thought maybe if we, you know, park, my husband and I could, you know, spark the flame. You can understand, can't you? I mean, don't you and your wife ever do crazy stuff like this?"

"No," he said.

"Couldn't you just give us a warning?"

"You didn't know that you're not supposed to have sex in public?" he asked.

"We were not having sex! We were *about to* have sex, but nothing had been, um, finalized yet. Officer, I beg of you, we have a child who would find his parents' criminal record incredibly embarrassing. Couldn't we just pretend this never happened?"

"Lady, I saw your bare ass scurrying around throwing clothes around. How can I pretend that never happened? Look, you seem like nice enough people, but I gotta take you in."

We saw a judge that afternoon who scolded us for our reckless behavior, ordered us to go to traffic school, and told us we were lucky he wasn't pressing public indecency charges against us. Jack and I straightened ourselves out, grabbed some lunch, then picked up Adam at preschool. "That was fun," Jack said.

I blushed, then peeked at Adam strapped into his car seat, playing with his Whoozit toy. "I know. Kind of exhilarating. I've never been wanted in the state of Massachusetts before."

"I beg to differ," Jack winked.

# Chapter 13

The following week, Aunt Bernice called. For the first time in months, she didn't provide an update on her pubic hair. Instead, she sniffed that she missed her sister, Rita. "You spend eighty yeyahs with someone, and you know exactly how they would have reacted to something, and when theyah not theyah to do it, you miss it," she explained.

"Did something happen today?" I asked.

"Something happens every day," Bernice said.

"Why so blue today?"

I knew something had to have happened. After all, this was a woman who described the woman who mugged her in the Publix parking lot as wearing a very elegant hat. Bernice said, "I got this flyah—everyone in the building got it—that said six dollahs a room for carpet cleaning, three room minimum. So I figyad for eighteen dollahs, I'll do both bedrooms and the living room."

"And?" I urged her to continue.

"These burly men got to the apartment, and they said it's going to be a hundred-twenty cawse I needed a deep cleaning. I said, 'Who needs a deep cleaning?' It's not like I'm such a big shot. I don't really know what happened next, but I paid them fifty dollahs and they cleaned my foyah."

"Your foyer?!" I repeated.

"Yes."

"They cleaned your foyer for fifty dollars?"

"Yes," Bernice replied.

"What happened to the six dollars per room?"

"That's what I want to know!"

"I don't understand what happened, Aunt Bernice. You paid them?"

"Yes."

"Why?!"

"I'm not shaw. They did a very nice job on the carpet. The foyah nevah looked so good. I thought they would get angry if I told them to go away. They were very big men."

I boiled with rage and heartbreak. My elderly aunt was baited-and-switched, then paid two thugs not to beat her up. I was beyond infuriated with this carpet Mafia.

"How did you pay?" I asked.

"Check," she said.

"Did you sign anything?" I asked.

"They made me sign a form when they were finished," she said. "I don't know what it said. I didn't have my reading glasses on, but they were pretty pushy about me needing to sign it before they would leave." She sighed. "If Rita were heyah, she would know exactly how to handle those kids."

"They were kids?!"

"They were young. Fordy, no more than fifdy."

"Do you still have the flyer?" I asked my aunt.

"Oh, Lucy, I don't think they have service in yaw area."

"Aunt Bernice!" I exclaimed. "I don't want to hire them. I want to call and demand your money back. They're preying on the elderly. I'm going to report them."

"Report them?" she asked.

"To the Better Business Bureau, the Elder Abuse people, and whoever else handles this sort of thing."

"Lucy, you're such an Erin Abramowitz."

My aunt is gifted in managing to convert anyone she likes to Judaism.

"It's Erin Brockovich, Auntie."

"Now there was a goil with celluloid breasts," she said. "But the way she saved those people from the dirty warter," she sighed. "A lovely, lovely goil. I wonda if she shaved her vaginer." I knew it couldn't last.

A few minutes later, I called Greg, the manager of the carpet-cleaning service, who abruptly told me that if Aunt Bernice signed the release form and paid his workers, she must have been satisfied with the work. I assured him that she wasn't. "Look, she's eighty-four years old, and you sent two giants to her house who wouldn't leave until they were paid fifty dollars to clean a foyer."

"She could've said no," he replied rudely.

"Do you advertise exclusively in senior citizen residences?" I asked. "Because this sounds a whole lot like preying on the elderly."

"Look, lady," he snapped. "Do you realize how cheap you sound complaining about fifty dollars? If your grandmother is half as stupid as you are, no wonder she didn't understand the terms of service."

"Excuse me?" I said in disbelief.

"What part of 'you're an idiot' did you not understand?"

"Have you ever cleaned anyone's carpets for six dollars a room?" I demanded.

"Not a deep cleaning."

"Have you ever done *any* cleaning for six dollars a room? I mean if someone were to audit your office, would they find one single invoice for a six-dollar-per-room service?"

"I don't have time for this shit, lady!" he said.

"I'm going to report you!" I said like a snitty school marm.

"Go right ahead. They'll tell you what I'm telling you right now—you're an idiot!" Then he hung up.

As it turned out, the Better Business Bureau did not tell me that I—or my aunt—were idiots, but rather that this kind of thing happens all the time. I filled out a rather unsatisfying complaint form, then called the Elder Abuse hotline. They were lovely, but said unless my aunt was taken advantage of by her caregiver, there was nothing they could do. I then spoke with a woman at the Department of Agriculture and Consumer Services, who said the agency would be more than happy to investigate within the next six months.

"Auntie," I said into the phone. "I have good news and bad news. The bad news is that we're going to have to wait awhile before this will be resolved legitimately. The good news is that I'm going to have fifty dollars worth of fun with these jerks."

"What are you going to do?" she asked.

"You'll see."

In my best southern accent, I called information. "Yes, Hollywood please. Can I have the number of Scarlett's Gentlemen's Club? Thank you kindly."

Next call: same southern accent. "Hi, I wanna be a dancer, and I'm wonderin' who I need to talk to." A young woman told me it was Goliath who handled the hiring. "And how will I know who Goliath is?" I listened. "Oh, built like a mountain with tattoos and a goatee, perfect. Thanks, honey. Now tell me, what time does Goliath come in today?" She told me he was in after noon, but that I shouldn't come in before three because he was always in a "real shitty mood" before then. "Aren't you sweet to let me know that? Thank you, sugar. Y'all are still near the ninety-five, right?" She confirmed.

Next call: same southern accent. "Hi, honey, we had a hell of a night here and we're needin' a full carpet cleaning. Y'all think you can get out here to help us out?" The dispatcher asked a few questions. "We had a beer spill, it's hella bad. I'm talkin' about a pretty large commercial space so I'm gonna need to make sure I get your manager out here to do the job." She said that she could send Greg. "Perfect, sugar. Now, he's gonna need to talk to Goliath, and he wants this done pronto. Can you get here right at noon? No later cause he needs to take his nap at twelve-thirty." She confirmed. "Great, now two things I gotta tell you about Goliath. I love him like a brother, don't misunderstand me now. But the man is hard-of-hearing so this Greg fella is gonna have to really turn up the volume, okay? Make sure Greg talks real loud and slow. And, Goliath is a sweetheart, but he's dumber than a sack of hair, so Greg may need to remind him a few times about the spill in the VIP lounge. He's real thick. Okay, great, lemme give you the directions."

The thought of nasty Greg shouting at Goliath, insisting that he clean the beer stain in the VIP lounge was gratifying.

But not fifty dollars worth.

Next I called the Harley-Davidson dealership. In my best New York accent, I said to the receptionist: "Yeah, uh I'm tinkin' about buyin' my husband a hog for his birtday. Where's your showroom at, ah?" She gave me directions. "And who's da sales managah?" She said it was Johnny. "How'm I gonna know dis Johnny person?"

The receptionist chimed, "Well, he's the only colored fellow here."

Good God, did people still say that? There wasn't an ounce of malice in her voice. It was just a normal word to her.

My next call to the carpet-cleaning place was answered by a different dispatcher. I could hear a dozen women's voices in the background. "Do you clean businesses?" I asked in my normal voice. " 'Cause we got a showroom that gets a lot of foot traffic, and it's starting to look a little shabby. We sure could use a cleaning." She said their manager, Greg, would be out doing a call that afternoon and offered to send him by at one. "Wonderful. Let me give you our address." Then, just for fun: "You're going to need to deal with our sales manager, so when you get here, just ask for Blackie."

I just knew that any man who ripped off old people had to be a bigot, too. If he had made it through an entire lifetime without a well-deserved ass-kicking from a southern black man, it was time to remedy that situation.

Finally, I made one last call to get information about the appropriate staff member at another Hollywood office building. Suzy, the lovely woman at the front desk, gave me the right person's name, directions, and the number of employees who worked there.

Last call to the carpet cleaner. It was the same dispatcher as last time so I hung up and tried again. This time I got a fresh voice. "Hi, I need one of your managers to come out and clean our lobby carpet. One of the guys got your flyer advertising six dollars per room, but he misplaced it, so would you do me a favor and bring another forty or so? We've got a lot of guys down here who want to get their carpets at home cleaned, so we want to put one of your flyers in everyone's box. In fact, first thing when you get here, give the flyers to me and remind me that Eddie wants them to go in everyone's "IN" box. I'm Suzy. Anyway, we'd love it if you could come out this afternoon, the later the better." She said that there was an opening at three-thirty. "Perfect. Tell me, what's the name of the manager you're sending out?" She told me it was Greg. "Great. I know Eddie will look forward to meeting him. That's Eddie Gold. And make sure you save a flyer for Eddie. If I'm busy I won't get the flyers in the boxes tonight, but I know Eddie will want one right away."

I was certain that Eddie would take a special interest in

the nonexistent six dollar carpet-cleaning special. After all, that's just the sort of thing the head of the fraud unit at the Hollywood Police Department would want to know about.

"Oh, dawling!" Aunt Bernice cried with joy. "You've given me such a laugh today. This is exactly the sort of thing Rita would have done if she were alive. "I have such a good story for tonight's bridge game."

I smiled, thrilled by both my ability to make my aunt happy and the sheer rush of mischief.

"Hey, honey, we're home," Jack said as he and Adam walked through the door. "Guess what we found today?"

"What?" I asked.

"I bought a junked car at a garage sale. It's an original VW Bug. Doesn't work, but the body's in great condition. We're gonna have some fun with that."

"What, may I ask, are we going to do with an immobile old car?" I asked.

"We paint the car!" Adam answered.

Jack confirmed: "When I was in San Diego, I saw this old car at the Children's Museum that kids would paint. They had open buckets of paint beside it at all times, and the kids flipped."

"You and Adam are going to paint the car?" I asked, envisioning the mess this would make.

"We're gonna make a party of it. We'll invite his friends from preschool and let them go to town. It'll be a blast." Ten kids with paint did not sound like a blast to me, but Jack seemed so thrilled, I didn't have the heart to discourage him. "Think about it, we can park it in the front yard and paint it a different theme for holidays. For Halloween, we'll paint it orange and make it a pumpkin. Thanksgiving we can make it into a turkey. We can make it into an Easter egg. Every month, we can do something different."

"I'm sure the neighbors will appreciate that," I said.

"Luce, this is why you wanted to leave New Jersey. Besides, you know no one can see our front yard unless they drive on to the property. We won't offend anyone's sensibilities." *Except mine,* I thought. I looked at my husband, filled with life and excitement that he shared with my son who was shouting about painting the car.

"The car is soooo fat, Mommy!" Adam told me. I wasn't sure if he was referring to the round top of the VW Beetle or if had learned some new ghetto jargon at preschool.

"Luce," Jack said, smiling at me. "I know it sounds crazy, but trust me, you're going to love it when you see how creative we can be with it. We can open the doors and make it into a Nativity scene next Christmas."

"Can we make it a menorah for Chanuka?" I said, warming up to the idea of my husband's wild happiness, if not the thought of having a piece of junk on our front lawn.

"I'll find nine huge electric candles and everything!" Jack said. The things that made this man happy.

"Okay," I shrugged, knowing that the damned thing was being towed over anyway.

Jack sidled up to me and whispered, "I checked out the backseat," he raised his eyebrows. "It's a tight squeeze, but on our own property, no harm, no foul."

# Chapter 14

By May, I no longer startled at the sound of breaking glass. In fact, I didn't even flinch. It was now simply part of the normal background noise at our home.

My mother's cousin had lived in London during World War II and said that the first time she heard bombs drop she would frantically duck and cover, but within weeks, the noise no longer alarmed her. She continued her strolls utterly unfazed by the distant explosions. This was how I felt in my home.

Unlike Maxime, Randy the glass sculptor began working as soon as he arrived at our place. Unfortunately, he developed a case of slippery fingers, which is a serious problem for someone who works with glass. At least twice a day, I'd hear the thunderous crashing of glass breaking in Randy's studio. He complained that not only were his creations being shattered, but that the windows in his house were cracked as well. We checked it out, and he was correct. Every piece of glass looked as though it had a cobweb in the center of it.

"It's strange," Randy said. "The first night I got here a window broke, then the next night the one next to it cracked. It's like someone comes around and smashes it with a rock. Look at the pattern here. There's some sort of an impact right at the center. It's freaky that they're all breaking in order too. It's like my place is having a tantrum or something."

I wondered if we had vandals or if perhaps Randy had pissed off a girlfriend. He would have to be a pretty fast operator to have a love affair gone sour the same day he arrived in town, but it wouldn't have surprised me too much if that were the case. He was, after all, *that* good-looking.

Maxime still hadn't produced a single work of art and wept inconsolably every day. Not that anyone was rushing to console him. Jacquie was gone most of every day, seemingly on a mission to single-handedly purchase the entire state of Massachusetts. Now Chantrell was crying, too. It appeared as though she and Maxime called off whatever relationship they had because she stopped visiting his home during Jacquie's outings. Her new routine was bringing her cello outside next to the vegetable garden and weeping into the soil. I don't know whether it was the salt water from her tears or the fact that she only played music for ten minutes, but Chantrell's zucchini garden looked a lot like undernourished jalapeños.

Our arts colony had become a creative vacuum for our guests, but Jack's painting was flourishing. He completed three pieces that were so dynamic, I hated to see him price them for sale. Not only was Jack filling canvasses, he invited Adam's preschool class over to paint the VW Bug. The kids dipped their hands in buckets of pastel color paints and were so thrilled to be able to leave their mark on the "crazy car" as Adam called it.

I heard the crashing of glass from Randy's cottage and wondered what he'd broken now. He hadn't completed a single sculpture to show for his entire month's stay with us.

I glanced at my watch. Thirty more minutes until I had to pick up Adam from preschool. I decided to lie down for a few minutes and recharge with a nap. And perhaps while

I was at it, I'd imagine what it would be like to feel
Randy's hot glass-blowing body pressed against mine during a senseless romp in the woods. I eased back onto my
fluffy comforter, closed my eyes and pictured Randy walking toward the house to borrow the dustpan so he could
sweep shattered glass from his floor. My eyes shot open as
I remembered that I needed to pick up Windex next time I
was at the store. Okay, back to Randy. I took a deep
breath, closed my eyes, and imagined him walking up to
the house in his well-worn Stanford T-shirt and torn Levi's
asking if I had an extra lightbulb. Hmmm, that wouldn't
work, I realized. I couldn't have a tryst with him in my
own house. Cut! I rewound the videotape in my mind and
watched Randy walking backward down the path toward
his own home. Action! I saw myself walking down to
Randy's house to bring him a lightbulb. *Argh! Enough
with the lightbulbs already!* Back to Randy and his well-
worn jeans and T-shirt. He opened the door and flashed a
smile. "Thanks for the lightbulb," he said. *Lose the goddamned lightbulb already!* Strike that. "Thanks for the
masking tape," he said.

"My pleasure," I replied demurely. A gentle breeze
blew back my hair, skillfully keeping it out of my lip gloss.

"Would you like to come in for lunch?" he asked, connecting his eyes with mine.

I looked at my watch and realized I was due at the
preschool in twenty minutes. *Earth to Lucy! This is a sexual fantasy. You do not have to pick up anyone at
preschool. You do not need to buy Windex. No one needs
friggin' lightbulbs. Walk in the house and allow this man
to seduce you!*

I did not look at my watch. Instead, I smiled coyly and
walked inside the glassman's house. "Can I offer you some
wine?" Randy asked.

"No, thank you," I said. "Too many calories." My eyes
shot open.

Why do I bother?!

I put on my jacket and shoes and drove to the preschool to get Adam. I looked out the window and caught a glance of Randy working in his studio. If only I could focus my attention for ten minutes, I could have some real imaginary fun with that guy.

"Darling, I am going out of my mind with this dog!" Anjoli announced through the phone.

"Hello, Mother," I said.

"Hello. Listen, I need to vent. I am simply seething with negativity."

"I'm fine, thanks for asking. Just heading to the preschool to pick up Adam."

"Not only am I going out of my mind with this neurotic animal, they're moving them in early! Do you understand what a devastating week this has been for me, darling?"

"Moving who in?" I asked.

"The girls!" Anjoli said as if I were an idiot for not knowing. "I saw the little giggle-gaggle Tuesday evening. They're going to be so noisy, I can tell. Mrs. Mccormick left instructions so the girls could move in any time—even during summer break—and found a way to circumvent the whole probate prices and get the property transfered quickly."

"What's going on with Paz, um Spot, I mean Mancha?"

"I took him to a floatation tank to help him relax, but the salt water irritated his chewed up paws and now they're all red and scabby."

"How awful!" I cried.

"Tell me about it, darling. It's hideous."

"Mother, I mean it's awful that your dog is in pain."

"He's never going to win any dog shows with paws that look like ground round!"

I sighed. "Do you ever fear that Animal Protective Services is going to take him away from you?"

"He has a gorgeous life, darling!" Anjoli shot defensively.

"Mother, you put him in a saltwater isolation tank. Didn't you think that might freak him out a bit? And it's so, so eighties anyway. Where did you even find a floatation tank?"

"At Alfie's house," she told me. "He bought it on eBay."

"Mother, I'm here at the school. I need to run."

"So, you're on your mobile. Go in and get him. I want to update you on Kimmy. I'm very concerned about this *professor* she's seeing. And the sorority thing has me in knots. It's going to ruin the quiet feeling of the block."

"The quiet feeling on the block?" I said, laughing. "PS Forty-one is on the block. How much of a quiet feeling does the elementary school provide?! Mother, I need to go in and talk to Adam's teacher. I'll call you later."

"I'm sorry, is he studying for his SATs this week, darling? I *need* to talk. I've made a lot of sacrifices for you. I think you can take time from your oh-so-busy life and listen to your mother who is in triple *crisis*."

"Mother, there's nothing I can do about any of this right now. I'm not sure I can do anything to be helpful, really."

"You can listen, darling. Let me be heard. Let me feel that I'm not so alone in this world."

"Where is this coming from?" I asked. "Do you really feel alone in this world?"

I watched a mother emerge from the preschool, holding the hand of little Tyler who I last saw with his nose in a bucket of blue paint.

"I have always felt alone," she began. "When I was growing up, my parents never *heard* me. They never saw who I really was. They had an idea of who a good Italian girl from New Jersey should be and tried to force me into that mold. But it couldn't be done. I would not become who I was not meant to be," she said dramatically.

Out came Whitney, who I remember placing her hands in dull yellow paint when she visited our home for car-painting day.

"Since then, I have always felt alone in this world, darling."

"Wow, Mother. I had no idea. Listen, Adam is going to have similar hang-ups if I don't go inside and pick him up. Let me call you back in a few minutes."

"I'm having a chemical peel I need to leave for in ten minutes."

"Okay, I'll call you later, then. Hang in there."

That afternoon, I left a message on my mother's voice-mail, then decided to take a nap with Adam. He smelled like peanut butter and vanilla cookies. His baby lips moved as if they were suckling. I stared at him for a half hour before drifting off to sleep myself. He looked exactly like his father. I couldn't take my eyes off of my baby who was growing up far too quickly for my comfort. In that time that I watched sweet Adam sleep, I never once thought about where I had to be next, buying Windex, or goddamned lightbulbs.

# Chapter 15

Looking back, it was ridiculous to think that my mother's crisis would last longer than a few minutes. When I called her home that evening she wasn't there. I left a message and decided to give her a try on her cell phone. I don't know if I expected Anjoli to be sobbing as she wandered aimlessly through the streets of Manhattan, but I didn't think she'd be raging at a seventies party with her theatre friends. In the background, I heard "Funky Town" and dozens of people singing along, "Won't you take me to . . . Funky Town."

"Hello, hello, who's there?" she shouted into the phone.

"Mother, it's me. You sound busy."

"Lucy, is that you, darling?" Anjoli shouted.

"Yes, Mother. I just wanted to make sure you were doing all right. Are you okay?" I shouted to make myself heard.

She laughed at something going on at the party. "Lucy, I most certainly am not fine. I'm fabulous. Haven't you heard?"

*Throughout my entire life, Mother.* "Listen, if you're okay, I'm going to let you get back to your party. Jack and I are heading out for dinner."

I heard a howl in the background. "Darling, Kiki is wearing the most retro outfit. Rainbow-striped bell-bottoms and an eighteen-inch afro. Kiki, that is absolutely hilarious, darling. Where did you get that wig?!"

"Mother!" I shouted, trying to get her attention.

"Hold on a sec, Kiki. My daughter is on the phone. She's concerned about my situation. It's sweet, really, but I keep telling her Mummy can handle her own life." Her voice now spoke into the receiver. "Darling, you are a gem for calling, but everything is under control. I just met these producers who are putting together an off-off-Broadway show merging two classics in sort of a southern Jewish dysfunctional marriage thing: Fiddler on the Hot Tin Roof. Isn't that fabu?"

Mother typically invests in gay shows like *Oklahomo!* and *The Queen and I*, but she was apparently starting to venture into the world of bizarre straight productions as well.

Anjoli continued, obviously cupping her cell phone for privacy. "Kimmy brought that Nick character to the party. I'm trying not to allow his presence to ruin my evening. Anthropology. Have you ever heard of anything as ridiculous?" My mother was all over the place, as was her usual party mode. "I dated an anthropologist once. He was a complete bore. How is Kimmy supposed to live in the manner I've taught her to become accustomed to if she takes up with this rock-digger?"

*Rock-digger?*

"Is he an anthropologist or archeologist?" I asked.

"You're missing the point, darling," she snapped.

*There's a point?*

"What's the point, Mother?" I asked, not sure why I was allowing myself to get sucked into this discussion.

"Those Ivory Tower types are all the same. They think they're better than everyone else. They're so smug and self-righteous," Anjoli explained.

"So are you and most of your friends, Mother. Why don't you give the guy a chance?"

"He gives me the creeps."

Then I got it. I was familiar with Kimmy's taste in men. It wasn't as though she was one of those beautiful women who picked loser after loser, one worse than the next. I was sure that Nick was not a scary guy. But that didn't mean my mother wasn't frightened. Any time she sensed that one of her primary relationships would shift due to the addition of someone new, Anjoli freaked out. The day before I married Jack, she begged me to back out of it, crying that it would "alter the balance" of our relationship. Upon this realization, I wondered if Anjoli had said anything to Kimmy before she jilted Geoff at St. Patrick's Cathedral.

When Wendy the babysitter arrived I couldn't keep my eyes off her tongue bar. It glistened as she spoke. She walked around our home commenting about how "rad" the artwork was. I had to agree. Jack was producing like a madman these days. When he found the VW Bug, he also bought all of this scrap metal and car parts, which looked like a pile of junk to me. I kept nagging Jack to get rid of it already, but he told me he was going to make a sculpture. Sure enough, we now have a truly unique life-size man made from hubcaps, a radiator, spark plugs, and miscellaneous other crap one finds at a junkyard. "This place is da bomb," Wendy proclaimed, her tongue lighting off and on with every syllable she spoke.

At dinner, Jack and I shared our concerns about the arts colony. "We've got a show in three months and no one's done shit," Jack said. "Maxime is depressed, Chantrell hasn't played a note in days much less composed anything, and Randy's trying, but everything keeps breaking."

"And how 'bout Jacquie?" I asked. "She's just a breath of fresh air, isn't she?"

"What *is* her deal?" Jack said, laughing. "That first night, I thought she was going to be terrific. What a bitch she turned out to be."

"What's with all of the shopping?" I asked.

"I know! She doesn't take a break!" Jack added.

Although Jack and I were frustrated that our artist community was a bomb (as opposed to *da* bomb), it was fun to band together against a common enemy—them. It was us against our guests. Jack looked more serious and reached for my hand as the waiter refilled our wineglasses. "Do you think there's something we could be doing differently?" Jack asked. "Seriously, I want to turn this around and have a good show for Labor Day weekend.

Leave it to a man to want to solve the problem. I was having such fun complaining and making fun of our nonproductive artists. Maxime, Jacquie, Chantrell, and Randy were worth their dead weight in gold.

"I don't see what we could do," I said. "You know what Anjoli always says, 'Grant me the wisdom to change what I can change, to not stress out about what I can't, and the wisdom to know the difference.' "

"I think that's the Alcoholics Anonymous serenity prayer," Jack said.

"Really? The way she and Kimmy are always spouting it, I always thought they made it up."

"Luce, seriously, what are we going to do? Right now we don't have an artist colony. We've got a bunch of squatters."

"I don't think that's fair to Randy," I said too quickly. "He's trying, but everything keeps breaking."

Jack raised his eyebrow. "You've got a thing for that guy, don't you?"

I gasped with denial. "Absolutely not! I just feel for him."

"I bet you do," Jack teased.

"I mean I feel sorry for him! He's trying his best."

Jack laughed. "Luce, it's okay. I can see the guy's a good-looking, interesting artist. It's no big deal if you're attracted to him."

*Really?*

"Really?" I asked.

Jack laughed. "Sure. Don't worry about it."

"Jack, are you just incredibly cool, or do you feel guilty because you're attracted to Chantrell?" I asked.

"The weeper? Not even close."

*Then who?!*

"Oh," I smiled. "That's good, because I think she and Maxime already had an affair."

"Gee, y'think?" Jack said.

*Who are you attracted to then?*

"So you're not attracted to Chantrell?" I asked.

*Then who?*

"Nope," he said as his food was placed before him.

*Then who?*

"Jack, are you attracted to anyone?"

"Very much," he said, smiling. It was clear he meant me.

"No, really. Are you just telling me it's okay to be attracted to Randy because you're attracted to someone else?"

"No, I'm telling you because I don't want you to get yourself all worked up feeling guilty over something that's completely normal."

"If you're telling me that it's normal for a happily married woman to find herself attracted to someone else, then you're telling me that it's normal for you to do the same."

"That wasn't the purpose of my comment, but yeah, I guess you're right. It would be just as normal for me as it is for you."

*Who is he attracted to?!*

"Oh," I said, smiling calmly. "Delicious salad dressing, don't you think?"

"I guess," he returned.

*Who the hell is he attracted to?!*

"Okay, as long as we're being so honest, yes, I do find Randy attractive. And you're telling me that you have no problem with that?" I took another bite of my salad.

"None," he said after sipping his wine.

"And why may I ask is that?!" I demanded.

"Because I know it doesn't mean anything."

*Who the hell is this guy pining for?!*

"So it wouldn't bother you in the slightest if I told you that yesterday I thought about Randy?"

"Nope," Jack said.

"I mean, I *thought* about Randy." I failed to disclose that a mother's sexual fantasies are often interrupted and derailed by the mundane.

"Nope, go ahead and put him on the wheel."

"The wheel?" I asked.

"Yeah, you've never heard of the wheel before?" Jack asked. I shook my head that I had not. "You know, the roulette wheel with eight different faces on it? You take a spin, see where it lands and then, well, you know?"

"Who the hell is on *your* wheel?!" I demanded.

"Luce, come on. I'm playing around with you a little here. You're the love of my life. I'd never fuck up what we've got. I was only trying to let you know that I'm not upset about your little crush on Slippery Fingers."

"I don't think this is at all funny, Jack! Actually, I think you're kind of being a jerk. When we were separated, you had two serious girlfriends. I had sex with one retarded short-order cook in a car wash in New Jersey. This is a sore subject for me. Frankly, I feel a little cheated by the timing on our whole reconciliation. I think you owe me one—at least." Jack looked startled. "If we're so happy and unthreatened, I should get to have a fling with Randy to even the score."

"Wow," Jack said, stunned. "I didn't know you were

still upset about Natalie. Luce, we weren't together then, remember?"

Jack and I had lived together as friends through most of my pregnancy and the first year of Adam's life. Natalie was his most serious girlfriend, but there was another. She ended their relationship after Jack was called away from their New Year's Eve party to assist me with Adam's delivery.

"Just for your information, she did *not* return to Scotland to care for her ailing uncle like I told you. She freaked out in the hospital the night of your accident and said she couldn't 'deal' with the situation because the doctor thought that she was your sister."

"That doesn't surprise me," Jack said.

"It doesn't?"

"Nah."

"Why's that?" I asked.

"That relationship was fading. When I came to at the hospital and you said she took off for Scotland, I figured it was bullshit. Her family wasn't even from Scotland."

"Oh," I said. After more than a year being reconciled with Jack, I just realized that I'd always felt as though our relationship was founded on a fault line. I had always assumed that if Natalie had not left so abruptly the night of Jack's car accident, he and I would never have gotten back together. I shared this with him and he smiled sympathetically.

"How come you never told me this?" he asked.

"I didn't realize it 'til just now," I told him.

"Well, let me set the record straight, Luce. Natalie and I would've ended anyway. The accident was a catalyst for it, but that relationship was going nowhere." Jack smiled, but saw I wasn't fully over the heartbreak of the past few years. "Luce, the moment I realized we could work things out, the only woman I wanted to be with was you."

I remembered our long nights when Jack sketched my Rubenesque body. I recalled how we worked with our marriage counselor, talking about our miscarriages and subsequent isolation from each other. I remembered everything we'd been through together from the time we met as grad students in Ann Arbor to parents and arts patrons in the Berkshires. Natalie, a heaviness I hadn't even realized I'd been carrying, became a mist, evaporating into thin air.

# Chapter 16

The next week Robin dropped by in a "May Flowers" theme sweater and a long denim skirt. She had a proposition, she said: "Let's have a lunch."

"Sure," I said. "Wanna try that new Thai place?"

"Oh," Robin sounded disappointed. "I didn't mean let's go out to eat. I meant let's have *a* lunch, as in we invite a few ladies to your place for lunch."

"A few *ladies*?"

"Don't say no before you've met them," Robin encouraged. She had been trying to get me to join the Junior League since we met, assuring me it was a very down-to-earth group of women who do a lot of charity work. I always thought of it as a middle-aged sorority that I wanted no part of. To be honest, I always assumed they wouldn't want me, so it was easier to reject them first on the grounds that they were snooty, pretentious, and judged people before getting to know them. "Give it a try, Lucy," Robin continued. "You have no idea what you're missing out on until you give it a chance."

"Why do we have to do it at my house?" I asked. "Do these oh-so-proper society ladies need to see my home before they decide whether or not I'm worthy of joining their little clique?"

"Oh dear," Robin said, discouraged. "It was my idea to have the lunch at your place, and it had nothing to do with the ladies checking out your house." I heard the crashing of glass from Randy's studio and his scream of frustration. *Perhaps I should go check on him.* "If I can be completely candid with you, Lucy," Robin said, pausing for me to confirm that she could. I did. "I thought it would be fun to, you know, people-watch at your place."

"People-watch?" I asked.

"Are you going to make me hit you over the head with it? You have two great-looking guys at the place and a kitchen window that provides an unobstructed overview of the guesthouses and their inhabitants. Let a few bored married ladies come over and ogle a little. It'll be fun."

"I don't know," I hesitated, wondering if my motives were pure or if I was simply hoarding them for myself.

Robin saw straight through me. "Come on, Lucy! You can't keep all of the neighborhood eye-candy for yourself. Be a pal and share with the girls. It's not like men don't have their innocent fun going to strip clubs and the like."

I decided not to share my demographic research, which suggested that a good twenty to twenty-five percent of strip club patrons were female. It seemed to stray from the issue, and was not quite ready for Junior League ears.

"Lucy, I have been in such pain for months with this ankle," Robin said, knowingly making me feel guilty that she injured herself at my house.

"It's *still* not healed?!" I asked.

"Not fully. Has yours?" Robin returned.

"No. I've stopped limping though, which is nice."

"Lucy, back to the luncheon. It would mean so much to me."

"Why? I don't get it."

"Last week, Renee, Abby, and I had lunch, and we noticed that the things we were talking about now were frighteningly more matronly than what we chatted about ten years ago. Can you keep a secret? On Monday, I saw a pubic hair growing out of the back of my knee! Abby had a Botox goof and the wrong part of her face is paralyzed, and Renee whitened her teeth too much, and they're now transparent. Poor thing had to get veneers."

"You had a pubic hair growing from your knee?" escaped disgustedly.

"Yes!"

"Look, I've obviously got my own issues," I said gesturing to my round body. "But ogling young artists isn't going to change any of that."

"No, it won't," Robin said, her tone growing more formal. "It will, however, make us forget about it for a few hours."

"Well, I guess there's no harm," I said. Before I could finish the thought, Robin thanked me. "I can't get sued for sexual harassment or anything, can I?"

Robin laughed. "How about Wednesday? I'll bring in the food so you won't have to do anything but set the table." With my confirmation, she whisked out the door with a lightness she hadn't walked in with. I thought it odd that a group of grown women would behave like adolescent girls, but shrugged and gave it no more thought.

Later, I called Earl at *Healthy Living* magazine and left a message: "Earl, hey, it's Lucy Klein. It's been a while since we chatted, but you expressed some interest in my writing an article about life on the artist community my husband and I started. We've got three artists here now, and it's been quite an experience. I'm not sure I'll be able to give you the upbeat, inspiring piece you may have had in mind, but I think I can write something compelling and truthful. Let me know what you think."

I hung up the phone and dialed Kimmy as I found a place by the window to perch myself and watch my pri-

vate television show. Jack and Tom were replacing the
windows at Randy's with shatterproof glass while Chantrell sat in a wooden chair, staring blankly at her vegetable
garden. It was noon, but Maxime and Jacquie seemed to
be still asleep.

"Kimmy!" I said as I heard her voice.

"Kisses and hugs, Lucy. Kisses and hugs!" she replied.

"You sound chipper," I said. If I were a tall skinny
blond former model, I'd be chipper, too.

"I'm in love," she sighed.

"Nick?" I asked. "The professor?"

"Yes." I could see her flopped back on her bright orange muppet-fur chair she bought last year when she re-
decorated her place to look like Austin Power's groovin'
love pad. In high school, I could always tell when Kimmy
was talking to (or about) a guy because she let the top part
of her body hang off the chair, draping down to the floor.
"He is so completely different than anyone I've ever met.
Would you believe that when he found out I'd slept with
several of his students on, you know, Spermquest, he wasn't
at all upset."

"Really?" I said, cynically assuming that he probably
bedded several female students as well.

"No, he said that in many cultures, it's very common
for the female to seek mates solely to procreate. He knows
that what we have is love and what I had with Jimmy, Ed,
Frank, James, Todd, Phil, and that other one was just an
attempt at getting pregnant. I think Nick even said that
some women kill the guy after they've had sex with him.
*That* I would never do."

"Kimmy, are you sure he wasn't talking about black
widow spiders?" I asked.

"Oh, maybe," she pondered. "Anyway, we're talking
about maybe getting married or at least moving in together."

"Does Anjoli know about this?"

"Oh yeah, she's totally excited."

"Good, good. So when do we get to meet Nick?"

"When school gets out. We'll come up for the weekend, okay? You are going to love him. He is so totally smart about people. He's always telling me what it's like in other places. And they're, like, places I've been to and everything. I never got to find out squat about those European cities while I was modeling. It was nonstop photo shoots and runways. When Nick talks about what he did in Paris, I'm like 'that was *so* not happening at Fashion Week.' Anyway, you'll meet him, and you'll love him just as much as Auntie Anjoli does. Kisses and hugs. Gotta fly."

The following week, Robin and her friends walked past a VW Bug painted black and silver like a spider as they made their way up to the entrance of my home. Jack even made spider legs that he attached to the sides of the car. One of the women lowered her oversized Jacqueline Onassis shades to get a better look at our lawn ornament. They looked polished and moneyed to be sure, but didn't appear to have that air of superiority I expected. Abby had a blond shoulder-length flip with wispy bangs peeking out from a tortoiseshell headband, and she wore a simple elegant sweater that looked like it must have cost about $500. Her two-inch-wide-heeled shoes were the same shade of olive as her sweater and had large silver buckles on the tops. Renee actually looked hip in that I-can-afford-to-shop-where-Madonna-does sort of way. She was just under six feet with short black hair and wore jeans with graffiti on them. Under her thigh-length, turquoise suede jacket was a simple ribbed white T-shirt that also had a triple digit price tag look. The only thing about this three-some that was uniform was the square-tip French manicured nails. Other than that, they defied my expectation of homogenous Junior Leaguers.

I trotted down the staircase to greet my guests, but before I reached the door, I heard women's voices squealing with concern. I opened the door to see Abby sitting on the steps with her shoe off while Renee turned her ankle in different directions asking if it hurt when she moved it. "Yes, yes, and yes," Abby answered with her New England old money accent. Why did people always twist an injured foot around to survey the extent of the damage?

"What happened?!" I said, moving toward the women.

"Klutzo over here fell up the steps," Renee shot, good-naturedly.

Abby smiled and sparred with her friend intimately, as if they were lovers. "May I remind you of *your* little tumble in Cancun last winter, Miss Graceful."

"I was drunk," Renee defended. Then looking at me, "I was shit-faced in Cancun. This one is stone-cold sober. Great piece in the front, by the way."

"Can I get you some ice?" I asked.

"Please, if it's not too much trouble," Abby asked. Renee and Robin hoisted their friend up the final two steps. Or at least, that was their plan. Renee suddenly lost her balance and fell back three steps to the ground. As I turned around at the sound of Renee's scream, I couldn't believe my eyes. Her graffiti pant leg was twisted in an unnatural position and Renee was clutching her knee.

"Make that two ice packs, please," Renee said.

I couldn't understand what was happening. The front steps were fully repaired. I understood how Robin fell on them when they were broken. I knew that anyone could trip and fall. But the thought that three women had now injured themselves ascending my front steps was unfathomable.

Thankfully this wasn't a litigious group. "Let us call to order the meeting of the hop-along support group," said Renee as she raised her bulbous wineglass. "To new friends, new injuries, and new sights," she said, smiling mischievously.

"Goodness gracious, which one is that?" Abby asked as she saw Maxime open his front door and stretch. It was not unusual to see him still in his pajamas at this hour, but, thankfully, he had recently shaved which gave him a devil-may-care look. Last week, he looked homeless. Jacquie brushed by him and shouted at him in French.

"That's Maxime, the French artist who doesn't do any art," I explained.

"And who's Fifi La Bitch?" Renee asked, delighted by the show.

"His wife. She shops pretty much nonstop, taking short breaks only to come home and fight with her husband."

Renee laughed. "You say that like it's something negative, Lucy. Insult me no further by frowning upon my lifestyle." It was clear she was being funny, but there was an indefinable something sad about her comment. Or her delivery. I couldn't figure out what it was, but something about Renee hinted that there was pain beneath the fabulous outfits and one-liners. She was like a crystal bowl filled with warm kettle corn. But when you lifted it up and checked the bottom, you could see a layer of burnt, unpopped kernels. The kind that make you flinch from the unexpected bitter taste. The kind that may cause you to chip a tooth.

"Abby, you speak French," Robin chimed in. "Tell us what they're saying."

She listened, knitted her brow, then held one finger up as if to tell us to wait. I decided to use this opportunity to bring the Chinese chicken salad to the table. As I served, Abby began translating.

"Okay, girls, here's the poop," Abby said. "She said that Maxime is a worthless slob who ruined their lives. She didn't go into details, however, she feels quite certain that they shall never be welcome in Lyon again. I believe it has something to do with a business deal." Abby rolled her eyes and added, "We all know how those can go sour in a heartbeat. Now she's saying something about a violinist."

"Cellist," I corrected. "Her husband and the cellist had an affair."

The room became still with discomfort.

"Oh," said Abby. "He seems to be very remorseful about it. He's telling her how sorry he is and that it wasn't her fault."

"Give me a break," Renee snapped. "I can see for myself that the guy isn't even speaking, so how do you expect me to believe he's apologizing?" I didn't have to wonder why Renee felt Abby's attempts were for her benefit. "Look, the guy just walked back into the house and slammed the door. That doesn't translate to remorse in any language."

# Chapter 17

As it turned out, Abby and Robin planned the ogling lunch to help cheer up Renee, who had recently discovered that her husband was having a long-term affair. Renee explained that Dan, her husband of twelve years, had agreed to end the affair and go to marriage counseling. But every time she looked at him she said she no longer saw a man. She no longer saw a marriage. She saw an affair. She imagined what Dan and his mistress did together. What they talked about. And whether he'd ever discussed their marriage with her. She wondered how she had been portrayed. Renee said that Dan swore up and down that he had never discussed her or their marriage, but then again, he also promised to be faithful, so she didn't know what she could believe anymore.

"Do you mind if I ask why you're staying with him?" I asked.

"We've got two kids," Renee sighed. "We have a routine. We have a life together." Her voice caught. "And I love him."

I had been where Renee was now and knew what a humiliating position she was in. My situation with Jack was different because we were technically separated so his relationships were not clandestine affairs, but that is of little comfort to a woman in love. I was tempted to tell her about how Jack and I had become estranged and found our way back to each other. Loathe as I am to admit, I wasn't willing to expose my own vulnerability. I could easily convince myself that I didn't want to turn the focus on myself. God knows, after a lifetime with Anjoli as a mother, I know how incredibly invalidating that can be. But the truth was that in our new home, in this new life, Jack's and my troubles were back in New Jersey. Even the thought of speaking them aloud seemed as if I was packing them in a box and bringing them along. I suppose we always do that anyway, whether we choose to or not. But to the extent that I could control it, I decided not to show these new friends the soft, scarred underbelly of my life.

"Things can turn around," I assured Renee. "Many couples go through rough times and find that afterward their marriages are stronger than before." There. All she needed to know was that there was hope, not that I had a similar experience.

The lunch went from being a silly escape to a weighty discussion of marriage, children, and midlife. I can't imagine a group of men ever becoming derailed from their mission of ogling beautiful women. But perhaps strip joints dim the light and blast music to make it impossible for men to engage in heady discussions about their relationships.

After I stopped laughing at the absurdity of that notion, I cleared the table and turned on the coffee maker. I peeked to see if Randy was outside, but he was not. His curtains were pulled back so I knew he was up and about, but I couldn't catch a glimpse of him inside.

After our marathon luncheon, Abby agreed to host the next at her home. Rather than recoiling at the invitation to their next Junior League meeting, I accepted. Reluctantly, but I accepted. These women seemed nice enough, troubled even, which in my book was an asset. As they hobbled out the front door, I told them how nice it was to meet them and watched as they passed the giant spider on my lawn. Jack and Adam returned home and crossed paths with the limping women. Renee told the others that Adam was "a doll," which automatically brought her up a notch in my book. Funny how someone complimenting your child makes you realize how very wise they are.

When I called Anjoli that evening, I caught her in the midst of Mancha's latest treatment for his trichillomania. Apparently, she felt psychotherapy was taking too long and Mancha's group counseling sessions were a disaster. Try being an undersized Chihuahua in a room full of Rottweilers, German Shepherds, and pit bulls trying to work through their own issues. During one session, the therapist returned from a trip to the restroom to find that another dog had dug a hole in a potted plant and buried Mancha.

"Darling!" Anjoli answered with excitement. "I only answered because I saw it was you. We're in the middle of giving Mancha a white-light bath, and it is absolutely fabulous. I might take one myself as long as I've got the practitioners here. You should see how peaceful he looks right now."

"A white-light bath?" I repeated, not really knowing what more to say.

"It's the latest in spiritual healing, darling," Anjoli explained. "They set out this lambskin mat and have the person—or in this case the dog—lie on it while rays of white light are focused from, oh, I'd have to say fifty, sixty bulbs. It's so warm and snuggly, it's all I can do to keep myself from tearing off *my* clothing and joining Manchita on the mat." She paused to consider the effects on her skin. "Do you think white light has UV rays?"

"So, he's under a heat lamp?" I asked.

Anjoli pooh-poohed my description. "You make it sound so pedestrian, darling. I'm not treating some jaundiced newborn. This is a special white light bathing machine where the slenderest rays of *white* light heal spiritual disease."

"Are you sure this is safe? How hot is he getting under there?"

"Darling, Mancha is a highly intelligent animal. Don't you think he'd protest if he found it uncomfortable?"

"Not if he's cooking, Mother! Do you even know what temperature he's under?"

"The practitioners do this on themselves every day, darling. It's sweet of you to worry, but—"

"How much do they weigh?" I interrupted.

"Excuse me," I heard Anjoli say to the white-light bathers. "Is there a risk of overheating with this thing?" I heard a male voice answer but couldn't make out what he was saying. My mother made noises of understanding and approval, then returned to me. "He'll be fine. You know I would never do anything I thought would hurt my little Manchita."

Three days later, Mancha had still not regained his vision. Anjoli noticed that when she took him for his walk in Washington Square Park, the poor thing walked straight into a tree instead of stopping in front of it to pee. "His ophthalmologist says he should be back to normal in a few weeks, darling. Please do not make me feel any more guilt about this than I already do, okay, Lucy? You know what I always say about guilt."

I finished the thought for her: "Guilt leads to punishment, and punishment resolves nothing."

"That's right, darling. How pleased I am that you remember."

How could I forget? Mother espoused this philosophy every time she had intentionally or unintentionally hurt someone, which was daily. When she had affairs with married men, she repeated that she refused to feel guilty because it would only lead to punishment. And punishment, of course, solved nothing. I always hoped that during the course of her hours of meditation, she would have an epiphany and decide to change her ways. She didn't need to feel guilty, but she might stop thinking of married men as library books that she could borrow for three weeks. Alas, this never happened, as her last affair I know about was with Adam's former pediatrician.

"I would imagine you learned quite a bit from having me as a mother," Anjoli said with some satisfaction.

"You'd imagine correctly, Mother. How are his spirits?" I asked.

"Whose?"

"Mancha's, Mother! How is he handling his blindness? Poor thing doesn't know it's temporary. He's probably terrified."

"Let's not be too dramatic, Lucy. He spends most of his time in my purse. It's not as though he's out burying bones or anything. His life remains as fabulous as ever. The only thing that I do find quite disturbing is the ridiculous glasses the doctor has given him to wear."

"Glasses?!" I shrieked, imagining a Chihuahua in wire-rim specs from Morgenthal Frederics.

"They're not glass, of course, darling. They're actually black cardstock with hundreds of tiny holes. They're supposed to strengthen his eyes or some such nonsense. He looks blind in them."

"He *is* blind, Mother. How are his paws? Is he still chewing them?"

"Yes," she said with exaggerated disgust. "He can't see a pothole when crossing a street but he can still manage to find his paws and pull every last hair from them. Can you imagine how silly this little dog looks with his Ray Charles glasses and scabby little paws?" I shuddered at the thought of this poster puppy for the canine telethon.

Hours later, Mancha's paw must have hit the redial button on Anjoli's cell phone because she was clearly unaware that I was on the line. "I don't care if it is semester break, you cannot play that music so loud." A young female voice sounded apologetic and asked if they could compromise and turn the music down in another hour. "You're playing music from the roof! The whole damned block can hear your party. This is a family neighborhood. Some of us have nieces and nephews who need to wake up early for school!"

*Since when does cousin Kimmy need to wake up early for school? She hasn't lived with Anjoli in eight years anyway. And when exactly did Greenwich Village become a family neighborhood?*

Multiple female voices began talking to my mother. It seemed friendly, except on my mother's part. "No, I most certainly would not like to come in!" she said.

"I would," said Alfie. I hadn't realized that he was with her until he spoke. "Come on, love. Let's go inside and meet the new neighbors," he suggested.

Anjoli grumbled and agreed. "Let me see if I have any sterilized cotton for Mancha's ears. The last thing my poor darling needs is to blow out his eardrums now." I assumed they had walked inside because the music became louder. A few minutes later, both Anjoli and Alfie were raving about the view from the roof.

"Why haven't we done a thing with *your* rooftop?!" Alfie cried. He seemed mortified that a group of college girls had come up with an idea that had eluded him for decades.

"Oh my God, that is *the* cutest dog!" said a young woman who spoke with the "Friends" accent. "Have you *ever* seen a dog with glasses?"

I hung up the phone and asked Jack if he felt like barbequing for dinner that evening. "It's so warm out tonight," I said. "It almost feels like summer." And with the optimism and joy that often accompanies the season of leisure, I suggested we invite Maxime and Jacquie, Chantrell, and Randy to join us.

"All together?" Jack asked, incredulously. "Jacquie and Chantrell at the same table together?"

"Act as if we don't know a thing and leave the ball in their court. What do you say?"

Jack shrugged and smiled. "If it'll make you happy, okay. Gimme an hour to get to the store. Shrimp and steak sound good to you?"

"You take care of that, I'll go down and invite our guests."

# Chapter 18

Amazingly, everyone got along beautifully at the bar-
beque, including Jacquie and Chantrell. Perhaps this was
because they now had something in common—they de-
spised Maxime. He didn't notice much, having sunk into
the depths of depression, but looked up every now and
then to force a smile. Randy was a pretty easygoing guy
and seemed utterly nonplussed by the fact that everything
he touched shattered.

In bed that evening, I asked Jack if we might consider
taking Maxime to a therapist. "The man is depressed!" I
said. "As his hosts, don't you think we ought to step in
and get him help? God knows his wife isn't going to do
anything but shop until it's time for them to leave. Can
you believe she invited Chantrell to go shopping with her
tomorrow?!"

"The mistress and the wife out shopping together,"
Jack pondered as he set down his book, realizing he wasn't
going to get any reading done. "Sounds pretty French."

I laughed. "When did you get a sense of humor?" I
asked. "Really, you were so dour when we lived in Jersey.
You're like a whole new person here."

"And this pleases you?" Jack said, smiling.

"Of course," I couldn't resist leaning in to peck him. "Remember when we took that lemon oil bath?"

"How could I forget?" Jack asked, laughing. But he hadn't been laughing when it happened. I had bought aromatherapy oil, which a woman at the health food store had said would be relaxing if I diluted it in a tub of hot water. It was soothing for about twenty seconds. Then our skin began burning and itching uncontrollably. Jack was more than a little angry about losing his top layer of flesh, but the rage he felt toward me was years of built-up resentment.

"What if that happened to us now?" I asked, hoping he would say that we'd pull together better and that he wouldn't blame me.

"Why would we take a lemon oil bath now?" he asked. "We know it'll burn the shit out of your skin."

*Men.*

"What if we didn't know, and we took a lemon oil bath together, and the same thing happened. How would we handle it?" I clarified.

"I don't know. We'd get out of the tub and rinse that crap off like we did last time," Jack asked.

"But you wouldn't be angry at me like you were, would you?" I asked.

Jack knew I was hoping for assurances that we would handle such crises with greater compassion for one another this time around, but he refused to play my game. "I think I'd be more angry at you this time, Luce, 'cause now you know how harsh that stuff is on the skin. Ach, that stinging," he said, clutching his arms with the memory.

"Seriously, what do you think we should do about Maxime? It's like 'night of the living dead' whenever he's around. Did you see how bloodshot his eyes were tonight? I think he cries pretty much all day."

"Let me talk to him man-to-man," Jack offered. "I'll see if I can get him to tell me what's going on."

Not to make sweeping generalizations about men, but I can pretty well guess how this conversation would go down.

> Jack: *Everything okay? You seem down in the*
> *mouth lately.*
> Maxime: *It is fine.*
> Jack: *Okay, just checking. See ya.*

The next week Aunt Bernice called with her past-due Snatch Report. "We're awl getting lazah-beamed. Sylvia, Ina, and Shifra were awl tawking about how hard it is to keep shaving aw pubic hayahs every few days and someone suggested we get a wax job. I don't go for awl of that hot wax nonsense. You kids are crazy with that pulling-it-out-with-wax business, but theyah's a new thing you can do with lazah beams that takes the hayahs awf and they nevah grow back."

"You're getting laser hair removal?"

"Whaddya think?"

"I think they use those lasers to open bank vaults," I said, flinching with the thought.

"Only when they've forgotten the combination," Bernice replied.

*Clearly, she's missed the point.*

What do you say to an eighty-four-year-old aunt who informs you of such plans? "If it makes you happy, Aunt Bernice, then I'm glad for you."

"You don't know how hot it can get down heyah," she informed me. I wasn't sure if she meant "down here" in Florida or "down here" in her nether regions, but decided to simply move on to a new topic—*any* new topic.

"What's going on in the condo?" I asked.

"Would you believe Fanny Lipshitz had a heart attack and died at her own birthday party?" Bernice told me.

"That'll make people think twice about throwing a surprise party for a ninety-year-old woman."

"She died *at* the party?" I gasped.

"Yeah, we awl yelled 'surprise!' and she held her chest and fell to the ground. We were pretty surprised, I'll tell you. The whole thing was so sad and a little bit confusing to tell you the truth. No one knew whethah we should eat the cake or what. What are you supposed to do when the guest of honah drops dead at the beginning of a party? Anyway, the whole *mishegas* reminded me of how Rita went at the Red Lobstah," Bernice sniffed. "I miss her so much."

"So do I," I said. But I knew it wasn't the same. Rita and Bernice were inseparable. I remember going to mahjong games, Jewish Women's Federation luncheons, and the Catskill Mountains with them. They were never apart, even when they were. They were the best of friends.

It was with the hope of meeting new friends that I attended the Junior League luncheon that Renee called to tell me about. "It's a good group, and they really get a lot of community work done. Try not to let the sea of theme sweaters freak you out too much, though. First time I went to one of these things, I counted fourteen of them."

"Fourteen theme sweaters?!" I laughed. "How many women were there?"

"About twenty," Renee said. "I hope I didn't offend you. You don't have a closet full of theme sweaters, do you?"

"Please!" I scoffed, though I'd really never given any thought to theme sweaters before. Now, I could never wear one for fear of appearing uncool to ultra-hip Renee. "You're forgetting I have a theme car on my front lawn."

"Ah yes, the Not-So Itsy-Bitsy Spider," Renee said.

I found the women of the Junior League to be absolutely lovely. They were warm and welcoming and announced me as their guest as though I was a foreign dignitary. I couldn't believe they were this excited to have me as a lunch guest. When the president told everyone about my upcoming novel, our arts community, and the Labor Day open house, the well-manicured hands clapped together so heartily, I almost had to check behind me to see if there was someone else they might be applauding. Abby stood to discuss delivering balloons to a member who had just returned from a year overseas, sending flowers to another member who'd just given birth, and hiring a musician to play at the bedside of a member who had been struck ill. These women were so kind and generous. And at the same time, as Renee predicted, they all wore theme sweaters. At least three-quarters of them did anyway. Robin was in a "Little Rabbit Foo Foo Hopping through the Forest." Abby sported the "Shoe Crazy" sweater with about two dozen embroidered high heel shoes covering the front and back. There was a soccer mom sweater with balls as buttons and netting down the sleeves, and one with different colored cocktails all over it. Most ironic were the two women seated next to each other. One was wearing a sweater with fish, jellyfish, and seahorses adorning it; beside her was her friend in a sushi theme sweater.

Renee leaned in to whisper to me. "How do you think it'd go over if I wore a drug theme sweater to the next meeting?" I giggled at the thought. "Really, I could sew a hypodermic needle to my arm, a couple joints on the front, and a few lines of coke with some rolled up bills next to them?"

"Stop," I said, laughing. "Behave yourself and sign up for a committee or something."

"How 'bout some prescription bottles sewn on to the collar? *As* a collar!" Renee continued.

With a very serious tone, I said, "My father died of a heroin overdose when I was thirteen."

Renee put her hand over her mouth in shock. "I'm so sorry," she began. "If I had known—"

"So I'm less inclined to do a drug theme sweater as I am, say, a slut theme sweater," I said. Renee caught herself before laughter escaped and disrupted the slide show of the "Meals in Heels" committee serving dinner at the Veterans Administration Hospital. "Think about it. It could be big," I whispered. "Not around these parts, but I think some younger women might go for it. You know, big C-cup breasts with perky nipples knit onto the sweater, a dangling rhinestone belly-button ring, and a dragon tattoo on the lower back."

Renee smiled mischievously and placed her hand on my arm. "I'm so glad you moved to the neighborhood. Now, back to this whore theme sweater. I think we're on to something, but it needs something more. Something that really says, 'I'm a whore!' "

"You don't think the exposed tits are enough?"

"Eh," she shrugged.

"How about some sort of sign that says something like 'Admission Free' or 'Slippery When Wet'?"

"Now you're talking," Renee said. "You know, Lucy, you're a bit twisted. I like that in a friend."

"Thanks," I said.

"Eh-hem," the president cleared her throat to signal us to quiet down. The admonition was not directed solely at us. Several others had started drifting off into their own conversations.

When I returned home, Jack and Tom were staring in amazement at our water heater. "I'm telling you, bro, I didn't do a thing to it," Tom said in a tone that suggested it wasn't his first denial of the repair.

"It couldn't just fix itself," Jack said. "I don't get it, Tom. You're telling me you haven't touched this thing?"

"Think about it, brother. I'm a contractor. This is how I

make my living. Why would I be tiptoeing around your place making home repairs and not billing you for it?" To alert them of my presence, I offered that perhaps Tom was in love with Jack. Both men's heads turned to me. Tom shuddered.

"Why would you say something like that?" Tom asked.

"Oh, Tom, lighten up," I said, shooing him with my hand. "We'll still love you, regardless of your sexual orientation. You can just come clean. You're in love with Jack."

"Stop it!" he shouted, more annoyed than I was comfortable with.

"What, am I not good-looking enough for you?" Jack asked, pretending to be offended. I was relieved he did not ally himself with Tom on this.

"Seriously, brother, knock it off," Tom said.

I continued, "If it's not you, then someone who knows home repair must be in love with Jack because there's a lot getting done around here that no one's taking credit for. Where's Adam?" I asked Jack.

"Inside with Wendy," he told me. "How was the Junior League?"

"Believe it or not, they want me to join," I said, before remembering that Tom's wife was also a member. "You don't think they'll have any problem with the fact that I'm bisexual, do you, Tom?" I joked. "Those are mighty fine lookin' ladies there at the Junior League, and I'm already thinking about who I want as my first *lover*."

Tom remained motionless. "Tom, she's kidding, man," Jack said, giving him a jolt to the arm. "Y'okay there?"

"Yeah, I'm okay, brother. I need to get used to you artsy-fartsy types and your humor."

I smiled. "Yeah, we need to get used to you contractor types and your homophobia."

Tom shrugged and smiled. "Yeah, I guess so. Listen, I haven't got a problem with gays. As long as—"

"They don't make a play for you, right?" I finished. Tom nodded to concur. I placed my hand on his shoulder for a Lifesaver moment. "Tom, not too many women find you attractive, so chances are gay men won't either."

He smiled, relieved. "You're right. Thanks."

# Chapter 19

To commemorate Adam's graduation from Miss Rhiannon's preschool class, Jack painted the Bug like Snoopy, complete with a tasseled graduation cap on the roof and red scarf draped around the tires. His latest creation lasted only two days. The kids from Adam's class had become accustomed to painting the car whenever they came to the house. Far from discouraging this, Jack made sure there were buckets of green paint beside the car and plenty of his old white T-shirts whenever kids came over. The sun shined through the cloudless blue sky onto our front lawn where three picnic tables sat covered with traditional red-and-white gingham cloths weighted by pitchers of lemonade. Mothers in sundresses helped cut sandwiches into small squares while dads gathered around Jack's grill to advise him on the best way to cook a burger. It almost looked normal except for the wild toddlers tossing paint onto a giant Snoopy head.

Jack and I met in graduate school in Ann Arbor, Michigan, where there is a boulder that sits on the corner of Washtenaw and Hill Street. It's been covered by hundreds of gallons of paint over the years. Sororities and fraternities paint it every few days. Casts of shows then paint over the Greek letters. Then art students come along and cover the rock with their creations. Underneath all the paint is probably a pebble. A team of archeologists will someday remove layer after layer of paint and be able to tell a story about the history of the University of Michigan, at least from the perspective of one rock. The same could be said for the car in front of our home. I just hoped that in twenty years, it would not grow to the size of a van.

Anjoli and Mancha came for the celebration, which meant we didn't have to hire any entertainers for the event. With "Honky" and her neurotic Chihuahua, there was no need to send in the clowns, jugglers, or Disney characters. Mancha had regained his vision, but still wore the paper glasses as a precaution. His ophthalmologist thought it would be a good idea for him to strengthen his eyes and partially block the sunlight on the bright Memorial Day weekend.

Of course, Renee gravitated right to my mother which simultaneously pleased and annoyed me. People loved my mother, and I understood why. She is exciting and beautiful. With her stories of being banned from several eastern European countries and having a misdemeanor charge in Prague, she made growing older seem like a fabulous adventure. At the same time, whenever friends adored my mother, I wanted to tell them that what they saw was not all there was to Anjoli. I wanted them to understand that she was also self-serving, self-indulgent, and completely self-absorbed. I didn't mind if they loved her, but I wanted friends to see her as a whole person. A real person, not a celebrity goddess. It was tough to complain about someone who everyone sees as perfect. It was hard to listen to friends dismiss my valid gripes and defend a woman they hardly knew. When I was in labor with Adam, the nurse asked how I was feeling. Anjoli had her back turned, so she didn't realize that the question was directed at me. Apparently, every time someone says "you," Anjoli assumes they're talking to her. My mother answered that she was exhausted and asked the nurse for a glass of mineral water. This is no major offense, of course. But I'd love it if a friend would roll her eyes in solidarity with me instead of defending, "that's just Anjoli."

Anjoli wore a silver silk camisole with tiny silver studs the size of pinheads covering it. It was like an extremely feminine suit of armor when she coupled it with matching silver pants. Jack said we should put an oilcan on her head so she could complete the Tin Man look, but he knew she looked stunning then, too. He could always be counted on to gently rib my mother, which may be one of the things I love most about him.

"Your mother is so cool," Renee confided in me as the party wrapped up. "She looks so young. How psyched are you to inherit those genes?" Truth be told, I think her flawless skin has more to do with intensive maintenance than genetics. "And her name, wow! It's like a combination of Angelina Jolie." Renee was smitten, but why should she be any different than the rest of the world? "If my mother was a dancer with the Joffrey Ballet," Renee started but finished the sentence with a sigh of awe. Renee sat at a picnic table that had a backdrop of our treehouse and kicked off her sandals. She leaned in to rest her face in her hand. "What your poor mother has been through with that crazy dog and the wild neighbors. She's really had a tough year."

My mother is a master. I know, technically, she's a mistress, but given her history with married men, I prefer to use the masculine form. How Anjoli managed to garner sympathy from Renee—a woman with real troubles—was beyond me. "I would hardly call Anjoli a victim," I advised Renee.

"I know!" she exclaimed. "That's what makes her so incredible. She's been through such an ordeal, and yet she manages to run a successful business, produce theatre, and keep herself looking so amazing."

When I stopped to see my mother through someone else's eyes, Anjoli really was pretty terrific. Yes, she's a self-centered pain in the ass, but she also possesses all of the wonderful characteristics Renee noticed. There were times I thought it was me who was the self-centered bitch for not simply allowing my mother to be who she is instead of constantly defining her by how she relates to me.

Renee ran her toes through the grass and kept her eyes on Anjoli, who was now holding court with the Junior Leaguers. They too seemed enthralled by her, nodding and smiling at her every word.

Adam waddled over to Anjoli and crookedly held out a plate for her. "Honky food!" he shouted. Mother was never into that whole bending down to talk to children routine. She looked down and told him she didn't eat hamburger, but asked him to leave the plate on the ground so Mancha could nibble on it a bit later. Adam looked perplexed. "Honky no want the buggers?"

She scrunched her face with disgust. "No, darling. Honky most definitely does not want any buggers, but thanks so much for asking."

I wasn't sure whether my motives were purely benevolent, or whether I was competing with Anjoli for Renee's affection, but I decided I would confide in my new friend about how Jack's and my marriage was on the brink of failure just three years earlier. That would show Renee who really overcame hardships. Compared to marital erosion, noisy neighbors and a neurotic dog would seem like small potatoes. Oh yes, and it would let Renee know that she's not alone in her Pompeii-like marriage. Sometimes I was more like Anjoli than I cared to admit. The cruel injustice is that I was somewhat aware of my character flaws, and was troubled by my deficits. Anjoli had the luxury of delusion.

"How's everything going with Dan?" I asked Renee,

who interrupted her sipping of a margarita at the mention of his name.

"Okay," she shrugged.

"Oh, I'm sorry if I'm overstepping. It's just that your situation reminds me of my own a few years ago." Renee raised both eyebrows as if to ask me how so. I lowered my voice and continued. "Jack asked me for a divorce three hours after I found out I was pregnant with Adam."

"Really?" Renee said, urging me to continue.

"I was getting ready to tell him the big news when he dropped this bomb on me and said he wanted out of the marriage."

"Wow," she said, but clearly meant *Go on*.

"Anyway, we spent more than a year living together as friends, if you can imagine that. It was horrible. I was still completely in love and willing to make it work, but Jack was out dating and moving on with his life as a single guy. He even got serious with this one woman. Took her along to the park with Adam. Brought her home to watch movies. It was hell."

Renee went from being amused to compelled by my story. She was no longer smiling, but looking wounded, as though any story of a fractured marriage hurt her personally. I decided to stop. As surprisingly freeing as I found this confession, it was having the opposite effect on Renee.

"So what happened?" she asked urgently. "I mean, obviously you're back together, aren't you? You're not still just friends, right? What ever happened to the other woman?"

I smiled and realized I was mistaken about her reaction. "Her type will always show their true colors when the chips are down. Jack got into a car accident and guess how long it took for her to dump him after that?"

Renee smiled naughtily. "A few weeks?"

"Try a few hours. Jack wasn't even conscious before

she tore ass out of the hospital. She asked *me* to break up with him for her, so she wouldn't have to wait around at the hospital."

"You're kidding?!" she shouted, unwittingly catching the attention of our other guests.

"I'm not. So I guess what I'm trying to say, Renee, is that things can turn around. Our marriage was over, but Jack and I are happier than ever now."

"Did you go to marriage counseling?" Renee asked.

"We did," I confirmed. "Listen, this is just between us, okay? I only told you because I want you to know that you're not alone. We've all been there, we just don't talk about it." I realized, of course, that by asking her to keep this information confidential, I was perpetuating the problem of women feeling isolated in their misery. Still, I wanted to maintain some control over my personal life.

"Wow, that's pretty incredible," Renee said. "I'm glad for you, but I'm not sure I'm going to get the same happy ending." She smiled. "Thanks for sharing that with me, though. I really appreciate it." She tapped my arm affectionately. "You're pretty amazing, Lucy Klein. But I don't know why that should surprise me. Look who you've got as a mother!"

As soon as Renee uttered the word, my mother's shriek could be heard for miles. The entire party stopped their conversations. Even the kids stopped bouncing in the inflated house to see what happened.

"Honky falled down!" Adam said and started crying.

Jack rushed toward her body sprawled in front of the house. Anjoli's hip thrust out and her right hand was on her forehead. It was too sexy a pose for a serious injury. "My hip, my hip! I've broken my hip," she shouted as a crowd gathered around her. She sobbed but also managed to blot her tears delicately away so her mascara would not run. "They say if you break a hip, you're likely to be dead the next year."

"I think that's only elderly people," Jack said.

Anjoli clutched her chest at the very mention of the word. "Well, I should be fine then. Help me up, darling." She stood and limped into the house where I offered to call a doctor. "I really *will* be dead within a year then!"

As it turned out, Anjoli did not break her hip, but she did have a nice bruise to show for her tumble up the walkway to the house.

Jack and I exchanged a concerned look. "Our injuries-to-artwork ratio is disturbing," he commented.

"I know," I said softly. "What is the deal?!"

# Chapter 20

The next afternoon my office phone rang. From the window I watched Anjoli sitting in the backyard sipping her tea and reading the newspaper as Adam tossed a gumball-sized rubber ball for Mancha to retrieve. They were perched in the area overlooking the guesthouses, all three of which were motionless with inactivity. I'd seen Jacquie and Chantrell leave for the mall that morning. Maxime had taken off for one of his eternal hikes in the woods an hour earlier, and Randy had driven to town to purchase materials at the glass supply shop. (Who knew there was such a place?)

After spending his entire life with my mother, Mancha was no ordinary dog. He watched Adam toss the ball and just stared at it through his paper glasses. "Get ball, Cha-Cha!" insisted Adam. If a Chihuahua could make facial expressions, I knew his would be one of *You've got to be kidding?* The dog had no instinct to chase balls or engage in any other such canine silliness.

"Lucy?" said a man's voice though the phone. I turned my head away from the window to focus on what the caller was saying. "It's Earl from *Healthy Living* magazine," he said. I sank into my hunter green leather chair which sat in front of my rustic, burled wood desk that

Jack made for me. I loved how it looked like a slice of tree with its undefined edges and tree rings on the surface. "Listen, sorry it's taken me so long to get back to you. I was camping in Juneau. Y'ever been to Alaska?" I told him I had not. "Beautiful country. Don't miss it. Really a sight to see. Anyway, I got your message, and I'd love to have you do a story for the 'Living the Dream' section. The piece you did on the flaxseed revolution is still getting letters." This *had* to be a lie. Even I was bored by my pitiful attempts at humor throughout that thoroughly dull piece. "So tell me what you've got goin' on there in your little corner of heaven?"

I sighed. "Earl, I've got to be honest with you. The dream has turned into a nightmare."

"Sorry to hear that," he replied. I peeked out the window again to see Mancha repeatedly reject my son's efforts to play with him. "What's going on?"

"First of all, not one visiting artist has created a single piece of art. The French guy has sunk into a depression and doesn't do anything, much less sketch. He had an affair with the cellist who doesn't play cello, but now goes out on endless shopping excursions with Maxime's extremely bitter wife."

"Maxime is?" Earl asked.

"Oh, sorry. Maxime is the French guy who used to do absolutely stunning sketches with thousands of ink dots the size of a needle prick. His wife, Jacquie, seemed like a breath of fresh air when she arrived, but quickly became a vitriolic demon of consumption. I'm serious, Earl, *all* this woman does is shop," I said, laughing at how absurd it sounded. "So Maxime took up with Chantrell for a few weeks. She completely abandoned her cello and her research on the effect of music on vegetables."

"Really?" Earl said, interested. "What effect is music supposed to have on vegetables?"

"I don't know. She was involved in some fruit and

flower research project before and wanted to expand it to vegetables."

"Sounds fascinating," Earl said.

"Except she doesn't play anymore, so the only definitive result we have is that complete neglect of vegetables leads to their death," I said. "She doesn't even water them anymore."

"Harsh," Earl said.

"But wait, there's more!" I said, imitating the tone of an infomercial hostess. "A month later, the glass sculptor arrived, and he's neither depressed nor unpleasant, but everything he touches shatters. Even things he doesn't touch! Every window in his house broke within weeks of his arrival. Don't you find that odd?"

"I'll spare you the joke about people living in glass houses," Earl said.

"Please do." I laughed. "So now, I have three completely unproductive artists and an open house on Labor Day that we've already advertised. The entire community will show up and see the artist colony where no art is made. It's a disaster."

"Sounds like it," Earl said, sympathetically.

"Oh, it gets better," I continued. "Every woman that passes through the threshold of my home gets some sort of leg injury. I sprained my ankle on a walk in the woods. My friend, Robin, broke hers. We've had knee injuries, twisted limbs, and bruises."

"Really?" Earl sounded piqued with curiosity. "Only the women?"

"Yes, not only are the men spared from injury, but they're assisted with home repairs."

"What do you mean?" Earl asked, intrigued.

"I mean that Jack and our neighbor Tom, who does handy-man stuff around the house, say that home repairs are getting done by themselves. Leaky faucets, bad wiring—all getting fixed without either of them lifting a finger!"

"Lucy," Earl said tentatively. "Can I propose something radical?"

"I think I can handle it."

"Have you considered the house might be haunted?" he asked.

"Haunted?" I repeated, incredulous. "Haunted like *Poltergeist* haunted? Haunted like 'I see dead people' haunted? Haunted like 'get out' *Amityville Horror* haunted?"

"Well, those are movies, Lucy," Earl said. "What I'm talking about is the more mundane haunting. You know, spirits stuck between worlds?"

I had grown up with this sort of talk, so it's not as though the idea of spirits stuck between worlds was something I'd never heard about before. It's just that this was Anjoli's realm. If anyone should have a haunted house, it should be her. She'd know what to do. Hell, she'd have a good time with it, throw a bon voyage party for the spirits or something. She'd have actors dressed like dead celebrities. It would be on Page Six.

"I don't know what to say," I told Earl. "I never considered it. I suppose anything's possible."

"Now that would be a story!" Earl exclaimed. "Even better than flaxseed, I'd say!"

"I'm not sure, Earl," I said. "I'm not sure I believe in haunted houses. I hope I'm not offending you, but it sounds a bit flaky."

"Oh," he returned with a tone that let me know I had, in fact, offended him.

"Earl, please. All of my life I grew up with a mother who was into every New Age trend. I've seen it all, and frankly, I like living in a world where reason and logic dictate my actions." I couldn't help laughing aloud. "Okay, maybe not reason and logic, but the whole paranormal thing just doesn't resonate with me."

"I understand, Lucy, but the fact is that it doesn't need to resonate with you to be real. Your house sounds like it's haunted, and whether you choose to respond to it or not is your decision. But if it were my place, I'd look into it and fast."

I couldn't believe what came out of my mouth next. "How would I even know if the house really is haunted?"

I could practically see Earl smiling on the other end of the phone as he delivered his easy joke. "Who y'gonna call?"

"Don't say it." I laughed.

"Ghostbusters!" we sang in unison.

"Seriously, Earl, who investigates this sort of thing? I mean, I don't want some charlatan coming in and charging thousands of dollars for a problem that doesn't even exist."

"You can buy ghost detection equipment on the web. It's fairly inexpensive," Earl said. I wondered why we were even having this conversation. There was no way my house was haunted. There was even less way I was going to order ghost-seeking equipment and hunt for spirits lingering in my home. I thought the guys who combed the beach for lost coins and watches looked ridiculous. I cannot even picture someone using a ghost detector.

"I need some time to digest everything you've said." I learned that dismissal years ago when a client said it to me. At the time, I thought it was a polite way of letting me know that my complex concept needed time to be broken down and properly appreciated. Now I know it's a nice way of saying: *This conversation is over.*

I went outside to join Adam and Anjoli who were still content in the backyard. "Reading anything good?" I asked my mother. She looked up and smiled. "Nothing more interesting than what you have to say, darling. What's the good word?"

Maybe the house was possessed. Who was this woman inquiring about me?

"No barking at lady!" Adam scolded Mancha who was

yelping toward the guesthouses. I looked down, but there was no one around. I was grateful that Mancha wasn't barking at Jacquie, our resident Cruella DeVil, who I suspect would want to skin him and make a pair of gloves for herself. Well, one glove maybe. Mancha yelped again and Adam reprimanded him similarly.

"That's been their little game this afternoon. Mancha barks and Adam tells him not to bark at the lady. It's really quite irritating, darling. I keep hoping one of them will do something different, but it's the same tedium over and over again," Anjoli said. She shrugged. "Kids, dogs, what are you going to do, right? They *are* cute, but not exactly stimulating, are they?"

Needless to say, my mother didn't knit booties, pinch cheeks, or do any other grandmother standards.

"Mother, do you find anything odd about the house?" I sat next to her. Anjoli lowered her reading glasses and asked what I meant. "I mean, do you think there's something wrong with the house?"

Anjoli waved her hand as if to dismiss my concerns. "All houses have problems. I've got old plumbing and a goddamned sorority house across the street. You should see the place. The oldest one of them is twenty-two."

"Honky, look at the lady!" Adam shouted, pointing at a grove of trees.

"Adam, I've said hello to the lady three times now, darling," she said in her sing-song voice. "I'm sure she feels properly greeted by us all."

"Say hi to the lady, Mommy!" he said to me.

"Hello, lady!" I shouted and waved.

Anjoli was growing impatient. "Why can't he watch TV for an hour?!"

"I think it's great that he uses his imagination for play," I said. "Miss Rhiannon says Adam is very bright and has conversations with his imaginary friends every day."

"And this is positive?" she whispered so Adam wouldn't

hear. "Back in my day, kids that did that were oddballs. It wouldn't kill him to watch a little "Sesame Street" every now and then. We didn't do this whole imaginary friend nonsense back when you were a baby. I popped you in front of the TV and came back when it was time for bed."

"The lady is flying!" Adam shouted as his gaze followed a path in the sky. Mancha joined him barking in the same direction.

"Mother! Don't you find this odd?!"

"Extremely, darling," Anjoli returned. "I think you're turning an otherwise normal little boy into a social outcast. Don't listen to that hippie teacher of his. Tell him that there is no lady and get him a video, or at least a truck or something real to play with so he's not incessantly chattering and disturbing people. He sounds like Rain Man over there."

Some of my friends tell me they can't stand listening to their mothers' constant cooing over their children. Mine just said she believed my son to be an idiot savant and suggested I remedy him with a ten-hour daily dose of Cartoon Network.

"Mother, I'm going to say something a bit strange for me, but I'm hoping that you, of all people, will understand." Anjoli nodded. "Do you think there's any bizarre chance that the house is, well, maybe slightly, um—haunted."

"Haunted?!" Anjoli said.

"I know it sounds odd, but there have been some strange things going on since we moved in," I explained.

"It doesn't sound odd, darling," Anjoli said. "It's not at all unusual for an old house to have visitors from the other side. It's impossible, though. Remember that when you moved in last year, I performed the space-clearing rituals that would rid your new home of any ghosts."

"Oh, yes," I said recalling Anjoli burning sage and chanting in every corner of the house. She took a class through the Learning Annex and was so thrilled with her newfound ghost-busting skills that she considered starting a side business. She gave up the idea after she found out how "exhausting" it was to rid our home of apparitions.

"So you see, darling, it's not possible to have ghosts unless you think my space-clearing rituals were ineffective." I said nothing. "You're not suggesting that my space-clearing didn't take, are you?"

It was then I realized that my home was absolutely, positively, without a shadow of a doubt, spooked.

# Chapter 21

"You think the house is *what*?" asked Jack as he began changing into a shirt for dinner. I love the way he looks after he scrubs every last bit of the day's paint off of his body, combs his wet hair to the side, and puts on a clean shirt for an evening at home. Honestly, I adore the way he looks as he's painting as well. Sometimes I go down to his studio and watch him. I stand in the doorway, and he doesn't even notice me there. He narrows his eyes with concentration, steps back, shakes his head, and returns to his stool to continue or correct his work. When I see him so engrossed in his painting, I know we made the right decision moving here so he could pursue his art. Haunted or not, I loved this house.

I sat on the edge of our bed and watched him button his shirt and start searching for his jeans strewn on the bedroom floor. "I didn't say I think the house is definitely haunted, just that it might be," I said.

Jack smiled. "Oh well, as long as you're not saying definitely." He laughed.

"Jack," I whined, urging him to take my suggestion more seriously. "Can't you even entertain the idea that something like this is possible? I mean, do we really know everything there is to know about life after death?"

After he buttoned his jeans, Jack sat beside me and addressed me without smiling. He placed his hand on mine and said he could not possibly consider that the house was haunted. "I'm sorry, Luce. I can't even go there. It's not in my nature to believe in that hocus-pocus."

"But the leg injuries, the personality changes, the complete black hole of art down there," I said gesturing to the guest cottages. "Do you really think that's a coincidence?"

"Yeah," he said. "I do. Look, I'm not saying you can't believe the place is haunted, but don't get mad at me if I don't agree with you."

His response took me back to our days in marriage counseling where Etta would remind us that we could be a stronger, more united couple when we accepted each other as individuals. That is, Jack could have his quirks and idiosyncrasies, and I didn't have to attach my identity to any of them. The reverse was also true, as he was now reminding me. I sort of missed our therapist back in New Jersey. Going to counseling forced Jack and me to sit down once a week and really listen to each other. We broke so many old habits like immediately defending charges that weren't even launched and blaming each other for failings in the relationship. And, of course, couples counseling also gave us a common language to speak—and a common person to make fun of at home. We had more laughs at the expense of our therapist and the way she habitually drew diagrams on her dry erase board. I even bought a white board and mounted it in the kitchen so I could do my impressions of Etta when Jack and I had a disagreement at home.

"No, I'm not mad at you, Jack," I assured him. "But I feel a little embarrassed that I'm even considering this, and it would be of great comfort to me if you also thought it might be a possibility."

"Sorry, hon, but I don't," he said. "It's too *Anjoli* for me."

"Fair enough," I returned.

"I won't stand in your way, though, if you wanna, you know, do something about it," Jack said. "I mean, if it makes you feel better to get the place, I don't know, de-spooked, I won't give you a hard time about it."

"You won't think it's silly?" I asked.

"Luce, I will think it's silly," Jack replied. "What I'm saying is that if you feel like you need to do something, I won't stand in your way."

I took a deep breath and suppressed the urge to try to convince him to see things my way. I wasn't even sure I saw things my way, and Jack was far more pragmatic a person than I. He hadn't grown up with Anjoli as a mother. My mother-in-law, Susan, had been Jack's den mother for Cub Scouts. She was a member of the Soroptimist Club in Winnetka, Illinois. She'd served as the PTA treasurer for all of the years her kids attended the local elementary school. If I was having trouble accepting the idea that our home might be haunted, how could I expect anything more from Jack?

"You're right," I said. "This is crazy talk. Of course, the house isn't haunted. I guess I want so much for there to be a reason for everything that's gone wrong. I was so eager to pinpoint a cause to our problems, but it's really rather ridiculous, isn't it? As soon as you said you'd support my de-spooking the house, I realized how flaky it sounded. *Haunted house*," I scoffed. "Forget I ever mentioned it."

"Forgotten," Jack said with a wink. "Now, let's eat."

The next morning, I woke up to the sound of the phone ringing. I rolled through my cloud of cotton sheets to see that Jack was still in bed, a rarity after six. The clock read 7:48 A.M., which made me smile with a sense of mischievous accomplishment. I'd completely exhausted him the night before.

"Hello," I said groggily. It was Renee in tears.

"Sorry to call so early," she sobbed.

I sat upright and took the phone into the hallway so I wouldn't wake Jack. "No problem. What's going on? You sound upset."

"Dan and I had a huge fight last night. He stormed out at midnight and when I woke up this morning, I saw he'd never come home."

"Whoa," slipped out. There seemed little else to say because the next questions seemed to have obvious answers. I dared not ask where he went, but did make a pitiful attempt to convince her that this may not appear as bad as it seemed. "Are you sure he didn't just wake up early to go, um, jogging or something?" These feeble attempts were always done as much for my benefit as the other person's. I hate to admit, but I am so squeamish with other people's discomfort that I try to make it go away as quickly as possible. Sure, I want to help my friend feel better, but I also want to escape the painful reality in which we are both trapped.

Renee laughed. "Oh, that's right, you've never seen Dan. Well, let me assure you, he's not out jogging. I might buy it if you said he got up early to get himself a dozen Krispy Kremes."

This depressed me more than anything. A woman in her forties with a few extra pounds—okay, we're talking about me—was as sexually marginalized as a pair of old tennis shoes, while Pudgy McButterball had a beautiful wife and a mistress on the side.

"Can I come over?" she said. Renee had always sounded so self-assured, it was unsettling to hear her sounding this vulnerable. I had already cast her as the woman who had it all together in spite of her marital problems. Now I would be forced to see her as a more complex, textured person, which terrified me to no end. Nonethe-

less, she was a friend and her needs would have to super-
sede my fears.

"Of course," I said. "We're just getting up. Can you
come by in an hour, and we'll put some breakfast on the
table?"

"Thank you," she sniffed. "I've got to bring my kids. Is
that okay?"

"Of course, I just set out the inflatable pool yesterday
so they can splash around in it."

"Eric will like that," she said of her four year old. "Jenna's twelve though, so she's far too cool for kiddie pools."
I could see Renee rolling her eyes with exasperation at her
high-maintenance adolescent. (Is that redundant?) "She
can bring a book or her cell phone. I just don't want to be
home alone 'cause I know I'll start crying and the kids
can't see me that way."

I always wondered about that parental choice. On one
hand, I understand the instinct to shield one's children
from unpleasantness. On the other, I wondered about raising kids who were unaware that their parents experienced
real emotions. When Jack's father left their family, Susan
put a smile on her face and never spoke a word of her ex-
husband. As a result, Jack grew up thinking all negative
feelings should be shoved under the bed, out of sight and
never to be spoken of. During our marital blue period—
the years that followed a series of miscarriages—Jack constantly dismissed my bereavement my telling me "don't
feel that way" or worse, "you shouldn't feel bad." It
caused a wedge between us that took years to remove. I
felt for Eric's future wife if Renee continued along the
same path as Susan's.

"Of course they can come over," I said. "But don't
worry about your kids seeing you upset. You're human,
and it's good for you to show them that it's okay to experience a full range of emotions."

"I don't know how positive it is for them to see me stuff daddy's clothing with pillows and stab him in effigy," Renee said, sniffing.

"Point taken," I said. "All I'm saying is you don't have to be a martyr. If you need to cry, your kids can handle it."

"Is Anjoli still there?" Renee asked. I confirmed that she was, wondering how it would go over once Renee found out that Anjoli was on the flip side of several affairs. My mother wasn't exactly secretive about her history, as she saw very little condemnable about her behavior.

When Renee and her kids arrived, Anjoli was setting the table in the backyard. I had debriefed her and Jack on the situation so neither would say anything that may inadvertently upset her. Jack had already commented on the fact that Dan never accompanied her to events, and Mother had a habit of espousing her self-acquitting philosophy on infidelity at every opportunity. I couldn't bear the thought of Jack innocently remarking, "Hubby's left you alone again, eh, Renee?" Even worse was the image of Anjoli sipping tea, pondering why married women don't look within for the answer to questions about why their husbands go astray.

"Not to worry, darling," Anjoli assured me. "I'm very sensitive to other people's feelings. In fact, at a workshop last weekend, I was told that I am an intuitive, always tuned in to the feelings of others."

"Really?" Jack said as he brought out a pot of coffee. He couldn't resist. "Let me ask you—what was the name of the person who told you this?"

Setting the silver down beside each plate, Anjoli tilted her head to look at Jack to reply. "It was the *leader* of the workshop," she said, impressed. Adam sat facing the guesthouses and sang a song as he jerked Elmo around by the neck to make him dance. Mancha sat quietly beside him as if he were ready to pounce.

"What was his name?" Jack asked.

"It was a woman," Anjoli replied, now actively dodging the question.

"Okay, what was her name?" Jack asked.

Anjoli shifted her eyes back down toward the table. "It was Camilla," she said.

"Really, so if I went to the website of this workshop, I'd see that the leader's name was Camilla?" Jack asked.

I shot him a look as if to say he was very naughty for trying to catch Anjoli in a lie. We all knew she didn't remember the leader's name. Why did he need to prove it? There was a part of me that wanted childishly to scamper to him and give him a high-five for having the moxie and wit to challenge my mother the way I never could. Another part wanted to stand by her side with my hands on my hips and reprimand him for teasing her. But I understood their relationship was one of playful antagonism, so I let them enjoy their repartee.

"Indeed you would, Jack!" Anjoli said, unable to contain her smile.

"Okay, let's go to my computer right now and look it up. What was the name of the workshop?"

"They don't have a website."

"No website?" Jack said. "How unusual. So how does Cynthia let people know about her workshops?"

Anjoli shrugged. "Couldn't tell you, darling."

"Ah-ha!" Jack shouted, catching the attention of boy and dog, possibly even the guests in their cottages fifty yards below. "You said her name was Camilla, but when I called her Cynthia, you didn't even notice, which means you never knew her name to begin with. You made it up when pressed because you couldn't admit the cold, hard reality that you didn't even know the name of this person who said you are soooooo sensitive to others."

"Listen, Perry Mason, I don't want to pop your bubble of theatrics, but you are way off base," Anjoli said with mock indignation.

"Am I?" Jack said, smiling. "Or is my mother-in-law a big, fat liar?!" He laughed and Anjoli could not help but join him.

"I am *not* fat, darling," she said.

"But you are a liar," Jack said, patting her back.

"Honky a liar!" Adam shouted, clapping his hands with delight. Mancha barked.

In the midst of our laughter, the doorbell rang, which cut us all off abruptly. My mother clapped her hands like a director and ordered us to change our tone. "We have sad people with *real* lying relatives with us now. Let's be sensitive and take it down a notch, shall we, darlings?"

# Chapter 22

Renee was surprisingly upbeat as she came through our front door. It was her daughter, Jenna, who seemed glum. "This is my friend Lucy," Renee said. The girl tried to be polite, but clearly she had her heart set on being somewhere else—anywhere but here. After breakfast, Jenna warmed up to us, though. Jack offered her twenty-five dollars to supervise Adam and Eric in the pool. Of course, our eyes would never leave the kids, but having Jenna as their paid entertainment allowed us to focus on Renee who whispered through her tea that she felt as if she was going to burst into tears at any moment.

With the kids out of earshot, Renee confided in Anjoli that she had heard from Dan before she left to come to our place. After breakfast, Jack excused himself to paint the Bug. He said that with the official start of summer, he wanted to do a surf-and-sand beach buggy theme. As he left, he showed us his sketch of blue waves of ocean splashing up the sides and an old surfboard he'd bought on eBay that he planned to mount on top.

"So he called this morning and said he wanted to let me know he wasn't dead or anything," Renee said, leaning in toward my mother and me. "I suppose that's something." Anjoli couldn't help releasing a sigh of exasperated annoyance. I said nothing, but urged Renee to continue. "I mean, I know he was with *her*, so what am I supposed to do? He swears he was at a hotel—alone."

The late morning sun baked the three of us under its bright rays, though it probably had a tough time fighting through the wide rim of Anjoli's straw hat and gauzy full-length dress. Ice from the tea pitcher had melted, and a bee buzzed around it, threatening to dive in to taste the honey settled at the bottom. The songs of the flitting birds made for a most incongruous soundtrack for the discussion below.

"And what do you think?" I asked.

"Oh, please," Anjoli said, rolling her eyes. "Renee's a smart woman. She can put two and two together, darling."

I was a bit surprised that Renee had opened up to my mother so easily, and wondered if she regretted it after hearing mother's harsh assessment. "You think he was with her too, don't you, Anjoli?" she asked.

"Darling, I know you'd like to believe otherwise, but clearly he's still carrying on with this woman."

"Mother, you don't know that for sure!" I said. *Unless it was you with Dan in the hotel room last night, in which case I'd have to slit my wrists with the butter knife right now.* "You have no idea what kind of person Dan is! He could have ended his affair just as he promised and may very well have been at a hotel alone."

Anjoli turned to Renee. "She's right, darling. I don't know your husband. I'm simply basing my assessment of his whereabouts last night on my experience with men, which, I might add, is vast. But Lucy is correct. I don't know Dan. You do, though. Does his story jibe with you?"

"I wish it did," she said. "I try to convince myself that his story is true, but it doesn't make sense. Why stay at a hotel? Why not come home and sleep in the den? He must have called *her*."

I couldn't figure out what bothered her more—the infidelity or not knowing. I can't imagine which would be worse.

"Look at me, Honky!" Adam shouted.

"How are they doing, Jenna?" I shouted.

"Perfect, Mrs. Klein," she returned. Jenna seemed genuinely happy walking across the pool to create waves for the boys.

"Maybe you should do a little something nice for yourself, darling," Anjoli shifted the focus back to our conversation. As if on cue, Randy walked up the front path to his house and turned to wave at us. "Like him."

"Mother," I said, laughing. "You're incorrigible. Don't listen to a thing she has to say, Renee. Her own marriage lasted something like forty-five minutes."

"Lucy's father was a drug addict," Anjoli said too lightly. She always delivered this as a blithe one-liner, failing to realize that it was like a body-slam to me every time she said it. "I wanted to go to the ballet. He wanted to get high and stare at a fishbowl." I've heard that characterization of their marriage no less than a hundred times throughout my life, and every time, it gets a laugh. I wish our house actually was haunted and my father's spirit could fly above her and dump an aquarium over her head.

"Anjoli, you've gone through so much," Renee said with a tone of adoration. *Come on, it's not like the woman built the pyramids. She had a brief marriage to my father who realized that the best way to go through life with Anjoli was with a hypodermic needle in his arm.*

"I am a survivor, darling," she said as if she was starring in a black and white film. "And so too shall you be, darling."

*Oh please!*

"You are such an inspiration!" Renee said. "You've helped me so much today." As she looked at me with her glassy brown eyes, I knew what was coming next. "You are so lucky to have a mother like Anjoli."

I glanced at Anjoli, who winked at me, feigning modesty. As much as I tried, I could never really stay angry with her for long. She meant far too well to ever really earn my disdain. Yes, she was selfish. Yes, she was exasperating. And yes, a part of me had to admit, I was a bit jealous of the spell she cast on the world.

"I know," I said.

"I'm dead serious, darling," she said to Renee, gesturing back down to Randy's guesthouse. "Have yourself a little fun on the side and see if that doesn't snap Mr. Ramada Inn out of his complacency-induced coma. He doesn't realize what a treasure he has in you, Renee. It's up to you to make him realize that if he doesn't wake up and start treating you the way you deserve, someone else will."

Renee glowed with Anjoli's praise. "He is hot," she said of Randy.

"No, no, no!" I interrupted. "Look, I agree with Anjoli that you're wonderful and beautiful and deserve better than the deal you're getting with Dan, but having an affair with Randy is not the solution." *Because he's mine!* If I had a dry erase board, I would have pulled an Etta, and sketched a triangle to illustrate the two people in a relationship and the distraction that takes time and attention away from the couple. "Having an affair with Randy isn't going to solve your problems with Dan." *Try Maxime!* "All you're going to do is delay the inevitable, and that's either reconciling your marriage or ending it."

"Darling, don't be such a killjoy. A good Randy romp, pun completely intended, will give her the confidence she needs, not to mention he looks like a fun way to spend the afternoon. Who says she needs to solve any problems with Dan? From where I'm sitting, he's the one who needs to beg forgiveness and make the effort to get the relationship back on track, if that's what Renee even wants!"

What did Renee want? We'd gotten so far offtrack with our discussion of extramarital affairs that we'd lost sight of what we were there to do—support Renee. Then again, she was laughing and enjoying herself far more than she would have at home, so I suppose we were being somewhat helpful.

"Renee, what do you want?" I asked.

"I'm not sure," she said. "I want him to be sorry, and I guess I really do want things to work out still."

"Let me share a little something with you, darling," Anjoli began. I could tell by the tone in her voice that she was about to disclose her role as the third party in marital triangles. I wasn't sure if this would change how Renee felt about Anjoli. In some ways, I hoped it would lower her a notch in Renee's esteem. In another way, I liked the dynamic we had going and feared losing it. "I've been the other woman." Anjoli paused to let this settle in and assess Renee's reaction. She was motionless, expressionless. For a moment, I wondered if she heard her.

Anjoli waited for a response, but got nothing from Renee. "Darling, I'm sorry if this is hurtful to you, but I am telling you because I can speak to the issue with some authority. If you want Dan back, you're in good standing. If he was going to leave you for this other woman, he would have by now."

Renee sighed. "This is a tough one," she said. "I like you Anjoli, but what you're telling me is that you're one of those women who's willing to have affairs with married men, and that I don't like. Don't you feel any sort of allegiance to other women?"

My mother sat on the bench next to Renee and put her arm around her. "I have loyalty to my friends. I would never sleep with one of *their* husbands, but I don't really know these other women, and until I met you, I never really gave them much thought. Darling, I know the right answer to your question, but I'd be lying if I told you that I've struggled with my choices. I haven't. I don't want to lie to you, darling. The truth is that no, I don't have any allegiance to the sisterhood of wives. But I do consider you a friend, and if you'll still have me as one, I can offer you a world of insight from behind enemy lines. You may not like everything about the way I live my life, but I think I've shown that I'm not a bullshitter. Take me for what I am, and I'll give you the straight scoop on affairs."

Renee considered this for a moment. "Anjoli, I'd feel so much better if you told me you were going to swear off married men forever. I mean, can't you see how horrible this has been on me?"

"Darling, I promise you this. I'll think about it."

"You'll think about it?" I asked, impressed.

"Fair enough," said Renee, who I could tell was dying to question Anjoli about her relationships with married men. "Tell me, why did you say I'm in a good position?"

It was time for Anjoli to hold court. "I'm sure he's given her a million excuses about the children and the house and so on, but the bottom line is that your husband is a self-serving jackass and if what he wanted was to be with this other woman, he would."

"But he did leave," Renee said. "Last night."

"He spent the night in a hotel room with a woman he wasn't fighting with, darling. He spent a few hours with a woman he's having an uncomplicated, shallow relationship with."

"Why would he risk our life together if he didn't love this woman?" Renee asked.

"He doesn't think he *is* risking it, darling," Anjoli said. "I'm sorry to be blunt, but what consequences has he paid so far for his transgressions?"

"Mother, are you suggesting that she make false threats about leaving?" I asked. "If she wants to rebuild the marriage, should she really be playing games like that?"

Renee's head went back and forth, listening to us. I looked at her in amazement that even on a day like this, her hair was jelled into a cool spiky do, and she had applied a thin layer of makeup. She had the gift of making a pair of jeans, a white T-shirt, and sandals appear as if they were a stylist's thoughtful selection. I had a low-hanging ponytail and wore a T-shirt Jack and I had gotten for joining the public radio station.

"Do they talk about their wives and their problems together?" Renee asked.

"Not with me, darling," Anjoli said. "To be perfectly frank, I'm not all that interested in their home lives. I'm not their guidance counselor. If they need a shoulder to cry on, they're looking for a therapist, not a mistress."

"Well, you *are* honest," said Renee. After a half hour of grilling Anjoli, Renee seemed exhausted and ready to move on to a new topic. "Okay, I've had enough chatter about my screwed-up marriage. Let's talk about something else."

"Well, Lucy thinks the house is haunted," Anjoli said.

"I don't actually think—"

"I did a space-clearing on the house when they moved in, but Lucy thinks it didn't take and the place is haunted."

"Mother, I didn't say I think it's haunted," I defended. "It's just that some weird things have been going on."

"I totally believe in that kind of thing," said Renee. "Especially with these older homes and in this part of the country. They burned witches here, you know?"

"I was a witch in a past life," Anjoli said. "Burned at the stake."

"Me, too!" Renee said, excitedly.

"I was a healer, but the townspeople were small-minded and, well," Anjoli stopped, and waved with her arms as if to say, *You know the rest.*

# Chapter 23

Renee and her kids were set to leave later that afternoon, but their departure was delayed when she made the mistake of asking Jack about his project. He explained that a VW Bug reminded him of the summers of his youth and by adding the surf-and-sand theme, he was recapturing a feeling of freedom he had as a teen. "Don't get me wrong," he said, glancing at me. "Life's good now, but there's a certain irresponsibility about the summer that I need to remind myself of these days. This is my way of saying to myself, 'Dude, school is out for the summer.' "

"God, I'd love to feel like school is out for the summer," Renee said. "I feel like I'm in friggin' detention in the middle of the winter."

Jack continued painting. "Yeah, Luce told me what's been going on. Sorry about all that. Care for a little art therapy?" he asked, holding out his brush.

"Do you mind?" she asked.

An hour later, Renee looked like a different person. Her pain visibly dissipated after painting in a way that it hadn't by chatting. I was impressed at how the paint fell onto her jeans as if by design. I am certain I would look like a drop-cloth after an hour of painting, but Renee's jeans looked purposefully adorned and incredibly hip. She also did a beautiful job on the Volkswagon, creating Van Gogh-like swirls of ocean waves.

"Love the jeans," I said.

Anjoli concurred. "If I gave you a pair of my dungarees, would you mind doing the same to mine, darling?"

Renee seemed startled by the request, but happily agreed. "If I can remember what I did," she said.

Moments later, Anjoli scampered out from the house in her light denim pants and demanded, "Do me right now, darling." I had to wonder how many times that phrase had been uttered by her in the past year alone. By the time Renee finished Anjoli's pants, I was in line waiting for my pair to be painted. Sitting in a lawn chair, I asked if she could "Pollock" my pants.

"Here," Jack began for her. "I had an art class come over and Pollock the Bug a few months ago. Let me show you how to do it." He held a dripping paintbrush over my thigh and let paint drizzle as he swept it inches over the length of my leg. When Renee finished, I was wearing a wet pair of blue jeans that seriously rivaled Alchemy. Anjoli wore Van Gogh sunflowers which suited her well.

Jack excused himself to check on Jenna and the boys and to rinse his brushes.

"Renee, you are talented!" I shrieked. "You know what?" I asked. When no one replied, I decided to continue anyway. "You should sell these!"

"She's not selling my dungarees!" Anjoli protested. "I adore these, darling. Wait until Alfie sees them. He will just about drop dead that he didn't come up with this idea."

"Not yours, Mother. She could sell hand-painted jeans. I'm sure they'd sell for a lot. How much did you pay for those graffiti pants you were wearing that first time I met you?"

She smiled. "Those?"

"What graffiti pants?!" Anjoli said. "I want to see the graffiti pants."

"Lucy, I made those," Renee said, blushing slightly.

"No you didn't!" I shouted. "I want a pair. What would you charge? I've got an old pair of jeans in my dresser."

Renee laughed. "I appreciate your kindness, but you really don't have to do this. Money isn't my problem."

"Renee, you are out of your mind if you think this is charity. I want a pair of those pants! While you're at it, I think you should seriously consider painting T-shirts. Now that summer's here, women need something fun to wear. I mean, we can't do theme sweaters all year round, can we?"

Renee was still with the thought. She was in the place between being flattered by the suggestion and considering it. She looked at Anjoli and asked: "Would you really buy these jeans if you didn't feel sorry for me?"

"Darling, let's not forget, it is I who asked for the pants to be painted." She paused, raised her eyebrows and explained, "I love these pants. I wouldn't ask you to do something to them unless I thought it would make me adore them even more. Really, I'm not that generous, darling."

But sometimes she was. And for a moment I wondered if this was one of those times.

"And I don't feel sorry for you, darling. Frankly, I'm too damned excited about how hot I look in these new dungarees to feel anything but joy," Anjoli said. "Seriously, I don't feel sorry for you. I feel sorry for your husband because he's obviously a fool to neglect a wife like you."

As Renee's car drove away, my heart softened a bit toward Anjoli. She wasn't going to win any Humanitarian-of-the-Year awards, but she had done something rare for her this afternoon. She gave something of herself.

Crossing paths through our driveway was Renee's car and a red Mustang convertible I didn't recognize until I saw a blond head bopping about on the passenger side. "Surprise!" shouted Kimmy, raising both hands over her head. "You said come visit, so here we are!" She laughed as if this were the funniest thing she'd ever heard as Jack, Anjoli, Adam, and I stood watching the car approach us.

In a pink "good girl" sundress, Kimmy flew out of the car before it fully stopped and twirled like Julie Andrews singing that the hills were alive. I would have thought she was on drugs or had fallen off the wagon if she didn't soon announce the cause for her delirium. She grabbed Nick by the hand and hurried him to us. "We are totally engaged!" I looked at Anjoli who forced a smile and congratulations.

"You must be Nick," I said, stepping toward him, awkwardly moving with uncertainty about whether I should shake his hand or hug him.

"Yes," he said, smiling broadly. Reaching out his hand, he introduced himself to Jack and apologized for coming by unannounced.

"We wanted it to be a surprise!" Kimmy said. "I proposed this morning and before we even went out to start looking for my ring, I was like, Nick, let's jump in the car and go see Auntie Anjoli and Cousin Lucy. Jack and Adam, too, of course. So anyway, we've been driving forever, but here we are!"

"*She* proposed to you," Anjoli asked pointedly.

Nick shrugged a laugh. "I would've done it myself, but when Kimmy asked, I figured, okay, this is how we're doing it. You know Kimmy always does things her own way."

His observation made me wonder if she might be pregnant with another man's child.

"Congratulations!" Jack offered.

Kimmy hugged everyone and continued, "Before we

speak another word of this, I have to know right now—
Anjoli, will you be my maid of honor?"

Anjoli had the look of a deer that was told that if it
smiled hard enough, the oncoming truck would stop.
Clumsily, she accepted. "Yes, certainly. I'd be, I'd be hon-
ored." She paused. "Darling."

"And Lucy, you're the matron, right?" Kimmy said.

"Of course I am," I said.

Kimmy shrieked with delight and said now that the
bridal party was settled, she needed to go to the bathroom.
She skipped and then leapt up the path to the front door.
But before she reached the front door, her ankle rolled inward and snapped. Nothing could faze this freshly engaged woman. She laughed and clutched her ankle as she
sat on the grass. "Whoa, am I poetry-in-motion or what?
Note to self: do not skip down the aisle."

What I loved about my marriage with Jack is how we
could have an entire conversation with facial expressions.

I popped my eyes and raised my brows as if to say, *Another woman injured her leg. Still think it's a coincidence?*

He shrugged as if to say, *Yes, I do, but like I said, if it
makes you feel better to get someone in to look at the
place, I'll be supportive.*

I pursed my lips to say, *Don't do it on my account. If
you're okay with living in a haunted house, I'm okay, too.*

As the sun set on the summer day, the six of us sat in the
backyard sipping champagne, toasting the new couple. I
tried to catch Anjoli's gaze every now and then to ask her
how she was handling the news. But she was in full performance mode, smiling, laughing, and celebrating the engagement. It was almost as if she didn't see me trying to
connect with her. Like an actor puts a fourth wall between
himself and an audience, Anjoli built a protective shield
between herself and the rest of the world.

"I love it when the sky gets pink like this," I said to no
one in particular.

"Here's to the pink sky," Kimmy said, raising her glass.

From Maxime and Jacquie's house, I saw a figure moving past the window. The front door flew open and Jacquie stood with her hands on her hips. "Keep it down up there!" she barked. "Some people are trying to sleep."

I looked at my watch. "It's eight-thirty, Jacquie. Come up and celebrate with us." A universal murmur of disapproval came from the group, including Mancha, who growled to let us know that Cruella De Vil should not join is. "My cousin just got engaged. Bring Maxime up and have a glass of champagne with us."

"If I wanted champagne, I would be drinking champagne!" Jacquie shouted. "What I want is quiet!" With that, she slammed the door loudly enough to wake the sleeping giant at the top of Jack's beanstalk.

I could tell I was really a mother now when my literary references were Disney films and fairy tales.

"Let her be," said Jack.

Chantrell opened her door and asked if she could join us. "Yeah!" Kimmy howled like Howard Dean after losing the Iowa primary. "The more the merrier." She went back into her house and returned with her cello. A few moments later, Chantrell swept her long red hair behind her shoulders and began to play for us. Maybe thirty or forty seconds was upbeat and celebrant. It then quickly descended into a melancholy, aching piece that would have been depressing enough without Chantrell weeping throughout every bar.

Again, I shot Jack a look as if to say, *This is not normal. She was so happy when she arrived.*

He looked at me and without uttering a word said, *Artists, what can you do?*

"You play so, um, nice," Kimmy said. "Do you know anything from, um, like *Fiddler on the Roof* or something?" Soon our engagement party soundtrack was "Anatevka," the song the heartbroken villagers sang as they were banished from their village by the Russian pogrom. I was sure Kimmy had meant something a bit festive, like "Match-maker, Matchmaker" or even "Sunrise Sunset."

"Darling, you have been such a love to play for us," Anjoli said to Chantrell. "But we have some family issues to sort out, you know, finances and the like, so if you don't mind." I had to say, Anjoli handled that quite gracefully until she made a shooing motion with her right hand.

After Chantrell left, Anjoli looked at me and said, "Darling, if I was ever inclined to think this place was haunted, now would be the time. That was a horror."

"She tried," said Nick. Jack reached for the champagne bottle and noticed it was empty. He went inside to get another.

"Jack won't hear of it," I said to my mother.

Turning to Kimmy and Nick, Anjoli explained. "Lucy thinks the house is haunted, which, of course, is impossible because I personally cleared the space."

"I don't think the house is haunted," I said. "I just think something is off. Every woman who comes to the house gets some sort of leg injury. Doesn't that seem odd?"

Anjoli defended her space-clearing. "I happen to know something about spirit inhabitants, and this house shows no signs of having visitors from the other side, darling." Anjoli turned to Nick and raised one brow. "You probably think this sounds incredibly flighty. Certainly they disdain any such talk in the Ivory Towers of Princeton."

"No, I think it's interesting," Nick answered. What was more shocking than his answer was the fact that he seemed completely sincere. "My dad did his fieldwork in Oaxaca. He specialized in Mexican *curanderos*, so I've always been fascinated by this kind of stuff."

"Your father studied witch doctors?!" Anjoli said.

"And tribal healing rituals," Nick said, not realizing he hit the Anjoli jackpot. "My family spent years in Mexico and went to all kinds of *curandero* healings. We never did anything normal like go to New Orleans for Mardi Gras. It was always to visit a voodoo doctor or attend some sort of ancient backwoods chicken sacrifice."

Jack and I stared at Nick, awestruck by the disclosure. He looked so normal—buttoned-up even.

"Isn't he the greatest?" Kimmy giggled.

My mother smiled. "Welcome to the family, darling."

# Chapter 24

Somewhere during dinner, Nick managed to convince my mother that if the house was, in fact, haunted, it was not due to any shortcomings in her ghost-busting skills. I liked him, but he did not fit my image of an Ivy League professor. He had the requisite salt-and-pepper goatee and thoughtful-looking face, but he seemed less clinically detached than I expected him to be, warm even. Nick spoke with admiring passion about tribal rituals that sounded far stranger than anything Anjoli had ever done. He was almost matter-of-fact about my entertaining the idea that the house was haunted.

"Come on, Nick," Jack said, slicing the apple pie Nick and Kimmy had brought from a local bakery. "You can't think a house can have ghosts."

"I can't?" Nick replied.

"Why can't he, darling?" Anjoli asked.

" 'Cause it doesn't make any sense," Jack countered. "Come on, there's no such thing as ghosts."

"Maybe," Nick said. "Maybe not. One thing I know for certain is that the longer I live and the more I learn, the more I realize that I know very little. Who's to say ghosts don't exist? No one's proven they do, but no one's proven they don't either, and until that happens, as far as I'm concerned, the jury's still out."

I didn't like admitting this—not even to myself—but the fact that a Princeton professor thought there might be some credence to the haunted house theory gave me permission to believe it myself.

"Really?!" Jack said, incredulously. He sat in silence for a moment, absorbing the thought. "Nah, it's too out there."

"How far out there is it really, Jack?" Nick asked. "You've got five intelligent people who think it's possible, and only one who's sure it isn't. It seems the really radical position is automatically to dismiss something you can't be certain of."

We all turned to Jack to catch his reaction. "Look, I'm not saying you guys can't believe in ghosts. It's not my thing."

"Not his thing, darling!" Anjoli scoffed. "Can you believe such arrogance?"

"I wouldn't call it arrogance, Anjoli," Nick said, diplomatically. "He's entitled to his opinion, like you are yours."

That night after we got Kimmy and Nick settled in the guest room, Anjoli and I surfed the Internet for ghost-busters while Jack went upstairs to read. Browsing a global network of information was difficult with Anjoli because she saw a million things that distracted her. Marketers are smart. They know that when a person enters "space-clearing," it's also a good time to hit them up for tarot cards, Wicca products, and essential oils. "Oh look!" Anjoli said. "Space-clearing salt is on close-out!" She insisted I click on the icon because we might need some for our house-clearing ritual. "Darling, rock salt is excellent for removing negative energy."

"Salt?" I asked.

"Yes, its cohesive qualities make it the ideal *sha chi* remover."

She sounded like she was on a TV commercial for spiritual Spray 'n Wash. *Sha chi got you down? No problem. Just use a little rock salt with extra cohesive qualities and say good-bye to evil spirits and negative energy. Thanks, rock salt!*

Looking at the myriad ghost-buster ads made me less sure that this was something I wanted to pursue. One site had a spooky music soundtrack. The other was decorated with tombstones. I felt extremely foolish for even considering this as an option. "Look at these prices, darling!" Anjoli said when she sensed my skepticism growing. "It's so cheap, you can't go wrong. Didn't you say that *Healthy Living* editor wants you to write an article about this anyway? It's a tax write-off!"

"I guess," I said. "Let's deal with this tomorrow."

"We can't wait another day!" Anjoli said dramatically. "This is a very powerful spirit if it was able to withstand my clearing rituals. Who knows what nefarious plan it has up its sleeve?" *Do ghosts have sleeves?* "Besides, I want to get back to the city by Tuesday, so we need to get the place cleansed tomorrow. Darling, you go to sleep. Let Mummy handle this. You know what pleasure it gives me to take care of you."

I went upstairs to find Jack in bed reading a novel. It was one of those typical guy paperbacks with a weapon against a dark black-and-red background. He looked up and asked how my hunt for a ghost-buster had gone. "Anjoli's handling it," I explained. "She says she enjoys taking care of me." We laughed. "Hey, you know what I just realized." Jack paused for me to continue. "We need to put our ad back on the Internet. We've got to start looking at new artists for our second season."

"I was thinking that too," Jack said. "Should we ask for psychiatric evaluations this go-round?"

"Very funny," I returned. "What are the odds of getting another Jacquie and Maxime?"

"Chantrell's no day-at-the-park either," Jack added. "What was the deal with that funeral dirge she was playing at dinner?"

"At a celebration of an engagement no less!"

"She's obviously been married before," Jack said, laughing.

I whacked him with a pillow. "Jack, seriously, let's talk about the schedule. If you post the announcement on the web tonight, can we reasonably ask for applications to be in by July fourth?"

"Why not? That gives people a month. It's not like our application is overly cumbersome. It's one page long, big deal. A few days to shoot photos of their work and get the all-clear from a mental health professional. I think that's plenty fair."

I smiled at his suggestion. "When did you get to be so cute?" I asked him, crawling in to be closer to him on the bed.

"I've always been this way," he replied.

"You were a grump for years," I said softly, kissing his forehead, then moving to his lips.

"I was great."

"You were a jerk," I kissed him again. And before we knew it, we forgot all about posting our request for applications online that night.


After Nick and Kimmy had breakfast, they said goodbye and headed back to Princeton. They promised to come back for our open house on Labor Day weekend, a promise I knew they'd keep. Nick sounded far too intrigued by the idea of our make-your-own culture that we'd created here on a few acres in the Berkshires. I liked him. He seemed just grounded enough to make a good, stable life with Kimmy, and yet wacky enough to keep up with the excitement she'd bring.

"Shelia will be here at three," Anjoli announced as the car drove away.

"Shelia?" I asked. Jack held the same puzzled expression, begging an answer.

As she tied her scarf around her hair to make a ponytail, Anjoli answered. "The woman who's going to finish the space-clearing I began, darling. Do you have any chicken liver?"

"Dare I ask what she needs with chicken liver, Mother?"

We walked toward the house, and she stroked Mancha's head. "Not for the space-clearing! For my baby. His nutritionist said he could be suffering from an iron deficiency. Chicken liver for a space-clearing," she scoffed. "Don't be ludicrous, darling."

Anjoli sat at the kitchen table while I loaded the dishwasher, and Jack took Adam down to his studio where he had recently installed a bouncing duck that a toddler could jump around in. "Have you ever taken him to a regular vet?" I asked my mother.

"Why would I do that, darling?"

"I don't know," I said. "Don't they need vaccinations?"

"I would never vaccinate Mancha!" Anjoli said, sounding appalled. "The mercury could upset his little system, darling. Plus, more goes wrong in these medical offices than anyone ever reports. I say if you want to stay healthy, keep far away from doctors."

"Mother," I said, as I realized my hand had been motionless under running water for quite some time. "I hate to have to ask you this, but did you have me vaccinated?"

"If I had it to do over again, I would spare you those awful shots, but yes, when you were a baby, I marched in lockstep with the doctor's orders," Anjoli said. "I suppose you're relieved about this, darling?"

"I am."

"So conventional," Anjoli said, waving her hand. "Anyway, darling, Shelia will be here at three, so I was hoping you could vacuum beforehand."

"Vacuum?"

"Yes, darling. Last night, I did some reading on the Internet and learned that negative energy can get stuck in the carpet. The more we can clean up before she gets here, the better off we'll be."

"Aren't we paying her to clean?" I asked.

"We can't expect her to vacuum, darling!"

There are times when I'm conversing with my mother when I have to stop myself and ask, *What the hell am I talking about?!* This was definitely one of them. "Okay," I said, inhaling deeply. "I'll vacuum before she gets here."

At 3:20 P.M., the doorbell rang. By then, not only was every inch of carpet vacuumed, Mother insisted that we lift all of the seat cushions and suction spirits from the sofa and loveseat. I found myself wondering if a simple vacuum cleaner bag would be strong enough to contain a ghost that managed to injure women's legs and to deplete artists of their creativity. Then I found myself wondering if I'd lost my mind completely by surrendering my home to an Internet ghost-buster found by a woman who had driven a dog to neurosis.

"A thousand apologies for my lateness," said Shelia. "Traffic was terrible." Somehow I had imagined her arriving by broom or magic carpet. At the very least, I'd expected her omnipotence to be able to avert mundane problems like traffic. Shelia wore a black sweatshirt with gold script lettering that read "Magic Happens" and a long black skirt with dark blue Chuck Taylor high-tops. She placed a square shoebox on my kitchen table and introduced herself, holding my hand too long and gazing too deeply into my eyes. When she spoke, I noticed her teeth were badly capped and her gums had freckles. I never knew gums could have spots, but hers did. Shelia opened her box and told us that she found Tibetan Tingsha bells extremely effective in purifying space. "My bells are hand-crafted in bronze, iron, and zinc by Tibetan monks," she said. I felt as though she expected some sort of reaction from me and couldn't help accommodating.

"Mmmm," I said, faking being impressed.

"They are individually ground and polished and adorned with ancient, mystic symbols," Shelia said, again waiting for a reaction.

"Really?" Anjoli said.

Shelia continued. "They are treasured for their ability to produce pure and cleansing sounds that release spaces of their *sha chi.*"

*All right lady, let's get this show on the road. I need to get dinner on the table in another two hours.*

She held the bells out for Anjoli and me to inspect. It felt as awkward as when waiters asked me to approve of the first sip of wine from a bottle. What was I supposed to say? "Lovely," I muttered. Soon Shelia was flitting around my house ringing her bells in each corner of the room. As the bells rang, Shelia shut her eyes and contorted her face as if spirits were traveling through her.

Jack, who had come upstairs to refill Adam's sippy-cup with juice, couldn't resist. "Are we trying to get rid of the ghosts or call them to the table for dinner?"

I wanted to run into his arms and declare myself on his side of this debate once and for all. I wondered how I let myself believe that this witchy bell-ringer could solve our problems. With a look, I told Jack, *You were right. This is truly ridiculous.*

Adam pointed at Shelia and said he wanted the drums. Apparently, the Tingsha bells look like an instrument from preschool music class. Adam thought it was time to reach in to the basket of music and sing, "*Sha chi*, go away, don't come back another day."

"Darling, go back to your studio," Anjoli scolded.

"Is this studio in the house?" Shelia asked, still ringing.

"Yes," I answered. "We've got three guesthouses and a studio in the back."

"I'll need to see them all," Shelia demanded. "Spirits can be very sneaky and hide. I need to ring every corner of every space if I am to fully cleanse the property of *sha chi*." I wondered if she charged by the corner.

She became more animated, swirling around the room with a childlike carelessness. One might think she was enjoying herself, except every few seconds, she stopped dead in her tracks and scrunched her face as if she were swallowing bad medicine.

"Are you okay?" Jack asked her.

"It's intense. *Sha chi* is leaving your home and using my body as a conduit to the spirit world," Shelia said.

Jack tried to contain his smile. "I hate it when that happens."

# Chapter 25

As we were making our way down the path to the guest cottages, I realized that it would be my first peek inside them since the artists moved in.

In a way, I hoped no one was home, especially Randy. How would I explain this witchy woman wanting to come inside to ring bells in each corner?

Our first knock was on the door of Maxime and Jacquie's place. It took a good minute for Maxime to answer, and when he did he looked as if we'd interrupted a nap. "Hi," I said, brightly. "This is my friend, Shelia, and you remember my mother, Anjoli, right?" He barely nodded. "I was wondering if we could come in for a sec and look around. Jacquie's not here, is she?"

"No, she is at the mall with Chantrell," he said before beginning to weep. "Excuse me for the tears. I cannot stop crying for months. If I sketched all the time I cried, I would have an entire exhibit by now."

As he spoke, my eyes scanned the living room in disbelief. I had seen fraternity houses that were cleaner than this house. There were fast food wrappers on the floor, stacks of newspaper, and a mountain of shopping bags in the corner. The smell of old food permeated the entire cottage. Despite the fact that Jack and Tom had installed screens, bugs had managed to find their way in to make an insect tornado around the uncovered garbage pail. I was certain that no self-respecting ghost was in this home, but asked to come in anyway.

"I hope Jacquie is shopping for Lysol," Anjoli said to Maxime. Without acknowledging her, he returned to the wooden bench at his table and buried his overflowing eyes in his palms.

As it turned out, my fear about how I would explain Shelia was completely unfounded. Maxime didn't seem at all curious about this strange woman who was dancing around his house ringing bells and contorting her face. He might not have even noticed because after Shelia finished, he simply looked up from his table and thanked us for stopping by.

Rattled by the mess Maxime and Jacquie had made of our guesthouse, I asked Anjoli and Shelia for advice. "I think I should call a therapist. This man is obviously depressed."

"Forget about the therapist, darling. Call a cleaning woman," Anjoli suggested. "Protect your investment before you worry about this deadbeat's mental health. You're going to get rats in that place if you're not careful."

"If you don't mind my saying so," Shelia began. "That guy and his wife need a good, swift kick in the ass. Didn't you say they are living here as your guests?" I confirmed. "You're not responsible for getting him a shrink or a maid. Tell him to clean up his act or hit the road." This was not the advice I expected of a self-proclaimed spiritual practitioner, but then again, she was in the business of evicting spirits, not coddling them.

I suggested we go to Chantrell's house next since I knew she wasn't there. Plus, I saw that Randy was home and hoped he might leave before we got around to his place. The cellist kept her home immaculate, but I was surprised to see the number of crucifixes hanging on the walls. There was a gold Jesus on the cross next to a plain gold cross in the entryway, and a painted Jesus on a wooden cross in the kitchen. In the living room there was a colorful needle-point cross framed in glass, an equally colorful Godseye-like cross done with rainbow yarn, and another made with twigs that appeared to have come from our woods. I could see a painting of Jesus in the hallway leading to her bed-room, but decided not to go down that path. No one could help noticing the tidal wave of Christ. Even Mancha seemed to be taking it all in, moving his beady eyes from one cross to the next.

Anjoli shuddered. "I feel so violated, darling," she said. "Who knew it was going to be a cathedral in here?"

While my mother felt violated by the abundance of cru-cifixes, I felt we had invaded Chantrell's privacy and was eager to get out of her home. Of course, I owned the place, but going in without her prior knowledge was something I hadn't thought through well enough. I felt as though Chantrell would be justifiably angry if she discovered we'd been in her home. I also had the feeling I was going to burn in eternal damnation. "Let's get out of here," I sug-gested to Anjoli. "Shelia, be quick about it and meet us outside."

"Have you gone mad, darling?" Anjoli protested. "We haven't seen her bedroom. I've got a hundred bucks that says she's crossed the mattresses over each other and is sleeping on a Posturepedic crucifix."

"Mother!" I scolded.

Shelia began ringing bells, ignoring my mother and my argument.

"Darling, why would you want to deprive me of such fun? I'm looking forward to seeing what other goodies she's got. What do you say we leave a little cross in the bathroom, right above the toilet paper, and write, 'Holy shit,' on it?"

I couldn't tell whether or not she was kidding, but with

Anjoli, it's best to err on the side of caution. "I don't think a devout Catholic would find that very funny."

"Oh, pooh!" Anjoli pouted to the sound of Tingsha bells. "Let's go check her underwear drawer to see if she's got panties with days of the week on them. Christ, that's so Catholic! I'll grab a marker and we can write 'Ash' over Wednesday and 'Good' before Friday. Surely, the girl has some sense of humor and would appreciate a little joke, darling."

As Anjoli contemplated her sophomoric pranks and Shelia rang bells in every corner of the rooms, I wondered about how this ultra-Catholic Irish woman reconciled having an affair with a married man just a few months ago. Sure, my hedonistic heathen of a mother ran around with the gold band crowd, but that was to be expected. How did Chantrell, the earthy musician with a thing for Christ, cat around with the Frenchman next door? I remembered that I should call Renee and see how she was doing—if Dan had agreed to go to marriage counseling as we had discussed. When we last spoke, Renee said she was going to insist that they get counseling or pack a suitcase for him, though I suspected that the last part was more of a throwaway line.

"Okay, we're outta here," said Shelia after about three minutes of bell-ringing.

*We're outta here?* I expected this from a cabdriver, not a spirit-remover.

"Show me the next place," Shelia demanded. "You know I'm going to have to charge extra, right? When I talked to Angie on the phone, she didn't say anything about all these corners."

Petting Mancha's smooth head, Anjoli stopped and looked up at me. *It's on me,* she mouthed. "Does baby want a treat?" She reached into the side pocket of her purse and fed Mancha a tiny brick-red pellet.

My heart pounded like drums at a virgin sacrifice when

we reached Randy's house. He came to the door in his white T-shirt and jeans, squinted and smiled at me, then looked at my mother and Shelia. "Hey, what's up, Lu?" he asked. *Oh, you know, nothing special. At the sound of your voice uttering my name—my shortened name at that—my nipples just sprang to life, and I'll need to change my panties. Same old, same old.*

"Hey, Rand," I said, mentally kicking myself for the ridiculous attempt to imitate his style. "This is probably going to sound a bit bizarre," I began. *He is smirking! Is he smirking or smiling? How does he get half of his mouth to turn up like that while the other half stays put? How full are those lips?* "But my mother's friend, Shelia, is taking a class on ghost-busting," I lied, rolling my eyes at the absurdity. "And my mother told her she could practice here because there are, um," my confidence waned as I spoke the next words. "There are, um, so many corners for, um, for her to ring her Tingsha bells in."

I was standing slightly in front of Anjoli and Shelia and hoped to God that they had enough discretion to refrain from making any quizzical facial expressions.

"Tingsha bells?" Randy repeated.

I raised my eyebrows and rolled my eyes so the women behind me couldn't see. "I told you it was an odd request, but she really needs to do our whole place or she'll get a bad grade on the assignment."

"Oh, it's not that," Randy said with a laugh. Was it my imagination or was he looking at me more than the other women? I suppose I was the one speaking to him, but it seemed as though his eyes broke contact with mine only rarely. "I just wonder why you're using Tingsha bells. My mom always burns the wands."

"Juniper wands?!" Shelia chimed in.

Randy nodded. "I think so."

"Those are only for cleansing. We need to get rid of the *sha chi* in here," Shelia said.

"There's no *sha chi* in here," Randy began. "I only see three beautiful women in my home." God save us from our girlish idiocy, but we all giggled. "Go ahead and do what you need, Lu. You know my place is yours."

I wasn't sure what to quiver about first. He said my name, not the other two so-called beautiful women. I absolutely loved the Lu business. And, my place is yours. Okay, technically, it's just an accurate representation of the ownership status of the property, but when he said it, I felt our bodies wrapped around each other's in a naked embrace. Good God, if I were glass, I'd shatter too.

"How do you know about all of this space-clearing stuff?" I asked.

"My mom is into all that New Age philosophy," he answered. "We're from northern California."

"Principles, darling," Anjoli added. "The spiritual principles which your mother follows have been around longer than any religion, so calling them philosophies is really quite condescending."

*Shut up, Mother!*

"Okay, I'm done," said Shelia.

"That was fast," slipped out. "I mean, you took less than a minute. Randy's got some serious *sha chi* here. Everything he touches breaks, and he works with glass! That's some serious stuff, Shelia. Maybe you should do another round."

Randy smiled. "I thought this was a school assignment."

"Well, that doesn't mean she shouldn't take it seriously, does it?" I returned without hesitation. "I think people should throw themselves into everything they do fully and passionately." *Holy fuck, did I just say that aloud?* "They should be conscientious and committed," I corrected.

"It'll be extra," Shelia said.

"Extra credit!" I said, bursting with nervous energy. I wondered if there was a New Age term for my neurotic

Jewish energy that seemed to have a life of its own. *Yid chi?* "Shelia, you're such a dedicated *student* that I know you'll want to go for that extra credit. Now spin your wand and do your thing."

"Bells," Randy corrected.

Shelia shrugged. "You're the boss."

"So are you," I blurted.

*What?! What did I just say?*

# Chapter 26

When Chantrell returned from her shopping excursion with Jacquie, she was not too happy about discovering that we had been in her home. I don't blame her, but her reaction was a bit much. She dropped her shopping bags as soon as she crossed the threshold and stormed back outside shouting. Anjoli, Shelia, and I came out from Randy's cottage to see what all of the commotion was about. "I want to know who's been in my house!" she shouted. Before anyone could answer, she shrieked again. "Don't stand there looking like fools. Tell me who's been in my goddamned house."

Anjoli muttered, "All of those crosses and she calls it a goddamned house."

"What's going on out here?" said Jacquie who had only been in her own home for a moment.

"Someone's been in my home, and I demand to know who before I call the police!" Chantrell shouted. A few shopping trips with Jacquie and she was a regular protégé.

"Chantrell, calm down," I said as I watched Shelia shuffle uncomfortably. Mancha sat upright in Anjoli's purse, an eager audience. "We were inside for a few minutes to make a few repairs."

*There, that should settle it.*

"Repairs?! What kind of repairs did you need to make?!" she demanded.

"Look, this is *my* home and I need to do maintenance on it," I said firmly. "None of your personal items were touched, so there's no need for the drama, Chantrell!"

She flew toward me with a hand raised in the air as if she were going to throw a punch. "This is the worst vacation I've ever had!"

"Vacation?!" my mother and I shouted simultaneously. "Now you listen here," I took over. "In case you've forgotten, you're living here rent-free so you can compose music and do your cockamamie cello research on vegetables. So far, you haven't put together two notes other than the 'ows' and 'ahs' that have been coming from you and Maxime."

With that, Jacquie gasped. "You swore that was over, Chantrell!"

*They discussed it?! When? Over red wine and cigarettes at an outdoor café with French accordion music in the background?*

"It *is* over!" Chantrell defended. "She's trying to take attention away from her breaking-and-entering."

Anjoli opened her mouth to yell at Chantrell, but before she could speak, we all gasped at the sight of a blaze of red hair falling down the front steps of the guesthouse. Chantrell screamed when she landed at the bottom and sobbed weakly. "My ankle," she sniffed. "It's broken, I can tell."

Before we could react, a thunderous crash of glass came from Randy's house. "Crap!" he shouted. He came outside with his hand wrapped in a paper towel to stop the bleeding. "What happened out here?" It was appalling to think that this wretched Irish woman's shouting jarred Randy to the point where he broke more glass. No one responded. We were interrupted by Maxime who came outside to announce that he was going to kill himself.

"Get me to a friggin' hospital already," Chantrell demanded.

"I'll take you to the hospital," Randy said as he moved toward Chantrell to help her up.

"Don't be ridiculous, Randy," I said. "Your hands are bleeding. I'll take her." I felt noble and good. Then I remembered that I'd be spending several hours alone with Chantrell, and I just felt sick. "Mom, will you run upstairs and tell Jack what's happened? Tell him I'll be home as soon as I can. Will you take care of Shelia please? And remind Jack that Adam has Kinder-Music this afternoon." Turning to Chantrell, "Oh, right, you need help getting up." I held out a hand.

"Why don't I come with you?" Randy asked.

*With me? Or with her? Can we rewind tape so I can see who that comment was directed toward, please?*

"That's sweet of you to want to help Chantrell, but I can manage," I said to Randy.

"I was thinking *you* could use a hand," he said. *Bingo.*

"Excuse me, but I am going to kill myself!" Maxime repeated. "Does no one care that I'm going to die?"

Jacquie walked inside and shouted to us, "Is there a morgue at the hospital? Take Maxime there for me, please." I was shocked. The woman actually knew the word "please."

I overheard Shelia tell my mother that there were multiple ghosts in my home and they were angry at our attempts to remove them. "It happens sometimes. You can't leave it like this or you're going to have a ghost revolution. Who knows how many of them are here?"

We waited about three hours in the hospital emergency room before Chantrell was seen by a doctor. I declined to go into the exam room with her, and instead asked Randy if he wanted to go on a Prozac hunt with me. "A what?" he asked, smirking.

"You saw how Maxime was acting," I said. "It would be immoral for me to be in a hospital and *not* try to steal some happy pills for him. He's my responsibility."

"Lu," Randy said softly, giving me that same look he did back at the house. Then he brushed my hair behind my shoulder. I felt a bit guilty that my hair had a fling. "You can't feel responsible for the whole world." *Oh my God,* I silently thought. *This man knows me.* "The artists, your mother, that friend of yours with the cheating husband," he said, conveniently omitting any mention of Jack or Adam. "They're all grownups who can take care of their own lives. You need to focus on yourself and your boy." *I couldn't agree more. Me and my boy. Oh, I think he means Adam, not himself.* "When was the last time you did something for yourself?" *Um, the last time I tried to entertain a failed lightbulb fantasy about you.* "Didn't you say you're a writer?" he asked. *Oh, we're talking about work?* "I've never seen you write. You never mention anything you're working on."

"I have a book coming out in November," I said, proudly.

"Nah, that's great. Lu, don't get me wrong. You're awesome, but I hate to see how much time and energy you take away from your own deal by babysitting everyone else."

Was he right? Was I too invested in everyone else's life and neglecting my own? Did this guy know me well enough to make such an observation?

"So, you don't want to steal pills?" I said, hoping to dodge the subject.

He laughed. "Lu, think about what I said," he said, placing his hand slightly above my knee. "I'd like to help you out."

Whoa! Direct hit. Was I imagining things or did he just make a vague and oblique offer to slam my naked body against the wall and pound himself into me? Or, um, something of the sort.

There was a thick cloud of sexual chemistry hovering in the hospital waiting room that evening. It didn't quite blend with the antiseptic, but I enjoyed it for what it was—a time when real life was put on pause and I could float in an alternative reality where dirty diapers and haunted houses were replaced by extended gazes and welling lust. I felt simultaneously thrilled and terrified. It was one thing to admire a hot young artist. It was an entirely different thing when he seemed mutually interested.

"Seriously, Lu, you've done so much for me," Randy continued. "Is there anything I can do for you?" His hand hadn't moved from my leg, and I was resisting the urge to push it beneath my skirt. I questioned my interpretation of what was going on. Perhaps he was offering to do some home repairs. Then he looked at me again and all of my questions were erased.

Swallowing terror, I responded with feigned ignorance. "You're very kind, but we've got a handyman who does all of that kind of stuff."

Randy's smirk let me know my pathetic attempt at neutralizing the discussion was transparent. "Have it your way, Lu," he said. "But if you think of anything you'd like from me, be sure and lemme know, okay?" Then he picked up *Men's Health* magazine from the table and began flipping from the back page to the front.

A few things bothered me about this interaction. First, I enjoyed it too much. Second, something about the invitation implied he'd be doing it as a favor to me. I didn't want a 'thank you' lay. Come to think of it, I didn't want any kind of lay from Randy. What I wanted was the feeling that he genuinely desired me, not that he'd be willing to sleep with me because it was cheaper than sending a hostess a fruit basket. It seemed meaningless to him. Even as I pondered it, dissecting every intonation and facial expression, he was reading a story about reducing cholesterol.

A haggard-looking nurse came through the hospital doors escorting newly-casted Chantrell on crutches. I wondered if her weary expression was from a lifetime in health care or an evening with Chantrell. "Bring the car around front," she snapped. "Do you honestly think I can walk like this?!"

Randy glanced at me to catch my next move. I felt as if I was on an audition. On one hand, I knew he would like to see me assert myself and decline the invitation to babysit this hostile witch. On the other hand, if Randy saw that I could handle myself, perhaps he wouldn't feel the need to take care of me. Although I hated that Randy felt sorry for me, I wasn't yet willing to let go of his pity.

"Come on," I said, standing from my seat, gesturing to Randy to do the same. To Chantrell, I added, "You need to get used to getting around on crutches. It's not far to the parking lot." I had no idea whether or not it was far because Randy had dropped Chantrell and me at the emergency room, but I knew that however far Chantrell had to struggle, it wasn't quite far enough.

"You can't be serious!" Chantrell said.

"Deadly serious," I returned. "And another thing. It's time for you to pull up the dead zucchini and start a new vegetable garden, one that will hear your cello every day. This is not a vacation, and it's time for you to come home from the mall and start composing some music!"

Randy winked with approval. I loved that I had earned it. I hated that I cared.

The side benefit of flirtation was that it charged me with passion that I could put toward legitimate use. The energy followed me into my bedroom, sweeping back my hair with a sensual breeze. Okay, there was no breeze. In fact, it was a stagnant, humid night, but something magical seemed to flow through me. I felt like an ad for perfume. I couldn't see myself, but I just knew I looked dazzling. When Jack glanced up from his book, he noticed it too. "Whoa!" He peered over his reading glasses and asked what had gotten into me. "You're like sex-on-a-stick, Luce," he said, placing the novel down on the nightstand. Without saying a word, I proved him correct.

# Chapter 27

The next day Anjoli was gone. Jack told me that she had left just after sunset the evening earlier, while I was at the hospital with Chantrell and Randy. Some senior citizens are afraid to drive at night, but, as is the case with most things in life, Anjoli is the opposite. She only drives after dark because she fears the sun will damage her skin through the windows. Wearing a wide rim hat blocks her vision of the road.

By afternoon, things had returned to normal. Well, as normal as things got around our house. Jack was in the front yard touching up his beach buggie as Adam napped beside him in the playpen. Maxime and Jacquie were fighting louder than ever. Chantrell was nowhere to be seen. And we could only tell Randy was in his home because it sounded as if an earthquake had hit a greenhouse. The temperature was holding steady at a full summer bake of more than ninety degrees, but thankfully it became a nice dry heat that carried the scent of jasmine through the air.

Renee stopped by, looking cheerful in her bold floral T-shirt that looked as though she had painted it herself, which as it turned out, she had.

"Looks like life is treating you well," I said, leaning in to kiss her cheek.

"It's actually kicking my ass." Renee told me that she had confronted Dan about his whereabouts the night he claimed to have stayed in a hotel, and he had refused to show her a receipt from the hotel. "He says he stayed at a Marriott, but I checked with all of his credit card companies and called both local Marriotts, and no one has a record of him staying there or charging a room," she said. "Worst part is that he refuses to admit he was with that slut and won't go to marriage counseling. Says he doesn't have enough time to spend with the people he knows, much less a stranger who's going to judge him. See that guilty conscience? Why would he think a therapist would judge him unless he had done something wrong?"

I couldn't disagree. I pulled my hair back into a bun as we spoke and asked Renee if she wanted to come inside where it was air-conditioned. She wanted to sit outside, but said she'd love a glass of ice water, an idea that appealed to me too. As I filled our glasses, I continued, "You look well, though. What's your secret?"

We sat in the back, overlooking the guesthouses. "I started going to marriage counseling by myself."

"By yourself?!" I quizzed.

"Yeah, that's what Dear Abby always advises, so I figured, what the hell, our insurance covers it. Why not?"

"How do you work on a marriage when one person doesn't participate?" I asked.

Her smile was absolutely perfect, which reminded me that she had overbleached her teeth and now wore porcelain veneers. "We talk about me and how I can only control myself and how I respond to Dan's infidelity. It's pretty helpful. I had my doubts, but I've got to say I've gotten a lot out of only two sessions." She paused to beam, then looked around and asked where Anjoli was.

"She left last night," I told Renee. "After the bell-ringer did her thing, Chantrell broke her ankle, and Maxime threatened to commit suicide."

"I love your place. My problems seem so mundane when I come here," Renee said, reaching into a shopping bag she brought over. "I'm sorry I missed her. I took her advice and started painting T-shirts," she said, gesturing to her own. *Um, it was actually my idea that you paint shirts.* "Look what I made for her." Renee pulled out a white form-fitting T-shirt with a black glittery figure enveloped in bold orange and yellow flames. It was beautifully frightening with a hint of tragedy. "Oh look," I said, noticing writing at the bottom: "I was burned at the stake in Salem and all I got was this lousy T-shirt."

"Do you like it?" Renee asked.

"Love it," I said. "I'm sure Anjoli will wear it with pride."

"Good, then I hope you'll like this one I made for you!" She pulled out an abstract of our home with a gray thundercloud hovering over it, like the Addams Family house. "Do you like it?"

"I love it." I did, but what I liked more than the T-shirt was how it pulled my friend from potential depression. She seemed to be taking the deterioration of her marriage as well as she possibly could.

"So did the bell-ringing work?" Renee asked.

"I think it made things worse," I told her.

"Are you going to try again?" Renee asked.

"I doubt it," I said. "The bell-ringer said that we had multiple spirits and we needed to have her back."

"Well, if you do, you better invite me this time. Have a heart, Lucy. My husband is cheating on me. The least you can do is let me watch the ghost-busters."

I promised Renee that there would be no future ghost-busting without her present. She said she had errands to run and left a few minutes later.

Though Renee didn't mind roasting in the summer afternoon heat, I went inside and sat at my desk. I dialed Bernice to say hello and see how the Florida summer was treating her. She said she had to go because her cousin Sylvia was over helping her set up for a house party for a city council member. "I really must have a problem with the fawcett because Sylvia keeps complaining about how noisy it is. I told her I'm not such a big shot that I need everything perfect, but she said it's driving her crazy."

"It *is* driving me crazy!" I heard Sylvia shout in the background.

"*Mamaleh,* I have to hang up. In twenty minutes, a couple dozen people from the building will be here, and I'm still in my muumuu."

"Okay, I'll talk to you later."

"Lucy," Aunt Bernice whispered. "You have to try the laser beam."

"The what?"

"Get your vaginer laser-beamed. It's like air-conditioning for your panties."

"Okay," I said, laughing. "Why don't we talk about this later?"

Next I called Earl at *Healthy Living* who answered on the first ring. "Hey, Earl," I said. "It's Lucy Klein. I didn't expect you to be there."

"So you were calling hoping not to get me?" he said lightly.

"I was wondering if you were still interested in having me write that piece for your 'Living the Dream' section?"

"Are things improving in paradise lost?" he asked.

"Not really," I said, hoping I could find a sunny spin to sell the story. "But I think I can offer some reflections on how we grow from personal challenges." *Did that bullshit just come from my mouth?!* "What I mean is that I'm starting to see how we've really had some great experiences here." *Great experiences? Could I be any less specific?*

"Oh yeah," Earl said, as he began typing in the background. "Like what?"

"Well, my husband Jack is really growing as an artist," I said, immediately regretting the meaningless cliché. "Our female guests are nasty and shop nonstop, and when Jack was taking out the garbage last week, he noticed hundreds of clothing tags, receipts, and shopping bags. It was really quite gross. I mean, some of the shopping bags and clothing tags were quite beautiful, but the overconsumption and hyperconsumerism was really quite pathetic. So Jack pulled me into his studio and dumped all of this crap in the middle of the floor and started carrying on about how these two women had become shopping zombies. One of them is supposed to be composing, and the other is supposed to be French. Well, the wife of a French artist anyway, so we expected a bit more from her creatively than buying up the local Banana Republic. Anyway, instead of getting pissed off about this—well, instead of *just* getting pissed about it—Jack made this unbelievable collage of bags, receipts, and tags. He pasted about a few hundred tags and receipts to the top of the mannequin and made a skirt of glossy shopping bags. It is gorgeous, really gorgeous."

"Sounds cool," Earl said, though I could tell he was wondering where I was going with this. "What's he going to do with his collage d'consumerism?"

"Oh, he'll sell it," I said, laughing at our own hypocrisy. "My point is that although the artist colony has turned out to be the Bermuda Triangle of creativity for our guests, it has been wonderful for Jack. And we've met some really lovely people." *Oy, I've just sunk to the "we've met some really lovely people" argument.* "There's this woman whose husband is cheating on her, but rather than sink into the depths of depression like the French sketch artist, she started painting T-shirts and jeans and is going to marriage counseling alone." *Where's my parachute? This pitch is going down.*

"Hmmm," Earl sounded uninterested. "What about

the ghosts? Did you ever look into it? I mean, *that's a* story."

"I actually did, Earl, and I've got to tell you, I don't think we're haunted. We had a woman come in and ring bells and as soon as she finished, the place got worse."

"What do you mean it got worse?" he asked, no longer typing.

"I mean Chantrell broke her ankle, and got insanely angry, Maxime threatened to commit suicide, and Randy broke glass I didn't even know existed," I explained.

"And that was right after she rang the Tingsha bells?" Earl asked.

"How did you know they were Tingsha bells?"

"Because I know what bullshit Tingsha bells are!" Earl exclaimed.

*Of course. How silly of me.*

"You know what you've done, don't you?" he asked. Without waiting for my reply, Earl told me that I'd aggravated the problem. "Your ghost is pissed now. You think you had problems before?! Ha, wait until you see a pissed-off ghost."

"The bell-ringer thinks there are a few ghosts," I said.

"After she got done with the place, I'm sure there are!" I felt like a child being scolded. "Listen, Lucy, don't mess around with this stuff. You need to call in the big guns. Promise me you'll do a story on this, and I'll get Effie in to work on your house."

"Effie?" I asked.

"Effie Hinkelmeyer," Earl said as if he'd just mentioned Pablo Picasso and I didn't recognize the name. "She's the world's leading space-cleaner and psychic. Effie is a consultant for the FBI and clears homes after violent crimes are committed in them."

"I'm confused," I said. "Wouldn't the FBI want to keep a crime scene intact?"

"I'm sorry," Earl said. "It's two separate things. She

helps the Bureau solve crimes, but she's also paid by realtors to clear out properties after people die or are killed in homes."

"This is all too icky and weird," I said.

"Lucy, I'll pay two bucks a word, make it the cover story, and pay for Effie to get rid of your ghosts," Earl offered.

"Deal!" I said, jumping at the idea of a cover story.

Earl explained what he saw as the scope of the piece, then said he'd be in touch later in the week with Effie's availability.

The whole thing felt a little silly to me, but I was willing to give it a try. Who was I to say our house wasn't haunted? If the FBI had faith in this Effie person, why should I dismiss her so easily? And how could I turn down five thousand bucks and a cover story?!

I went down to Jack's studio to tell him about my new assignment. I found him doing a painting on a truck tire that he said was a commentary about the cyclical nature of life.

"I'm not sure I get it," I said, tilting my head to look at it from a different perspective.

"I'm not sure I do either," Jack said. "Oh hey, Anjoli called while you were on your office phone. She wants you to ask Renee to paint a design on a sunhat for Mancha."

# Chapter 28

Nearly two weeks had gone by since Jack had posted on the Internet our request for applications from artists. We hadn't received a single application. After the same period last year, we had received almost fifty packages of art samples, photographs, CD-roms, and heartfelt essays. "Are you sure it's up?" I asked Jack.

"I checked a couple times," Jack assured me. "The site's getting hits. Be patient, Luce. It's probably taking longer this year 'cause we're asking for character references."

That was Renee's smart idea, one we certainly should have incorporated last year. We decided it would be overstepping to ask for clearance from a mental health professional, but were definitely looking for a few buzzwords this time around. Jack and I agreed that someone needed to vouch for the applicants' "commitment" to his or her art. We'd love to find artists with a "pleasant demeanor," but would settle for an "even temper."

As Jack changed into his swimming trunks and applied sunscreen, he told me he was grateful Adam's friend Spartacus was hosting his third birthday party at Splash City water park. Spartacus's father is a retired pitcher for the Red Sox and shared with Jack that he and his brother, John, had always thought their names were dull. They wanted names for their sons that reflected the family strength and athleticism. So the Sorvik brothers named their sons Spartacus, Hercules, Zeus, and Rambo. Thankfully, their families bore no girls. Our son Adam—appropriately named after the guy whose Garden of Eden didn't quite work out—waddled into our bedroom naked holding his swimming diaper. The problem was that he was spouting a trail of urine from his room to ours. "Dude, you gotta take that to the can," Jack said. We both stood paralyzed watching the stream shoot upward then down onto our blue carpet. After a while, Jack turned to me and muttered, "That is the longest piss I've ever seen anyone take." We looked at each other, the unspoken question was clear: Who would take care of the mess? As Jack and I silently begged each other to clean the pee, the phone rang.

"Whoever the call is not for has to clean the pee," I shot.

"That's so wrong," Jack protested. "It's never for me."

The phone rang a second time. "It could be for you. It's the weekend, maybe it's your mother."

"Odds are it's your mother or her dog calling, Luce. Let's flip a coin."

"We should make *him* clean it," I said pointing to Adam.

"Yeah, you clean it, little man," Jack suggested as the phone rang a third time.

"Hello," I said, answering the phone. "Oh hi, Mother," I said, smiling and gesturing to Jack that he was on pee cleanup.

He blew me a kiss, then gave me the finger. Picking up Adam's bag of diapers, clothes, sippy cup, and birthday gift, Jack left, gesturing to the rug. "We need to take off, Luce," Jack whispered. "We're all meeting at the front gate so we gotta run."

"Lucy, are you listening to me?!" Anjoli demanded.

"I'm sorry, Mother," I returned. "Jack and Adam are just leaving for a party and I was saying good-bye. I missed what you were saying."

"Excuse me, darling, but who was it that gave you undivided attention throughout your entire life?"

I sighed with resignation. "No one did, Mother. Perhaps that's why I'm such an insecure, needy nutcase now."

Anjoli burst into laughter. "You are hilarious, darling. I must say, you can deliver lines with such dryness, it makes them that much funnier. I have to give your father credit for that. He was a womanizing drug addict, but a damned funny one. Sometimes I really miss him. Anyway, I'm calling see if you can come to the city this week and talk to the girls."

"What girls?" I asked.

"The college girls who live in the old MacIntosh house. They're driving me out of my mind with all of their comings and goings."

"Their comings and goings?" I asked. "What does that mean?"

"Darling, my home is my sanctuary. Every time I look out the window, one is coming, another one is going. It's dizzying to have all of that activity going on right outside my front door. It's like living across the street from a beehive."

"And what am I supposed to do about this?"

"I need someone to talk to them, darling. It's very confusing for Mancha as well. He's plucking his paw fur more than ever before. You simply must intercede on my behalf."

"You want me to go over there and ask them to regulate their comings and goings because the activity across the street is making you dizzy?" I asked, hoping she would realize the absurdity.

"Thank you, darling."

"Mother, I have agreed to no such thing. Since when

are you sitting at your window anyway? I thought your life was far too fabulous to be sitting by the window watching what your neighbors are doing?"

"My life *is* fabulous, darling. I took a workshop on oxygen meditation last weekend, and the instructor said that, in order to connect with our core spirituality, we had to breathe deeply outside or near an open window. You know that gorgeous bay window I have overlooking West Eleventh Street? Naturally, I sit on my lavendar chenille pillow and meditate there. You would think I could get twenty minutes of peace sitting there, but no. Every few minutes, one of these little pep squad tarts shouts out, 'Hiya, Mrs. L'Fontaine!' I don't know what revolts me more—the Mrs. L'Fontaine business or the yokel greeting. I mean, really, who says, 'Hiya'? Somebody really ought to tell them that we are not in Kansas anymore. Maybe that's how they talk wherever they're from, but this down home 'Hiya, Mrs. L'Fontaine' is not going to cut it on my block."

"You're upset because they're friendly?" I asked.

"Don't be so naïve, darling," she replied. "Remember that night that Alfie and I went to extend the olive branch at their little roof soiree?"

"I thought you went to complain that their music was too loud."

"Whatever," she dismissed. "My point is that I introduced myself to everyone as Anjoli. I don't even recall telling them my last name, but the next thing you know, they're addressing me like Eddie Fucking Haskell spoke to June Cleaver. Don't be fooled by their faux deference, darling. It's hostile. They only call me *Mrs. L'Fontaine* to focus attention on our age gap. Friendly? Please. I'd rather they be honest and pelt rotten eggs at my window."

"And that would help your oxygen meditation?" I asked.

"I prefer active aggression to passive aggressive behavior any day of the week, darling. Now, when can you talk to them?"

"Talk to them about *what*, Mother?" I asked. "I'm supposed to drive from Massachusetts to tell friendly college girls to stop saying hello to my mother? I would sound like a lunatic. Frankly, Mother, I think you've really lost it this time."

"I most certainly still have it, darling!"

"Mother, here's a crazy idea. Why don't you meditate in your backyard?" The woman is one of the few New Yorkers who actually has a yard. It's four-hundred square feet of off-street courtyard with terra cotta tiles and a small herb garden, but by Manhattan standards, she lives on a ranch. There's a teak wood table, six chairs, and a recliner—certainly enough room for a person to sit cross-legged and chant for serenity.

"Why should I let these girls dictate where I meditate?! I will not be a prisoner in my own home, darling."

"A prisoner in your own home?" I repeated.

"It's so Martha Stewart, darling," Anjoli said. "What will be next, a metal wristband to detect my every move?"

"Don't you think your reaction is a bit dramatic?"

"I most certainly do not! I have to set firm boundaries with these little cupcakes or the next thing you know, they'll be—" Anjoli trailed off.

"What, telling you to have a good day?" I asked.

"Don't think that wouldn't irritate the hell out of me, darling. How presumptuous people are telling others what kind of day to have."

"Maxime is threatening to commit suicide," I said, switching gears.

"Who?" Anjoli asked.

"The French guy," I reminded her.

"What French guy, darling? France is full of French guys. Might you be willing to narrow it down for me?"

"The French artist living at the house. You know, the

one whose wife shops nonstop? The guy who doesn't sketch anymore."

"Oh him," Anjoli recalled. "He threatened to kill himself while I was there, remember? I was there for that whole scene with the pianist who broke her leg. And you think *I'm* being dramatic? Your home is a regular freak show."

"It's been that way my whole life," I said.

She ignored the comment. "Well, clearly if he was serious about killing himself, he'd be dead by now," Anjoli said. "The man doesn't follow through on anything, so I wouldn't worry about it, darling. He's obviously looking for attention. Now, when are you coming home to get these girls to stop their shenanigans?"

"I don't understand why you need me, Mother," I said, still not really sure what her problem was with the college girls. "Why don't you just go across the street, say something rude, and alienate yourself from them?"

"I couldn't do that, darling! They idolize me. Yesterday, Kathy told me my skin was an inspiration. Her friend Jasmina agreed that my skin is flawless, better than theirs even. They even asked me what skincare products I use. They love me."

"Sounds horrid, Mother!" I gasped. "How do you live under such conditions?"

"Very funny," she replied. "It's irritating. If I wanted to chat with my neighbors, I'd live in Ohio. They're inhibiting my lifestyle."

"Gee, I'd think with the influx of young straight guys to the area, they would help your lifestyle." My comment was followed by complete silence.

After a moment, I heard a voice in the background that proved my mother was not lying. These girls were indeed taunting my mother with friendly greetings. "Hello, darlings!" my mother shouted back. "Did you get the Dr. Hauschka day cream?" She paused, presumably listening to their response. "Oh, I know. It's so hydrating and don't we need it in the city?" Another pause. "Absolutely, darling. No, no, no, only during the day. It's too heavy for night." Pause. "I don't care what the woman at the counter says. You look at her skin then look at mine, and you decide who you're going to listen to, darling." Short pause. "Of course, no problem. It's my pleasure."

The skincare chat with her neighbor had ended, yet Anjoli did not return to our conversation. "Mother, are you still there?" I asked. "Mother?!" She did not reply. In the background, I heard her humming a tune from *Avenue Q*. "Mother, hang up the phone!" The next sound I heard was Mancha sniffing the phone. "Hit the red button, boy," I instructed. "The red button that says 'off'," I said, hoping it was not true that dogs were color-blind. And illiterate.

When Jack and Adam returned from Spartacus's party, my husband looked like he'd just survived a shipwreck. Not only was his T-shirt soggy, but a sleeve was entirely torn off. The front was ripped as if by a knife. Jack's hair was drying upright and his lip was swollen and cut. He limped favoring his right leg and clutched his neck in pain. Adam, on the other hand, appeared unscathed. "What happened?" I asked, unable to contain my grin.

"You should see the other guys," Jack said, joining me in the fun. "Luce, I don't know what got into me. One dad started getting really competitive with Steve, and the next thing you know we're all trying to outdo each other in the Extreme Machine."

"The Extreme Machine?" I asked, laughing.

"It's basically a tidal wave. You gotta be eighteen to go in it. What they don't tell you is that you shouldn't be any older than eighteen. Anyway, it was an ass-kicker the first time around. I should've stopped after that, but about five guys started really getting into it, and I got carried away. It was like a wolfpack mentality. We all lost our minds for about two hours. Every one of us trying to show how tough he was."

"Well, what do you expect from a retired baseball player?" I said, shrugging. I moved toward him and began rubbing Jack's neck. "Do you want me to get the Motrin?"

"Steve wasn't the one being competitive," Jack corrected. "When you're a former Red Sox pitcher, the rest of the world's competing with you, not the other way around." I wondered for a moment what it would be like to be one of the Steves of the world. To be like Anjoli, Kimmy, and Randy, where things fell into your lap because your lap was *the* place to be. "Ouch, Luce, I can't turn my head!" Jack shouted. He scrunched his face in pain then repeated that he was unable to turn his head from its current position of looking over his right shoulder. "Can you get me the hot pad, babe?" As I was halfway down the hall, I heard Jack ask himself if any of the other dads were feeling the pain.

"Luce!" Jack shouted. "It smells like piss in here. Did you clean the rug this morning?"

Gulp.

# Chapter 29

Earl arranged for Effie the ghost-buster to come to our house on July fourth. She explained that she didn't work on religious holidays, but had no problem with national ones. In fact, she said it was quite appropriate for her to give us independence from our lingering residents on the day we celebrate our nation's sovereignty.

I drove Adam to Renee's house about a half hour before Effie was due to arrive at my place. Her mother was going to babysit her grandchildren and my son while her daughter attended our domestic exorcism and her son-in-law supposedly spent the day at the office. Renee's home was a study in eclecticism with a Chinese rug, mission-style woodwork, and a mixture of pop art and renaissance-style tapestries covering the walls. With her touch, it looked purposefully quirky. If I tried something similar, it would look schizophrenic. Renee brushed by her traditional-looking mother and kissed her on the cheek, rattling off reminders of where to find games, first aid, and emergency phone numbers. Her childlike enthusiasm eclipsed her typical cool demeanor. Renee rubbed her hands together gleefully as if she'd been waiting her entire life to witness a ghost-busting. I found her choice of tank top to be rather telling of her current personal status. She wore a ribbed men's undershirt often called a "wife beater" that she had painted with thick lilac and pink flowers. I wondered how much of the real Renee I was seeing these days. Was she really taking her trials incredibly gracefully, or simply doing an exceptional job of painting?

When we arrived back at my place, Effie was already there talking to Jack. He wore an expression of a man begging to be dismissed from the sideshow I'd brought into our home. His look asked me if he had to stick around for the ghost-busting. "Effie, hi, I'm Lucy Klein," I said extending my hand. "You've met my husband, Jack, I see. Jack, honey, you should go work on that thing, so we can go to the fireworks tonight."

Jack smiled, relieved. "You got it. Yeah, if I get to it right away, I'll finish right in time." He scurried off faster than if he'd woken up from a one-night stand with Marg Schott.

"Let's get started then, shall ve?" Effie said with a thick eastern European accent. Her appearance matched her voice in that it was exactly what one would expect from a ghost-busting psychic. She was short and thick with a dark purple dress with winged sleeves. Every time she lifted her arms, she looked like a bat in flight. Effie began clapping in couplets as she walked around my living room. Renee and I exchanged a look, wondering if she had already begun or was getting warmed up. I was thankful we didn't have those clap-on lights or the place would look like a disco.

"Are you, um, doing it?" Renee asked. Effie turned her head to us, revealing that her eyes were closed, and nodded affirmatively.

"Okay, next room," Effie said moments later.

"That was it?" Renee asked.

"What vere you expecting? I vas to rise up like the vitch in *Vicked*?"

"Kind of," Renee said, laughing.

Effie began making her way to the kitchen where she stopped dead in her tracks. "They're here."

"Who, the ghosts?" I asked.

"No, the caterers for your party," Effie said. "Of course, the ghosts." She began clapping again, then froze. "This is vierd." You know that when a ghost-buster who sounds as if she's from Transylvania claims that something is "vierd," it has to be off-the-charts bizarre. "This has not happened to me before."

"What hasn't happened?" Renee asked eagerly.

"One of these ghosts is very pushy. Usually, they clear out when I clap and do my incantations, but this one says she vants to talk to you. The man says it's time to go, but the voman is yelling now. She says she vill go novhere vithout first speaking to Lucy. She's very pushy. She seems to be in a very bad mood."

"What?!" I gasped. "She called me by name? She said she wants to speak to the owner of the house, or did she name me specifically?"

"She says Lucy," Effie said.

"The ghost said she wants to speak with Lucy?" I asked, incredulous.

"Do you know a Rita and an Arnold?" Effie asked.

"Oh my God!" escaped from my lips. "Look, I know Renee said she wanted more drama, but I'm happy just getting rid of the ghosts. I don't need a whole production to feel like I'm getting my money's worth. The magazine's paying for this anyway, so don't feel like you need to—"

"Rita asked if you vant a glass of pink vine to settle your nerves," Effie said. This was unbelievable. My Aunt Rita always had a bottle of "pink wine" open and poured herself a tall glass after a day teaching kindergarten, saying that it settled her nerves. How did this Effie woman know that? Is this sort of stuff on Google? Was her son blogging? How did Effie even know about Rita? As I continued my silent questioning, Effie said Rita was coming through her.

"She's what?!" I said.

"I knew this would be good!" Renee chirped.

"Lucy, *mamaleh*, don't be alarmed," Effie said, now sounding distinctly like my Aunt Rita. Rita always told people not to be alarmed. She never said, "Don't panic" or "Stay calm." It was always, "Don't be alarmed."

"Okay, Effie, the joke's over," I said.

"Effie's gone now," Effie—or Rita—said.

"Please stop," I begged. "This really isn't funny."

"Don't be alarmed, Lucy. I only want to tawk to you about this ghost-busting nonsense. Why can't Arnold and I stay put? We're very comf'table here and now you come along and try to get rid of us." Renee interrupted and asked if I knew who this was. "Zip it unless you want another turned ankle," Rita said.

"Aunt Rita!" I yelled, now fully accepting that my aunt was the one spooking my house. It was Rita who walked with a limp after she was afflicted with polio as a child. She was more than a tad cranky and shopped compulsively. As wholly incredible as it seemed, clearly it was my Aunt Rita who was causing all of the trouble with my home and its guests. "If you wanted to stay here, why have you been abusing everyone?! None of the artists have been able to create a thing since they've arrived. Every woman who's visited has left with a limp. Interesting women have become crazed shopaholics. Why would you wreak such havoc on the place if you wanted to stay?!"

"That's my way, *mamaleh*," she said. "I wanted a place that reminded me of home and my home had a cranky woman who limped. You know I couldn't stand being forgotten, so I decided to give a little piece of myself to yaw life. I tried to live inside you for awhile, but you weren't crabby enough. Limp or no limp, you were always too damn happy. Same with that friend of yaws, Robin. But Jacquie, now there was a body ripe for the taking. And she could really hang in there with my shopping sprees. It hasn't been all bad. You haven't appreciated the home repairs Arnold's been doing?"

"Uncle Arnold's been working on the house?!" I said, incredulously.

"He was always handy," Rita said.

"What about the breaking glass?" I asked.

"Listen, I'm new at this. I wasn't perfect in life, why should I be in death?"

Then switching voices, Effie's mouth began to move again. "Hello, sweetheart. Don't be too angry with Rita."

"Uncle Arnold?" I asked. This was too bizarre, even for my family.

"You have termites in the attic," he informed me.

"Why are you two here?" I asked.

Switching back to the voice of Aunt Rita, Effie continued, "Why not here? You love the place, why shouldn't we?"

"I don't believe this," I said. "Effie, this is obviously some sort of scam you've got going. So, you can do impersonations of my aunt and uncle. It doesn't mean I buy any of this."

"Listen, big shot," she snapped. "When you were born, Arnold hung a mobile over your crib when my brothah couldn't figure out how to do it. Too smacked up to figure it out." *Smacked up?* "When you visited us in Merrick, you ate Kraft Macaroni and Cheese at every meal and liked it extra milky. When you were in fourth grade, you confided in me that your teacher, Mrs. Fried, didn't like you and I told you that you only had to be with her for the rest of the year, but she had to live with her miserable self for the rest of her life. Convinced now?"

*Holy shit.*

Renee nudged me after my body froze. ""Y'okay, Lucy?" she asked.

"This can't be true," I whispered.

"You must have left a little room for the possibility if you were willing to bring in Effie," she reminded me. Effie was now sitting at my kitchen table with her face buried in her hands, muttering that they had to leave. She seemed to be using her normal voice, but she appeared drained and frail. My aunt could do that to people. Then switching back to Aunt Rita's voice, she said, "We promise to behave, *mamaleh*. Arnold and I agreed that we'll be quiet from now on. I've had my fun."

"It was fun for you to sprain my ankle?!" I asked.

"I said I'll knock it off!" she shouted, making me feel guilty for asking the question. She was a pro at that, too. "Where are we supposed to go?!" Rita said, sadly.

"I'm sorry, but you can't stay here. Your presence is a distraction, to say the least," I said. I couldn't believe I was carrying on such a ludicrous exchange. "Why don't you go to Florida with Aunt Bernice. No one will notice another two dead people there."

There was no response. "Aunt Rita?" I called, looking around. I didn't know why I was looking around since I never actually saw her and I wasn't fully convinced that any of this was real. Effie began shivering and her eyes bolted open.

"Are you okay?" Renee asked as she made her way over to warm Effie with her arms.

"That's never happened before," Effie said.

"Come on, Effie," I said. "You can knock it off now. Earl put you up to that, didn't he? It was a good one, really," I said laughing. "But you can come clean now. How did you know all that stuff about my aunt and uncle?"

"They have gone," was all Effie said.

"I know," I returned. "She died last year and he went a few years earlier."

"I mean your house has no more spirits. They have left," Effie said.

"This is so cool," Renee said, making her way to the fridge. She took a pitcher of lemonade and began pouring it into three glasses for us. "Do you think Jack wants some?"

"Renee!" I shouted. "Forget about the lemonade. I want to know how she pulled this off. Come on, Effie, the joke's over. It was funny, but now I want to know how you did that!"

Effie wiped her brow, clearly fatigued. "It has never happened like this before. Never do spirits use my body like that."

Turning to me, Renee said, "You said she was pushy."

Effie continued, "Never do customers complain after their house has been cleared. Be happy. You have a clean house and you have a story for the magazine."

So that's what this was all about. Earl had instructed Effie to make a dramatic presentation so I would have good material for my article for *Healthy Living*. He always struck me as more ethical than that, but these magazines survive on advertising dollars which depend on sales, so everyone does what it can to attract readers. In any case, I didn't believe a bit of what had just occurred, so I would not be able to write an article about it for Earl. He would just have to send his freak show to another writer's house. As sleazy of an editor he turned out to be, he was still a pretty nice guy and wouldn't give me a hard time about my being unable to write an article on the house-clearing. Besides, I had a dozen new ideas for articles and wanted to get started on writing them as soon as I could. Perhaps I'd even skip the fireworks that evening and start drafting ideas.

# Chapter 30

Three weeks later, I'd pitched, sold and written three magazine articles and drafted an outline for my next book. When I spoke with Earl, he was so earnest about not being responsible for Effie's production that I felt guilty for making the charge. "Lucy, we're friends," he said, hurt. "I would never trick you like that for a story. I would never trick anyone for that matter."

"Come on," I said, lightly. "I'm not angry. I just want the truth. How did she know all that stuff about my aunt?"

"I have no idea," he said. "I'm sorry you don't believe me, but I had nothing to do with Effie channeling your aunt." He then moved on to talking to me about the story on holistic healing for pets. Earl did not scramble to convince me he was telling the truth, which convinced me that he was. It seems the less people try to convince you of their sincerity, the more they actually did so. I had a friend who worked at Macy's in college and said you could always tell the people who were returning stolen merchandise because they talked too much. Their story went on just a bit too long. The legitimate returns simply placed the items on the counter and waited for their money back. Honesty was quiet whereas guilt was fidgety.

"Earl, I'm going to ask you this one more time, and I want you to know that if you tell me you put Effie up to pretending to channel Aunt Rita, I will not be mad," I promised. "There will be absolutely no hard feelings. Do you understand?"

He sighed. "Okay," he said. *I knew it! I knew he set this whole thing up. There was no way my Aunt Rita and Uncle Arnold were living, um, not living at my house and possessing the guests. Thank goodness the world makes sense again. Crazy editors, I can understand.* Earl continued after he sighed. "I'm getting a little tired of this conversation," he finished. *What?* "*Okay, I'm getting tired of the conversation?!*" Earl's delivery remained steady: "When you're ready to talk about the piece, gimme a call. In the meantime, I've got an issue to put to bed and a lunch date I'm already late for." Before I could apologize, he hung up.

August was thick with humidity. Every step I took felt as though I had gum stuck on the bottom of my shoe. I stayed indoors where it was air-conditioned much of the day, and went to Renee's pool to swim with Adam. As I sat at the kitchen table overlooking the guest cottages, I was amazed at the difference a few weeks made. I sipped at a sweating glass of iced tea and watched Maxime and Jacquie playfully interacting with each other. The formerly depressed artist was actually tickling his formerly bitchy wife, and she seemed delighted by it though she was swatting him away as she laughed. Maxime had completed several ink sketches of his wife, and remarkably, Jacquie and Chantrell together. The women seemed utterly unaffected by their past love triangle. Or perhaps it wasn't so past and it had taken on another incarnation. Whatever had conspired between the three of them was more than I needed to know. As long as there was peace at home, I was happy. Chantrell came to sit outside and play her cello, and Jacquie waved to her brightly. I overheard Maxime thank Chantrell for her suggestion of using diluted mud to create "earth ink." He ran inside the house and returned with sheets of white paper that he showed her. From where I was sitting, I couldn't see what he'd made, but could surmise that he was showing her what he'd done with his new medium. Chantrell's eyes lit when she saw it.

Jacquie caught me watching their interaction, but instead of yelling at me as I'd grown to expect, she waved her arm for me to come down and look at Maxime's drawings. She pinched her thumb and index finger together and kissed them to tell me how magnificent she thought they were. The day after Effie came to visit, Jacquie became a new person. Rather, she returned to her old self, the woman who had walked through our doors on Valentine's Day with red wine and reminiscences. A few days after the despooking, Jacquie knocked on my door and asked if we could talk. She apologized for her behavior and explained that she and Maxime had an extremely stressful few years where they acquired more debt than they could possibly handle. Jacquie believed this is what caused her disposition to sour and apologized profusely. Their financial situation had not improved, but something inside her had, she explained after she promised to be a more gracious tenant.

As the three were looking at Maxime's new work, Randy came outside in his bare feet and cotton shorts. As I reflected on the last three weeks at the house, I realized that Randy hadn't broken a single glass object since the day Effie visited.

The time had come to admit the truth. The bizarre reality was that my house had been haunted by Aunt Rita and Uncle Arnold. Though completely illogical, it was the only explanation. As wonderful as it was to have a house filled with laughter, art, and peace, I couldn't help feel a bit guilty about evicting my aunt and uncle's spirits. As a child, when I visited their home, they never sent me back to Anjoli's when I misbehaved. Rita had offered to change her ways. Maybe I should have given her a second chance.

Where would they go? What would they do? *Is* tomorrow another day for the dead?

As Adam and I drove to Renee's house to swim, my cell phone rang. After I answered, I didn't hear anything. "Mancha, is that you?" I asked. I heard nothing, not even Anjoli talking in the background. "Mother!" I shouted. "Anjoli, are you there?!"

"Hello, darling," she said. "What can I do for you?"

*What can she do for me? Who was this imposter?*

"Mancha just called me," I said. "I guess he was calling to say hello."

"Darling, I have some very exciting news about the baby," she began. "Are you sitting down?"

"I'm driving," I told her. "What baby? Do you mean Mancha?"

"It is about, well, the dog formerly known as Mancha," Anjoli said.

"Mother, what are you talking about?"

"Darling, don't get all wound up. I have only good news to share," she said. Then nothing.

"Okay, what is it?"

"First, J.Lo has been completely healed of her hair-pulling disorder."

"Jennifer Lopez has a hair-pulling disorder?"

"That's the second piece of news, darling. When I saw that J.Lo had finally stopped chewing on her paws, I took her to a vet immediately, and he said that she was a girl all along! Isn't that a hoot?! Naturally I went out and bought the cutest pink rhinestone collar to go with her new gender and when the KAT girls saw it, they told me about this pop star, Jennifer Lopez, who goes by the nickname J.Lo, who once wore an engagement ring with a pink stone. So I figured it was a sign that the baby's true name was J.Lo."

"Okay, back up a minute here, Mother. The dog stopped pulling his fur out of his paws, so you decided to take him to a vet?"

"The only time to see a traditional doctor is when you're well, darling."

"And he told you Mancha is a female?"

"J.Lo, darling. Her name is J.Lo."

"You didn't notice that she was female before? I mean, wasn't the absence of a penis your first clue?"

"Oh no, darling. J.Lo was fixed, so when I thought he was a boy, I figured they had simply cut his penis off during the procedure."

"They don't cut the—" I sighed, exasperated. "Never mind. Well, it's a good thing he, um, she's stopped the fur-pulling."

"Now I can start thinking about dog shows again, darling! It's funny, I think J.Lo is happy that we know she's a girl. She holds herself a little different now. She's got a little more attitude."

"So it sounds like you're getting along better with your neighbors," I said.

"They are the sweetest," Anjoli returned.

"I thought that was the problem."

"They've grown on me. I'm giving a talk on skincare at the house on Thursday night. They say I'm an inspiration. You know how I am. If I can inspire just one person, I have to do what I'm called to."

"Skincare is your calling?"

"Don't be ludicrous, darling. I'm not so one-dimensional. My calling is total beauty. Skin, hair, clothing, makeup— the full package. Darling, that reminds me of something I need to discuss with you. It's a bit heavy. Are you sitting down?"

"Still driving, Mother."

"I went to see Kendra last night and it was devastating." Kendra is one of my mother's oldest friends. They shared their first apartment together in Greenwich Village in the late fifties, before my parents met. They went to poetry readings, dance performances, and lectures together.

They were inseparable. Kendra was Anjoli's maid of honor, and when Kendra's husband came on to Anjoli, she turned him down flatly. She told me that Jim was not her type, but she couldn't fool me. Even at twelve years old, I could see that Jim was an extremely handsome and successful guy. That was exactly Anjoli's type. The part of her that declined the invitation was the teaspoon of decency that kept her from screwing her best friend's husband. Kendra now had cancer. Not the kind of cancer where you go in for surgery and chemotherapy, then fight your way back to health. The kind of cancer where you're in a hospital bed at home, waiting to die. "She wasn't even conscious," Anjoli sniffed. "And tubes in the nose, a needle in her arm. She looked horrible."

"I'm so sorry," I said. "I know how you love Kendra." They were the sort of friends who could go years without seeing each other, but when they caught up, they picked up right where they left. After Kendra and her family moved to Westchester, she and my mother didn't see each other as often as they did when they both lived in the city, but she always held the top spot in my mother's heart.

"It got me thinking about my own mortality," Anjoli said. *Of course it did. We couldn't have another person dying without somehow making you think about yourself.* "So I've prepared a living will of sorts so you'll know how I want things handled should I ever become incapacitated." As I pulled into Renee's driveway, I checked my rearview mirror to check on Adam. He had fallen asleep. I stayed in the car and continued with Anjoli.

"So, do you want to be kept on life support?" I asked.

"Oh, I don't know about that, darling," she said. "Those things are so complicated. It depends on the situation. There are times when it's completely appropriate and others when it's totally hopeless. I'm sure you'll make the right decision based on the circumstances. What I do know is that if you let me grow chin hairs, I will haunt you so bad I'll make your Aunt Rita look like an amateur."

"What?"

"I'm not finished, darling. I'm setting up a Schwab account that will cover the cost for weekly manicures and pedicures, leg waxing, and hair-coloring. You should have seen Kendra's roots! I know my Kendra and as soon as she comes to, she's going to ask for a hand mirror, then promptly drop dead. And that daughter of hers is so damned self-righteous she isn't even considering what her mother would want. Kendra was an extremely vain woman. I was only trying to do what Kendra would want when Little Miss Know-It-All burst into the room and started yelling at me to leave Kendra be! The nerve, darling."

"Wait, I'm missing something here," I said. "Why did her daughter yell at you? What were you doing?" I asked, bracing myself for anything.

"Plucking her chin hairs," Anjoli said. "I know Kendra, and cancer or no cancer, she would be mortified to see herself looking that way."

"Mother, you're a piece of work."

"And so was Kendra. Don't be so judgmental. I used a tweezer, it's not like I was yanking them out with my bare hands. For Christ sake, the woman had a three-inch hair coming from her chin. She looked like a Chinese chef!"

"Okay, so what you're telling me is that you're leaving behind a living beauty will?" I asked. "And if you should ever become seriously injured or sick, I should just wing it on the medical decisions as long as I make sure your toenails are polished?"

"Exactly, darling. It's in the file cabinet in my office. It's clearly marked 'For Lucy.' "

Most people have emotional baggage from their parents. I am lucky enough to have a mother who puts it in file folders and labels it for me.

"Mother, I'm in Renee's driveway. I've got to go."

"How lovely. Be sure to say hello to her for me. Tell her I've been thinking of her."

Most parents encourage their children not to lie. Like absolutely everything else in life, my mother does the opposite.

# Chapter 31

After a day of splashing in Renee's pool, we returned to the house to look at applications for next year's resident artists. When I told Renee about last year's lot—including stages of orgasm in paint—she insisted that she come over and sift through the applicants with Jack and me this year. On more than one occasion, she confided that the bizarre amusements of our household were her only entertainment as her own marriage was imploding. In other words, we were good for a laugh. I knew to take her remark as a compliment as I felt similarly toward her. I loved hanging out with her because she dared to pull off sophomoric pranks I never had the courage to do. Once when we were pulling into the supermarket parking lot together, she saw an able-bodied young woman park in a handicapped spot. "Look at her!" Renee said in disgust. "Who the hell does this little bitch think she is?" I had to admit, as the niece of a legitimately disabled woman, I did find the young woman's arrogance off-putting, but Renee hopped out of my minivan and started surrounding the car with shopping carts. "You go inside and tell me when she gets in the checkout line," Renee said to me before darting off. By the time Renee was done, she had surrounded the car with more than forty carts. As we slouched in the front seat of my van, Renee and I giggled like teens as we watched the navel-pierced twit wobble in her platform shoes as she exasperatedly returned the carts.

On the August evening that Jack and I set aside to review artist applications, we had already arranged for Jenna to babysit. We knew from last year's experience that reading essays, looking at slides, and listening to CDs was an all-night affair. As soon as we finished dinner, the three of us went down to Jack's studio where he had been collecting applicant packages. I loved the rich scent of jasmine and honeysuckle that surrounded the property in the summer. It reminded me of the tall wall of bushes I had to pass on my way to the playground in summer camp.

The first application contained a CD from a guy who combined his ethnic heritage into a musical genre all its own—Celtic salsa. We loved his music, but since he needed housing for a five-man band we had to decline.

A woman named Grace from Amsterdam sent us slides of a room where she glued three million clear plastic straws to the walls. She placed them perpendicular to the wall surface, one beside the next, creating the look of foam mattress. When we looked at the first slide, I couldn't see the straws at all, but they were clear in the close-ups. The shots taken straight-on looked like honeycomb, while the pictures taken from the sides looked like crystallized ice. Grace's essay explained that she enjoyed experimenting with texture, which explained why her next slides were of pieces made from sewing pins, nails, and broken glass. I almost accepted her on the spot so she could put to use all of Randy's fumbles.

Laura Jackson from the Bronx sent slides of sculptures she made from a collection of wire hangers that would make Joan Crawford freak out beyond anything seen in *Mommie Dearest*. She explained that she used nothing more than a set of pliers and hangers to create pieces ranging from simple, elegant figures to perfect reproductions of bridges. She did use orange paint to accent the Golden Gate. The Brooklyn Bridge was painstakingly well-detailed. She made sure we could appreciate this by enclosing a photo of the actual bridge.

Clint Treadwell of Munich sent slides of sculptures he made from shredded newspaper. It was actually pretty cool. I would never think to create balls from old newspaper, but he demonstrated his ability to do so best with a sculpture of a poodle. "Doesn't anyone paint anymore?" Jack asked.

"I was thinking the exact same thing," Renee added. Before opening a package from an Austrian minimalist, we opened another bottle of wine and compared our stack of "definitely nots" to our "maybes." So far we had thirty-two rejects and seven contenders. As we checked again for the contents of the minimalist's package, we realized that he had actually enclosed nothing, taking minimalism to the extreme of stupidity. We had to wonder if this was his idea of a goof on us, or if he thought he was being clever.

One guy sent us a DVD of something so strange it defied description. Men's clothing was stuffed with pillows. The figure was lying on the ground with a white pillow head coming from the collar. On top of the man's head was a safe that had fallen on it and kept him from getting up. Projected onto the white pillow was film of a man's face who was muttering obscenities. "Stop looking at me, motherfucker!" he said. So we did, and put freaky boy's application in the reject pile.

By midnight we agreed on Grace and Laura, but could not come to a consensus on the third artist. I liked the newspaper shredder, but Renee said that his essay gave her the creeps. Jack and I desperately wanted a harmonious second season so we eliminated anyone Renee said she thought may be mentally unstable. Since we had another few weeks to decide on our third pick, Jack and I decided to call it a night and send our invitations to Grace and Laura in the morning. Rather, later that morning.

As the sun pierced through our bedroom curtains, I groped for the telephone receiver as it rang persistently. "I didn't wake you did I, darling?" Anjoli said urgently. I looked at the blurry digits on my clock. As my eyes began to focus, I could see it was just after seven. "You know how I detest mornings, but I've been waiting all night to tell you the news." Before I could ask, Anjoli continued: "Kimmy and Nick set a date and it is right around the corner." I wondered why this was such big news. "The wedding will be over Labor Day weekend, so we have a little over three weeks to prepare, darling."

"Labor Day?!" I shrieked, sitting up in bed. Glancing toward Jack's side of the bed, I was grateful to see he had already risen and started his day. Otherwise he would have had the most shrill alarm clock. "Mother, does she realize that Labor Day is our open house? I can't miss it. This is a huge deal for Jack and me. It'll be the first time we open our artist colony up to the community. It's already in the local calendar section of the paper, and stores are hanging flyers about it in their windows. Did you both forget that this is the biggest weekend of my life?!"

"And it's about to get bigger, darling," Anjoli said with a drumroll delivery.

"What do you mean?" I asked. I hated how my mother teased in her delivery. I always had to ask, "What do you mean?" or somehow encourage her to go on with the rest of her news. Instead of getting right to it, she gave a seemingly endless preamble that left me wondering if she'd forgotten the point all together and had simply drifted off on to another topic.

"Kimmy and I went to the Needle Park Gallery for her dress today and we were talking about what type of dress would fit with the ambience we wanted to create," Anjoli began. Perhaps this would be a good time to explain that the Needle Park Gallery, despite its name and location, is the hippest bridal dressmaker in Manhattan. In order to get an appointment, women have to submit a headshot for consideration because as the designer, Mingi X, was quoted saying in *Vogue,* she does not waste her talent on ugly brides. I believe the exact quote was something like, "To preserve the integrity of my art, I must hand-select women to wear my gowns because my work becomes polluted when worn by ugly brides." Instead of alienating potential brides, Mingi found that her hideous comments launched her into superstardom. Brides from across the country hired professional makeup artists, hairstylists, and photographers so they could show Mingi that they were pretty enough to wear a Needle Park bridal gown. Needle Park wasn't even called Needle Park anymore. The East Village had been so gentrified over the last ten years that heroin addicts had to relocate to make way for kids to play on the jungle gym. Yet the pretentiously unpretentious Mingi opted to name her dress shop after an outdoor heroin shooting gallery. Instead of being repelled by this, women from even the most wholesome states sent giggly notes to Mingi, begging to be initiated into the ranks of the Needle Park brides. They promised to make the pilgrimage to New York for their fittings, and agreed to sign a contract allowing Mingi to destroy any wedding photographs that weren't flattering to her dresses. "Anyway, darling, naturally after taking one look at Kimmy, Mingi accepted her application and even waived the file review fee. Such a sweetheart, that Mingi. She's making a hat for me that will match Kimmy's dress. Not that I didn't qualify for a dress, of course, darling. I may yet be a Needle Park maid of honor, but I have to feel out Alfie and see if he'll be crushed if he doesn't dress me for the wedding."

"How sensitive of you, Mother," I said.

"And guess who else is going to be wearing a Mingi original to Kimmy's wedding?"

"Me?" I asked tentatively. I wasn't sure I wanted this nasty woman, sighing with exasperation as she measured my hips and waist.

"Oh," Anjoli's voice fell. "No, darling. I didn't think you were into that whole scene." I wasn't, but it would have been nice to be the one rejecting the idea. I wondered if my mother thought Mingi would turn down my application. Then I shook off the entire, ridiculous notion of having to apply for the right to pay top dollar for a dress named after a rehabilitated druggie park.

"Good," I said. "I don't have time to come in to the city for fittings with the open house coming up. Oh right! Tell me how we're supposed to handle my being in two places at once on Labor Day."

"Don't you want to hear about J.Lo's dress?"

"J.Lo's dress?" I repeated. "Ah yes, the dog. You're getting a dress made for your Chihuahua? Did Mingi agree to this?"

"Agree to it?! It was her idea, darling." *Unbelievable.*

"That's terrific then. The three of you should look very coordinated."

"You don't feel left out do you, darling?" Anjoli asked. "If you want Mingi to whip up something for you, I'm sure she'd do it for me. We won't let her see you until all the papers are signed." *Ouch!* It took a long time for me to come to peace with my weight. I wish the rest of the world would hurry up.

"Don't bother, Mother. Renee's going to cut a hole through a canvas tent so I can put my head through it. I'll just wear that."

"She is so creative," Anjoli said.

"Anyway, tell me about this Labor Day wedding."

"Oh yes, how could I forget, darling?"

*Because you're a flake, Mother!*

"Kimmy and Nick have decided to have their wedding on Labor Day weekend."

"I know *that!* How am I supposed to be her matron of honor if we have our big art show that weekend?"

"Because Kimmy and Nick's wedding will be at your place. That's how, darling," Anjoli said with great satisfaction.

"We're having an art show," I reminded her.

"This will be part of it! Think of it as performance art, darling. Everyone adores watching beautiful people get married. I bet you double attendance when people hear that a model is getting married on your commune."

"Mother!" I shouted, not knowing where to begin. I took a deep breath and tried to reason with her. "Jack, Maxime, Chantrell, and Randy have worked really hard to make this show a success. If we throw a wedding in the middle of it, it'll detract from their work. Besides, do Kimmy and Nick really want a bunch of strangers at their wedding?"

"As long as they bring gifts," Anjoli said, laughing. "Seriously, darling, if you're worried about money, I'll pay for all of the champagne and hors d'oeuvres. Plus, consider how much exposure these artists will get if I infuse the party with our fabulous guest list. We'll make your open house *the* place to be on Labor Day weekend. The townspeople will feel like absolute bumpkins if they don't show up."

# Chapter 32

Oddly, I was the only one who objected to Kimmy and Nick relocating their wedding smack dab in the middle of our first open house. Jack agreed with Anjoli that hosting a wedding would be a huge draw. And bringing two hundred well-heeled guests from the city couldn't help but result in art sales for everyone. Randy immediately asked if he could design an abstract glass bride-and-groom ornament for the cake top. Chantrell offered to play her cello for the bridal procession, and Maxime insisted on creating the invitations. I never thought a wedding invitation done entirely in ink dots would look quite as elegant as it did. Even Jacquie got into the act. At first, I assumed her contribution would be shopping for party supplies, but she stunned us all when she announced that she was a classically trained opera singer and belted out an absolutely spectacular "Ave Maria."

The next day, I woke up to the sight of Jack and Adam dressed in white undershirts, backward baseball caps, and unusually large medallions made of fake gold and rhinestones. "Is today Anderson's hip-hop birthday party?" I asked.

"Gangsta party, woman," Jack corrected. As he smiled, I saw that my husband had wrapped a front tooth in gold foil. He picked up his water gun and tucked it into his low-rider pants and instructed Adam, "Word to your mother." Whatever the hell that meant. "You best start gettin' dressed, woman," he said to me.

There was something more than a bit ironic about a ghetto theme party in honor of a five year old named Anderson P. Barrington IV held on a multimillion-dollar estate so large that the invitation included a map. Not a map of how to get to the Barrington estate—a map of how to get from the driveway to the "Sunny Garden." Apparently, Anderson P. Barrington III provided legal representation for Forty Cent, a cheap imitation of the half-dollar megastar. Forty agreed to entertain the kids for an hour.

I couldn't even imagine why Adam was invited to this party. We'd never met the Barringtons. When we received the invitation last week, Renee was at the house helping Jack paint the car. She informed me that every family in town with children ranging from newborns to high schoolers would be attending the Barrington bash. When I told her it was Jack's turn to take Adam to the party, she gasped. "You *have* to go!"

"I took Adam to Devin's fire engine party three weeks ago, and I still hear sirens blaring in my head," I reminded her. "Don't I deserve a break?"

Renee took a serious tone and explained, "This party is going to rock in ways that people like you and me can't begin to imagine. Bebe told me that MTV was going to make a surprise launch of its new G-rated music television station *live* from the Barrington party!" I could not care less about MTV or its new kid station, but I found Renee's excitement contagious. I began wondering if I should attend. "Plus, if you don't go, Faidra will take it as a huge snub and you'll be on her shit list forever. Believe me, you do not want that. She had a huge falling out with Felicity Griswold six years ago. Do you know her?"

I ran through my mental Rolodex. "No, never heard of her," I told Renee.

"Exactly," she said, folding her arms smugly. When Renee sensed that I was unmoved by the threat of social Siberia, she changed tactics. "It will be a total blast, hon. Go for me, won't you. Dan has to work all next weekend and I don't want to go alone."

"Okay," I agreed. "How are things going with you two?"

"He's working *all* next weekend," she replied. "And he worked all this weekend. It's amazing that he isn't running the place by now."

"Renee," I said, extending her name to scold her cynicism. "Maybe he *is* working."

"I called his cell phone company and said I was his secretary, and had them fax me a copy of his phone bill for the last month. He makes a lot of calls to the same number, the home of a Cindy Phoenix. Could you puke at the name? His credit card statements show that he's having some pretty swanky dinners on the nights Dan said he was working. Remember working late on big projects?" Renee asked. I nodded. "Remember where dinner came from? Subway sandwiches or someplace like that, not Phillipe's Bistro."

I said nothing because there was nothing to say. It was clear Dan was still having an affair and had no intention of calling it off. I wanted to ask her what she planned to do about her philandering husband. I wanted to tell her she deserved better than this. But before I could open my mouth, she shifted gears and continued to urge me to attend the Barrington bash. "You could pitch a story to *Parenting* magazine about over-the-top birthday parties," she urged. "I mean, when was the last time you went to a backyard party with pin the tail on the donkey and frosted sponge cake?"

I laughed. "I once went to a kid's birthday party where Barney showed up drunk off his ass and fell into the swimming pool. He actually hit his head pretty badly and had to be taken away by paramedics. The mom called in a shrink to do a post-party therapy session so the kids wouldn't suffer long-term damage."

I agreed to go to the party, and truth be told, I was looking forward to it all week. When I saw Jack and Adam dressed and ready to go that morning, I wondered what I would wear to match their gangsta ensemble. I opted for a yellow sundress and was eternally grateful for the choice when we arrived. The only mother who was pimped out was Faidra who looked as if she borrowed Janet Jackson's Super Bowl jumpsuit. Clearly, the unspoken rule was that Faidra was the belle of this ball and the other mothers better not even try to compete. How any woman could wear black leather on an August day was beyond me. I have to admit, though, she didn't break a sweat. I wouldn't be surprised if there was some sort of surgical intervention to ensure that Faidra would never do something as human as perspire. Renee told me that she had every type of cosmetic assistance available, including the bleaching of her butt hole.

"What?!" I gasped when Renee whispered this to me at the party. "Why would she do that?"

"I guess to make it look more youthful," Renee said, shrugging.

"Who's looking at her asshole?" I said, incredulous.

"It's apparently pretty common."

"It is *not* common!" I exclaimed. "Come on, tell me you're kidding."

"I'm not kidding, Lucy. Faidra Barrington has a bleached ass. Actually, I think it's a laser procedure."

"Jesus," I sighed. "That's good grooming." I made a point to remind myself to squat over a hand mirror later that evening and see what all the fuss was about. It infuriated me that men could walk around feeling perfectly good about their appearance whether they had a unibrow, triple chin, or skin flaps hanging off their eyelids, but stunning women like Faidra felt the need to have an unblemished butt hole. The world is insane.

Not only was the world insane, this party was crazy. The closest parking spot was more than three blocks from the house. We found our way to the "Sunny Garden" by following the pounding rhythm of a band calling itself PG-Unit, the warm-up band for Forty Cent. The Barringtons had a stage set up that looked as if it were an actual rock concert. They had a 2,000 square foot wood dance floor surrounded by dainty tables covered with white umbrellas you just don't see in the hood. The irony of this party was too delicious. Adam and Jack looked cute dancing, but others were more amusing. As I sat under a parasol, gossiping about Faidra's asshole with Renee, I watched Phil MacInerny, the local elementary school principal, gyrating his hips and pumping his arm up and down like John Travolta in *Saturday Night Fever.* I always enjoy the sight of white people trying to show how hip they are by self-consciously copying moves they think black people would do.

Faidra flitted by every table with her freshly dyed burgundy hair that was flipped above the shoulder like Marcia Cross's character, Bree, from "Desperate Housewives." She kissed Renee on both cheeks and introduced herself to me, telling me how pleased she was that Jack, Adam, and I could attend. Her manners were astonishing. Well over four hundred people were at this party and she remembered the names of the people connected with me as soon as she heard my name. "You're the family that turned the Adler place into an arts colony. Anderson and I are very much looking forward to your open house on Labor Day weekend. We're collectors," she said matter-of-factly. "Anyhoo," Faidra continued, handing us two red bandannas. "You are both Bloods, so put these on your heads before the water balloon battle with the Cryps later." Pointing at the red bandanna on her own head, she said, "I'm a Blood too, so let's kick some booty together, bitches," she said with a demure giggle chaser. There was something extraordinarily lovable about Faidra. Despite her pearly white asshole and insistence that we dress like gangsta girls, she was warm and sincere in a way I didn't expect.

Robin joined us at the table and waved her red bandanna at Renee and me. "I guess we're Bloods together," she said, leaning in to kiss me. "It's been too long. We need to get together soon," Robin said to me.

Glancing across the lawn, Renee took inventory of who was there and what color bandannas Faidra was handing them. "I think all of the Junior League gals are Bloods," Robin told her as she noticed Renee's eyes scanning. "And all of the guys from Anderson's law firm are Cryps." Renee and I burst into laughter as Robin smiled.

"I have *got* to write an article about this!" I shouted.

Just then, I heard the familiar beginning of the Forty Cent song, "In Da House": "In da house it's always y'birfday. We gotta party like it's your birfday," he sang. *We've got to party like it's your birthday? No wonder this man needs good legal representation!* Forty wore low-riding jeans and no top and was most definitely sweating. His ripped abs and muscular arms were so shiny they looked almost as if they were oiled. If I squinted, I could see a trail of black hair trickling down from his charcoal black belly button down into his jeans. After the crowd finished hooting and hollering, Forty greeted the guests and brought little Anderson on stage to wish him a happy birthday. We all had to give a "shout out for Shorty" and repeated several chants Forty led.

"I thought Shorties were women," Renee whispered to me.

"Forget everything you once knew," I whispered back. "Sounds like it means 'kid' today."

Forty said he wrote a song especially for Anderson and his homeys, and shouted into his microphone, "How many y'all Shorties here was titty-fed? Lucky, mother-suckers, getting all that free titty." He immediately launched into a song where the chorus was something about mother-suckers. Forty held out his mike and urged the audience to shout back at him, "Lucky mother-suckers." Absurdly enough, they did. No one seemed at all outwardly fazed by the fact that their kids were being taught borderline obscene lyrics that make nursing babies seem like sex-crazy boob fiends.

"Am I hallucinating, or does this guy keep calling our kids mother-suckers?" I finally asked.

"This is classic Faidra," Renee said.

"Well, I have to agree with Lucy that this is wholly inappropriate," Robin added. "I'm going to say something to Faidra."

Forty continued, "If you love that titty, say, ho!"

"Ho!" replied a mob of self-conscious white people trying to prove how hip they are.

Faidra rushed by us, heading toward the house with a sense of urgency. I may have even seen a bead of sweat peeking out from under her bandanna. Robin held out her manicured hand with a diamond that caught the sunlight in such a way that it looked as if her hand just launched fireworks. "Faidra," Robin said. "We need to talk about these lyrics!"

Faidra brushed by our table, looking back to reply. "Not now, girls. There are some kids snorting confectionary sugar in the kitchen. Be back in a second."

# Chapter 33

The night after the Barrington hood bash, I drafted an article on how kids' birthday parties have gone from neighborhood gatherings with cake and ice cream to ostentatious mega-events with pop stars and faux cocaine. It was supposed to be a humorous piece, but I found myself growing heavyhearted at the thought that some kids were sacrificing their childhood rite of passage to make way for their parents' show of affluence. Three days later, *Parenting* bought the piece and assigned a follow-up two-part series: blow jobs at Bar Mitzvahs and sex at Sweet Sixteens.

The phone rang. Aunt Bernice called to ask if I would like a laser treatment next time I come to Florida. "Turns out, I refudd so much business that I get a free lasah job, but what do I need with it now that my vaginer is as smooth as a baby's?" Why she felt the need to give me the status of her pubic hair every time we spoke was beyond me. "Thank you for sending that adorable T-shirt your friend Ronni painted. I'm the hit of the Hallmark with it on."

"Oh, you're the hit of the Hallmark even without it, Aunt Bern," I replied.

"True," she chirped. "Why isn't Ronni selling these gorgeous creations at boutiques?"

"Renee," I corrected. "Her name is Renee,"

"Whatevah her name is, that goil has talent."

As much as I adored Aunt Bernice, talking to her made me miss Aunt Rita. Rita would have had some negative comment to balance Bernice's sunshine. She would say the T-shirts were ugly. She'd add that the paint smelled so bad it was giving her a migraine. As lovely as Bernice was, half of her was missing without Rita. I understood how she felt. There was an empty space in my home now that Rita and Arnold were gone—and they were *haunting* my house. If only Rita could have been a well-behaved ghost. But why would she be different in death than she was in life?

Before I could pick up the phone to call Robin to ask her about the next Junior League luncheon, I heard Jack shout from the attic. Hoping he hadn't hurt himself, I ran to the ladder leading up to the attic and asked if he was okay. "Come up here, Luce," he said. As I ascended the rungs, I asked what the problem was. "Look at this," he said gesturing to the walls. I looked puzzled. "Look closely," Jack said. I stepped close to the walls to see that the wood beams and walls were lumpy and torn. "Termites," Jack said. "It's pretty extensive. We're gonna need to get the place tented. We'll need to move out for a few days."

"Can it wait until after the open house?" I asked.

"Yeah," Jack said. "Why don't we get the place looked at, then take off for a few days if we need to get tented. Maybe leave Adam with Bernice and cruise down to the Bahamas or something."

"It's going to be sad to see them go," I said of our visitors. "Where will Maxime and Jacquie go?"

"I don't know," Jack said, shrugging. "They seem to be the type that always land on their feet. Ya know, we bought this place less than two years ago. I think the guys who did the termite inspection need to cover this." With that, he began climbing down the ladder. "Come on down, Luce. Where do we keep the house stuff?"

"In the bottom drawer of the file cabinet," I told him as the phone began to ring.

"Hello," I said, answering the call.

"The wedding is a fiasco! Kimmy can't settle on a dress, darling," Anjoli launched. "Honestly, she is so high maintenance."

"Hello, Mother."

"Darling, I am in *crisis*. We spent all day in that gritty little hot box Needle Park looking at design after design after design, and absolutely nothing pleased madam." I could see my mother rolling her eyes at Kimmy's world-class divatude. "Finally, Mingi started shouting at us in Chinese or whatever language she speaks. When she finally calmed down, she told us that no one rejected her dresses and kicked us out. Can you imagine being asked to leave a dress shop?"

"Mother, you're forbidden to return to several eastern European countries," I reminded her.

"Precisely why being banned from her dinky little bridal sweatshop is so insulting, darling," Anjoli said. "I think the woman is a complete fraud. Do you know what she said?" Not waiting for a reply, she continued, "She said we weren't nice. Not *nice?!* Who the hell wants to be thought of as *nice* anyway? It's such an insipidly pedestrian compliment, it's practically an insult. I thought she was one of us."

"One of *us?*" I inquired.

"An artiste, darling," Anjoli clarified. "Someone who didn't have an interest in being characterized as *nice*. For God's sake, the woman said she didn't allow ugly brides to wear her dresses. I respected her for that honesty. Now it turns out that she's a simpy little mouse cake like all the rest interested in dealing with people who are 'nice' and 'good' and other such blandness. *Nice!* Who the hell wants to be *nice?*"

"Mother, if it makes you feel any better, I don't find you the least bit nice."

"You're such a love," she said, sniffing. "So get ready for my next piece of news. Are you sitting?"

"Mother," I said, sighing. "I have never once fainted on account of your news. Why do you always ask if I'm sitting?"

"Oh, I don't know, darling. Does it really matter? Does every word I say need to be hyperanalyzed by you?"

"I suppose not," I dismissed. "Okay, I'm sitting. I have my smelling salts by my side and a handmaiden ready to assist me should I keel over from the shock of Kimmy's wedding dress news."

Anjoli burst into laughter. "Your delivery is just like your father's, darling. God, I miss that man. Why he had to leave this plane is beyond me. It wasn't as though he was so spiritually evolved."

Mother saw death as a graduation from earth. Whenever people passed away, Anjoli nodded her head somberly, declared them evolved souls, then darted off to Pilates. "Were you able to change Mingi's mind?"

"Change her mind?!" my mother gasped. "I wouldn't dream of it. It's beneath me and beneath Kimmy to grovel for the approval of anyone, much less a hyped-up seamstress."

"Oh, did you want me to call her?" I asked.

"Ha!" she laughed. "It's beneath you too, darling. How did you ever get such low self-esteem with me as a mother? Anyway, Kimmy decided she's going to forgo the whole wedding dress thing altogether. She says it's too mainstream." There were certain words that were emotionally loaded in my family. "Mainstream" was one of them, along with "pedestrian" and "common."

"So what's Kimmy going to wear, a pantsuit?"

"Think again, darling."

"Um, a skirt?"

"One more guess!"

"A tuxedo?"

"That's clever, but more your style than Kimmy's. Ready to give up, darling?"

"Yeah, tell me."

"Are you ready?"

"Mother, I need to go in a minute. Either tell me or don't tell me," I bluffed. I was dying to know after such a build-up, but couldn't stand to let my mother know how effective her game was.

"Nothing!"

"What do you mean nothing?" I asked.

"I mean she's not going to wear one stitch of clothing, darling. Nothing, nada, neit."

"Are you telling me that Kimmy's going to get married naked?"

"Well, there's more to it than that," Anjoli said, enjoying herself. "You've heard of body painting, haven't you, darling? It's all the rage among the kids these days. Apparently, all the girls at the Playboy Mansion adore body paint."

"Oh yes, how could I have forgotten? Last time I was hanging out at Hef's place, I got painted like a mermaid before I posed for my centerfold."

"Very funny, darling. My little friends at the KAT house told me about it. You don't mind if I add them to the guest list, do you?"

"Will they be dressed or painted?" I asked, half serious.

"Dressed, of course. It takes a while to do a good paint job. I imagine Jack will be busy for two to three hours on Kimmy's body."

"Excuse me?" I said, hoping I had misunderstood.

"I said that it will take Jack between two to three hours to paint Kimmy's body, especially considering the glitter glaze she wants on top. You know how brides are, they always wants that little extra sparkle."

"Yes, but it's usually on their eyelids, not their nipples, Mother. I'm sorry, but Jack cannot paint Kimmy's naked body," I said.

"Why not?! He's always working on that car of yours on the lawn. How is this any different, darling?"

"I've never feared Jack would get sexually aroused by a VW Bug, Mother! Why does she have to get married in the nude anyway? First she jilted her groom, then she married herself in a gown made of disco-ball mirrors, and now after having screwed half the Ivy League, she decides to marry an anthropology professor in nothing but a coat of paint?!"

"And glitter," Anjoli added.

"The point is that this is not normal!"

"Who wants to be normal?" Anjoli shrieked. "Normal is boring. Normal is insipid. Normal is a complete bore and I, for one, think it's fabulous that Kimmy marches to her own tune. Why do you begrudge her this? Look at you, living in an artist colony, you're not exactly Donna Reed, and thank goodness for it, darling. I'm proud of how unique my girls are."

"Okay," I said, not defeated, but accepting of my role in this world. For the first time in my life, I felt at peace with who I was in relation to the rest of society. I was the daughter of an adulterous, narcissistic mother and a dead drug-addicted father. I now lived in an arts colony with a husband who would paint my cousin's naked body for her wedding. Meanwhile the aunt who did not haunt my house would undoubtedly be on-call to offer Kimmy pubic hair removal tips. In that moment of agreeing to allow Jack to paint Kimmy, I felt at home with myself for the first time in my life. "I'll ask Jack if he's comfortable with this, and if he agrees, it's fine with me."

"He's an artist, of course he'll feel comfortable with it,

darling," Anjoli said. "Do you think he could do me, too?"

"You know, Mother, call me pedestrian, but having my husband 'do' my mother is a bit more than I can handle."

"That's fine. Alfie would be devastated if I didn't let him sew up a little number for me anyway. Plus, the attention really should be on Kimmy for her wedding. The last thing we need is to have everyone talking about how fabulous my ass looks. Absolutely no cellulite whatsoever."

# Chapter 34

"Let's all give a warm round of applause for the Meals in Heels committee and Pennies for Peace," announced Cecile as the room full of Junior Leaguers politely clapped. "And of course, our newest member, Lucy Klein, and her family will be hosting their first open house at their arts ranch in two short weeks," she continued, winking playfully. There was genuine excitement in the community about our Labor Day weekend. I hoped the fact that we were simultaneously hosting a nude wedding wouldn't cast me as the neighborhood pariah, but this community seemed extremely welcoming of families that were a little off the beaten path. Faidra was still in good standing after Anderson's gangsta party, even after she confirmed the rumors that Forty Cent was caught naked in the Jacuzzi with seven waitresses from the catering company after the party. I liked that Faidra didn't hide from her scandals. She seemed stronger for not needing to deny the truth. Kids were snorting sugar. Entertainers were entertaining fourteen boobs in her hot tub. Why deny it? Just deal with it. I wondered if that type of serenity came from inner peace or from outrageous wealth. I liked her and told Renee I wanted to invite her to our next luncheon at my house.

Cecile continued, "Lucy, would you like to say a few words about your event?"

Nervously, I stood. I hoped my voice didn't catch and the women wouldn't see how terrified I was to speak at the meeting. "Hi," I began. I held up a stack of orange flyers with information about the open house printed on them. "You've probably seen these posters around town. Anyway, my husband, son, and I are new to the community, but we fell in love with the area two years ago and decided to buy a place and fulfill our dream of starting an artist colony. We've got three artists who will be showing at the open house. Well, four when you include my husband." I laughed nervously. "Maxime and his wife are visiting from France. He does ink sketches using a pinpoint pen. It's really pretty incredible when you see them. Everything he does is in disconnected dots, but at first glance it looks like they're all connected." I stopped for a moment and took a sip of water. "Chantrell plays cello and will be performing live there as well as selling her CDs. Randy does glass sculptures, and I really couldn't even begin to do him justice if I tried to describe him. I mean, I couldn't do justice to his work. His *work* is gorgeous. Then there's Jack. That's my husband, and he paints. Some of you have been to my house and seen how he changes the car on the front lawn. Anyway, his work is really beautiful, so I hope you'll come by and check it out. Oh yes, and my cousin will be getting married at the open house. It's kind of a performance art piece." I paused, then looked out at the women. "I know this may sound bizarre, but I think I'd better tell you now rather than have you be caught off guard, but my cousin is getting married naked." The crowd murmured. They repeated what I said in the form of a question. "Well, she'll have body paint," I explained. "And, um, glitter."

Cecile brightened. "Oh! Body paint is very in right now," she said. Shockingly, the women began nodding in agreement.

A woman raised her hand. "Will there be someone there to paint the guests' bodies, or is it only for the bride?"

Renee nudged me under the table. She could barely contain her smirk.

Robin pointed a finger in the air. "Can we set up a booth to collect canned foods for the homeless shelter?"

*That's it? Some women wanted to get painted and others wanted to collect canned food? Where was the burning at the stake?*

"I'll see if I can get a few people to do body painting," I said.

Cecile added, "You can charge. I know I'd pay, wouldn't you, Deb?" Deb nodded affirmatively.

"Okay," I said. "And yes, of course you can collect canned goods, but maybe since no one knows to bring food, you can just take up a cash collection at a booth."

"Good point," Cecile said. "Okay, any other announcements?"

"One last thing," I chimed in. "As you can see, I'm wearing a stunning painted tank top and jeans with the same floral pattern." I gave my body a Vanna-like motion. Renee looked shocked. I've never seen her face so completely motionless. "One of our very own members painted these for me, and is starting her own business hand-painting clothes. You can give her your favorite jeans or she can supply them for you."

"What are you doing?" Renee whispered through gritting teeth.

"Emancipating you," I whispered back.

"This is humiliating," she said. "No one wants my—"

"Who would like to order a set for themselves? We're taking orders today and they'll be ready by Labor Day so we can all come to the open house in our painted outfits. Won't we be adorable?" Every hand in the room shot up, not out of pity, but pure exhilaration. "Now, those of you with daughters will want to get Mommy and Me outfits, and let's not forget that the holidays are just around the corner. What a unique gift idea, no?"

"You are out of your mind," Renee said, now smiling.

"That's why you love me," I said. "Let's not forget to call Faidra. She will kill you if she's the only one who wasn't offered painted jeans."

By the end of the luncheon, Renee had collected orders and payment for forty-eight pairs of jeans and sixty-four tops. As we walked to the parking lot, Renee wondered how she would fill this colossal order. I offered, "Just do the sets that need to be done by Labor Day first and get to the gifts afterward."

"Good idea," she said. "Still, it's a lot."

"I guess you'll be working long hours like Dan," I said, not sure if the mention of his name would deflate the high we both felt. It did, but just a bit. "You know, Renee, we still haven't found our third artist for the new season. If you wanted to move out, we've got plenty of room for you and the kids in the new guesthouse."

"Mmmm, I'd be sleeping in Randy's old bed," Renee said, smiling. "Tempting. Remember how I told you that I've been going to marriage counseling without Dan? I've got to say, it's working."

"Oh good," I replied, somewhat disappointed. How could she feel her relationship was improving when her husband was clearly still cheating on her? "So you feel like your marriage is better now?"

"No," Renee said, opening the door to her car. She hopped in and fastened her seat belt. "But I'm getting better, so I may take you up on that offer yet."

"Meaning what, Renee?"

"Meaning, I'm starting to get a little sick of this shit from Dan. I am a beautiful, talented woman with good friends and a suddenly successful business," she said. "When I ask myself why I put up with this crap, I can't think of one good reason. I mean, I used to tell myself it was for the kids, but what am I teaching them by tolerating this? I love Dan, I really do. I wish I didn't, but I can't lie. I still love him, but the bottom line is I love me better."

I smiled as I watched her put the keys in the ignition and start her car. "That's an exit line if I ever heard one," I said. "Drive safely and let me know what you want to do. We need to figure out what to do with the third bungalow by Labor Day, fair enough?"

"Lucy Klein, you've been more than fair," she said and drove away.

I returned home to an empty house. Jack had left a note on the table that said his brother had an unexpected layover overnight at Logan Airport. He had taken Adam and said they would be back the following afternoon. As if on cue, there was a knock on the back door.

Freshly showered with his hair still wet, Randy was at the door in his signature plain white T-shirt and jeans. "Hey," he said casually. "Hate to bug you, but my light burned out down there and it's starting to get dark out." As he stood against a backdrop of purple streaks of cloud, I thought surely I was having another sexual fantasy. But it seemed so real.

"You mean you need—" I started but couldn't finish.

"A lightbulb," Randy said.

"You need a lightbulb?" I repeated like an idiot.

"Yeah, you got one?"

"I do," I said, sounding far too much like a wedding vow than an affirmation of possession of a lightbulb.

"You think I could get some from you?" he asked. *Wow! He was bold. Jack and Adam were out of town for all of ten minutes and he was trotting up to the house asking if he could get some.* "I really only need one. I can go to the store tomorrow and buy a pack."

"A pack?" I asked, my body in a heightened state of arousal.

"Of lightbulbs," Randy reminded me.

"Oh yes, lightbulbs, right. I can give you some. I can give you some lightbulbs," I said, hoping I didn't sound flustered. "We've got plenty of lightbulbs around here. We're like lightbulb central." *Stop talking!!!!*

"Where are the men of the house?" Randy asked as he followed me to the kitchen pantry. He stood inches from me as I climbed up a stepladder and reached up to the top shelf for the bulbs. I could feel the heat from the front of his body warming my back like a blanket. I wanted to turn around and throw myself into his arms and slide down until we were face to face, then feel his thick lips press against mine for that irresistible sensation of a first kiss.

"They're in Boston for the night," I said. "Here we go, one hundred watts. Let there be light." *Oh dear God, shut me up.*

"They've abandoned you, huh?" Randy said lightly.

"I wouldn't put it that way," I said, stepping off the ladder and back down onto the pantry floor. "Jack's brother is flying to Heathrow and got laid over unexpectedly."

"Don't you wonder why he didn't take you along?" Randy asked.

Stepping back out into the kitchen, I turned to Randy and smiled. "Because he loves me."

"That bad, eh?"

"Nah, his family is great, but Jack knows I don't want to schlep out to Boston to see Dave and stay in some airport hotel overnight." Opening the fridge, I asked, "Where are the others?"

"You mean Maxime, Jacquie, and Chantrell?" I nodded affirmatively. "They went to a movie together."

"The three of them went to a movie together?" I said, raising my eyebrows. "What's the deal with those three? On second thought, the less I know, the better."

Randy laughed and closed the fridge door. "Why don't you let me cook for you tonight?"

"Oh, well, um, I—" *Smooth.* "I don't want to trouble you."

"It's no trouble," Randy said. "You've let me stay here all this time. It'll be my way of saying thanks." *Again with the friggin' gratitude.* "I cook a mean veal piccata."

"I think anything with veal would qualify as mean," I said. *Great. The man offers to cook a gourmet meal and you start spewing PETA talking points.* "What I meant was that we don't have any veal around the kitchen."

"How 'bout chicken breast?" he asked.

"It's really not necessary," I began, knowing I needed to extricate myself from this dangerous liaison. There was something in the air that felt a lot like a seduction. "I was just going to grab a quick—"

Randy interrupted by physically sitting me down in my chair and holding his finger over my lips. "Lu, I think you're so used to taking care of everyone else, you've forgotten what it feels like to have someone do something for you." He opened the fridge and removed a package of chicken breast.

*Huh?*

"I wouldn't say—" I began before Randy cut me off again.

"Shhhhh." He held his finger now over his own lips. Unwrapping chicken breast and placing ingredients on my countertop, he began looking for a pan. He came to my chair and knelt before me. "I see how Jack takes you for granted. I'm going to pamper you tonight."

After having harbored lustful feelings for this exquisite man for months, my heart should have been racing with the exhilaration of fear and joy. Instead, I grew annoyed and worried. I was annoyed because Randy knew nothing about my relationship with Jack. My husband did not take me for granted in the least. It felt as though he was reading a passage from the *Disingenuous Lothario's Seduction Manual*. He was clearly using the routine designed for married women. Mothers in particular. The assumption that I was neglected was insulting to both me and Jack. His words also made me worry that we were out of Pampers.

"Randy, I appreciate the dinner, but I've got to tell you, Jack does *not* take me for granted," I said.

"Then where is he?" Randy asked.

"I already told you. He's in Boston."

Randy smirked cockily and returned to the stove. He placed garlic and white wine in a buttered pan and asked if we had capers. Okay, I guess that was the end of the conversation. I suppose I set him straight, I thought.

We sat on the back deck eating chicken piccata and sipping white wine to Celia Cruz's greatest hits. I must have been swaying to the music a bit because Randy asked if I wanted to dance with him. A bit tipsy and a bit curious, I agreed. The moment our bodies touched, I knew I'd made a mistake. It was uncomfortably comfortable. Our bodies fit like pieces of Adam's foam floor puzzle we had done together a few days earlier. Adam. That's who I needed to think about. Adam and Jack—the important guys in my life. I began to pull away to return to the table when Randy pulled my waist, drawing me closer to him. "There's something I've been wanting to give you for a long time now," Randy said, his face now inches from mine.

Knowing he was about to kiss me, I wanted to discourage him. "I don't want you to give me anything more than you already have, Randy." I pulled away and finished. "Dinner was delicious and that's more than enough." Before I could turn away, he pulled me in to him again and began kissing me so aggressively, I actually pulled a muscle in my neck trying to free myself. I stepped back, but he persisted. "Randy!" I said, breaking loose. "Stop it!"

He looked at me as if he'd never heard such words before. He probably hadn't. "What do you mean?" he asked.

"What I mean is that I'm a married woman. A happily married woman, so I can't go around kissing other guys. Those are kind of the rules when you get married."

He knit his brows with a look of confusion. "You seemed like you wanted it," he said. "The way you're always watching me from your window. I thought—" he trailed off.

"Who said I was watching you?!" I shot, now angry with his presumptuousness. I wish I hadn't posed this question as it opened the door for him to reply, "Your eyes stayed locked on my every move. You ducked every time I looked up to wave. You hosted a luncheon where ogling me was the entertainment." Thankfully, Randy spared me the list of overwhelming evidence that I did, in fact, have an ever-so-tiny crush on him. But the crush had lifted. No guy is good-looking enough to support this type of arrogance. I only hoped he would drop it, so our next two weeks together wouldn't be excruciatingly awkward.

"Gee, I'm sorry," Randy said. "I guess I read things wrong. I always thought you were a woman I'd like to hang with, and I sort of got a vibe that the feeling was mutual, but I guess I was wrong."

*He always thought I seemed a woman he'd like to hang with?! Maintain stern look on face. Do not giggle or float dreamily off into the evening sky.*

"You certainly were," I said, with as much huffiness as I could muster. Admittedly, it wasn't much, but I think I maintained an air of righteous indignation. I didn't want to be too uppity, though. After all, he wasn't all that mistaken, really. "Listen, no hard feelings, okay?" I offered. "To be perfectly honest, I'm kind of flattered. You're a great-looking guy and if I weren't madly in love with my husband, hanging out with you would be a mighty tempting proposition."

"Okay," he said, flatly, likely still in shock. "Sorry 'bout that." Randy turned around and left. And that was it. No drama. He just disappeared back to his house, leaving me with two servings of his excellent chicken piccata.

# Chapter 35

When Earl found out about Kimmy and Nick getting married at the open house, he immediately asked me to write a story about it. How my cousin's naked wedding had anything to do with healthy living was beyond me, but the magazine paid well and I enjoyed working with Earl so I gladly accepted. When Kimmy had married herself, I wrote about it for *Glamour*. I suppose it was my lot in life to write about my cousin's bizarre nuptials.

Since Aunt Rita and Uncle Arnold had left, I wrote almost nonstop. Before I finished one article, I had ideas for three more, all of which were miraculously accepted by magazines I'd never worked with before. My batting average had never been better. Not only was my creativity at an all-time high, the visiting artists were all working round-the-clock producing pieces for the open house, which was just days away.

The day before the event, Renee asked if the offer for her to be our third resident artist next season still stood. "I'm leaving him," she told me as we assembled displays on Friday evening. I didn't know what to say. Do you congratulate someone on a divorce? Though it was clearly the best choice for her, it was still a loss. Her voice caught as she recalled telling Dan that she was filing for divorce.

"I've tried to repair this marriage, but it's killing me," she said, not dramatically, but with an awareness that tolerating his infidelity was taking its emotional toll on her. "Every time he comes home, I wonder whether he's been with her. And every time I torture myself with this question, I'm forced to face the fact that by putting up with this shit, I'm telling myself that it's okay to treat me this way. And it's not. God, I love him so much, though. I wish he would've stopped seeing her when he promised to and gone to counseling with me months ago. I know we could've worked it out, but I can't rebuild a marriage on my own, you know?"

Of course, Jack and I had already agreed that if Renee and her kids wanted to spend the following season with us, they would be more than welcome. I was both elated and saddened for her.

The big day finally arrived. Anjoli chartered several buses for Kimmy and Nick's wedding guests, who were, much to their disappointment, the first to arrive. They didn't seem to realize that when you're with a group of two hundred, the concept of being fashionably late became irrelevant. As caterers began pouring champagne, they quickly got over it. At noon, it was balmy without any sign of the oppressive heat we expected.

I recognized the KAT girls immediately. Not simply because they were all young and adorable, but because they surrounded Anjoli and J.Lo like an entourage. A dozen young women with trendy hair and perfect outfits walked to the backyard where tents and tables were set up and wait staff was placing canapés on clear Lucite trays. I was amazed at how the young women could balance themselves on such narrow heels on grass and unpaved dirt, but they walked it like a runway.

Anjoli and J.Lo wore matching emerald silk dresses with pillbox hats. J.Lo sported a necklace with a purse that was an exact replica of her carrier. I later learned this was where Kimmy and Nick's rings were being safe-guarded.

Anjoli's Queen Team, five gay men in black T-shirts and jeans, followed Alfie into the house where they would set up their body-painting station to decorate the bride. Thankfully, Jack had been relieved of this duty.

About a half hour later, a white stretch limousine pulled up to the house, passed the VW Bug (which Jack had painted white and decorated with tulle and flowers) and delivered Kimmy in her white bathrobe. She held her hand over her head and waved. "Hugs and kisses everyone," she shouted from the back deck, making sure we all saw how fabulous she looked without a stitch of makeup on. "It's me! The naked bride," she announced with a giggle of excitement. How does one even respond to that? *Hi, naked bride!*

By three o'clock that afternoon, our backyard was packed with everyone I'd ever seen in town, the entire Junior League, and some people I'd never met. Watching people mill about the tents, Jack and I stood close to each other and drank it in. "Pretty cool, huh?" he asked. "Remember when this was all a pipe dream?"

I smiled as I recalled the image of Jack and me excitedly sketching our artist colony on napkins at Steve's Lunch in Ann Arbor. Now, not only was it real, but hundreds of guests had come from as far as New York to see our artists' show. The sun beat on my shoulders and the familiar scent of honeysuckle wafted through the air. Adam held court in the air jump we had rented for the children of guests. Part of this was our genuine desire to provide a partylike atmosphere, but a more cynical side of us had hired babysitters and entertainment so parents could deposit their kids far away from the naked bride, and focus on spending their time viewing our residents' work. For the sake of our guests, we hoped people would buy the art in large quantities. I was especially concerned about Maxime and Jacquie as they seemingly had nowhere to go and no money to support themselves after they left our place. Unfortunately, Jacquie had maxed out their credit cards during her Rita-inspired shopping sprees. Several of the stores accepted her returns, but most did not because she had used or worn her purchases.

Chantrell wore her hair in two tight French braids, a tribute, I believe, to her two new best friends, Maxime and Jacquie. She sat on a plain wood chair and played classical music as guests milled about, filling our yard to capacity. Jacquie and Maxime sat peacefully in front of their white canvas tent, ushering guests in to see Maxime's sketches in ink and mud. Faidra and Anderson, who had purchased several of Maxime's works, were intently discussing something with the couple. My eyes scanned to the most crowded station of all—Randy's. Savvy salesman that he was, my favorite glass sculptor had created dozens of original perfume bottles, giving the female guests a reason to linger around his tent. Every Junior League member was clearly recognizable because she was wearing a T-shirt painted by Renee and toting a small purple shopping bag that Randy had purchased especially for his customers.

An excitement filled the air. It was the thrill of looking at original art. The adrenaline rush of new purchases. And the feeling that something exciting was yet to come. The anticipation of a naked wedding is not easy to describe. There's the giddiness associated with the most ordinary weddings, but an added element of sexual titillation when the guests know the bride will be wearing nothing but paint. Oh, excuse me, and glitter.

I went to Kimmy's dressing room—or should I call it a preparation room—to see how off-the-charts stunning she looked. It was amazing. Alfie and his assistants used different shades of white to create shadows and accents so realistic, one could barely tell that her dress wasn't made from actual cloth. In the ultimate touch of irony, they painted a high-neck collar on her gown, giving it a Victorian look. The glitter was barely noticeable, though the bodice had an inexplicable shine. This area also included painfully detailed painted laces which looked as though they were actually holding together the bodice and tied at the bottom. I couldn't help glancing down, curious to see how they handled the issue of her pubic hair. I couldn't help it. Aunt Bernice's weekly Snatch Reports had made me increasingly pubecentric. As I later learned, Bernice had offered her free laser treatments to Kimmy as a wedding gift. Apparently, the Florida salon Bernice and her friends patronized had sister salons in New York. All that could be seen was the slightest sliver that separated her vaginal lips, tastefully decorated with clear rhinestones. It kind of looked like a change purse.

Kimmy's northern hair was brushed up to the top of her head with loose tendrils of curls cascading down above her shoulders. Again, Queen Team made great effort to ensure that every pearl was in its perfect location, and not a strand of hair fell into the painted-on gown. If *Playboy* ever decided to do the ultimate antithesis of itself, a bridal issue, Kimmy would be the cover girl. And I, no doubt, would write the story.

"Kimmy, you look gorgeous," I said, awestruck by the incredible job Rafael had done on her makeup. It was perfectly elegant with subtle touches of kinky white to give it the quirky tie-in one needs when walking down the aisle in virtual nudity. The insides of her lips and a tiny section of her eyelids were pearlescent, posing a stark contrast from the earthen pinks on the rest of her face.

"Thank you!" Kimmy beamed. "My weddings are such fun, aren't they?" Indeed they were. This was Kimmy's third trip to the altar and, if all went according to plan, it would be the first time she wound up with a husband.

Anjoli burst through the door, clutching J.Lo, announcing there was a *crisis* at the show. Knowing she was dismissed from these, Kimmy turned away and gave her full attention back to her personal Fab Five. "Darling, some imbecile brought her dog, and the vile little Schnauzer is trying to hump little J.Lo!" The dog was shivering in my mother's arms, visibly shaken by the assault. Anjoli patted J.Lo's forehead with a damp napkin and encouraged her to take deep, stress-reducing breaths. "You must ask this Faidra person to take her dog home immediately."

I shuddered at the thought of a bunch of kids watching a Schnauzer humping a miniature Chihuahua in a Vera Wang original. Thankfully, I had made sure the kiddie tent was a good distance from the rest of the show so no little ones would ask mommy if they could put rhinestones on their coochies like the pretty bride did. The unforeseen benefit was that I shielded them from their first episode of *Dogs Gone Wild*. I noticed that poor J.Lo had lost her pillbox hat in the dreadful transaction. "Did the kids see what was going on?" I asked.

"No, thank the divine energy for that, darling!" Anjoli said, now stroking a calmer J.Lo. I could see Alfie and his friends trying to contain their laughter. "Well, they saw it, but they thought the dogs were dancing! They thought it was part of the show. You know that I'm very open-minded on issues of sexuality, but I don't want my little J.Lo used as a prop for their discussion on masturbation."

"Is it masturbation if another dog is involved?" Alfie asked.

"Of course it is," Rafael said, shooing with his hand. "What do you think, he needs to be alone with dog porn?"

Alfie feigned outrage and placed a hand on his hip. "It was just a question. No need to be bitchy."

"Darlings, this is no time for jokes!" Anjoli exclaimed. "Tell that woman that a wedding is no place for her dog."

"Mother, you brought J.Lo," I reminded her.

"J.Lo is the ring-bearer!" Anjoli said. "J.Lo is part of this family. J.Lo is wearing Vera Wang! That dirty little Schnauzer has no business here."

"Can't you just keep her in your purse?"

"She can't walk down the aisle in my purse, darling!"

"Why not?" I asked. "I'm walking down first then you go right afterward. Why can't you just take J.Lo with you? The rings will get there just the same. Does she have to toss rose petals or something like that?"

"Don't be ludicrous, darling," Anjoli answered. "That's the flower girl, and we'd never do something as pedestrian as that. J.Lo needs to make her own entrance and it needs to be before you walk down the aisle."

"It does?"

"It does."

At this point, Kimmy turned to us to voice her agreement with Anjoli. "Lucy, I don't think you fully appreciate how hard Auntie Anjoli has been working with J.Lo to get her prepped for this."

"Prepped?" I asked. "The dog has to walk a straight line."

"The timing is everything, darling," Anjoli explained. "J.Lo has the most graceful gait *and* she knows to stop and turn toward the audience once she reaches the altar."

*The audience?*

"I saw it the other day, Lucy," Kimmy said. "You are going to be so totally stoked when you see J.Lo strutting her stuff. She even knows to make eye contact with guests on both sides of the aisle. She's pretty amazing. I hope I have a dog like J.Lo some day."

"Oh, Kimmy, I'm quite certain you will." I headed for the door, conceding defeat. "Kimmy, it's your day. If this is important to you that J.Lo walk down the aisle, I'll go ask Faidra to take her dog home or tie him to a tree or something."

"Or put him to sleep," I heard Anjoli suggest as the door closed behind me.

When I returned to the yard, it was like Carnival in Rio. Not that I've ever been to Rio, but this is how I imagined it might be. People were running around with multicolored balloon sculpture hats and painted faces while Chantrell—and three new musicians who had mysteriously appeared—had changed the repertoire to Latin jazz. The constant hum of conversation and laughter filled the air, frequently punctuated by the clinking of champagne glasses. I found Faidra surrounded by a sea of floral T-shirts, telling the ladies that she had just invited Maxime and Jacquie to stay at their estate indefinitely. As she saw me approaching her group, Faidra smiled brightly. "I know why you're here," she sang.

*I live here*, I didn't sing back.

"Confucius has a thing for J.Lo," Faidra teased.

*Huh? Oh, right, Confucius the Schnauzer.*

"They say it's only puppy love," I said, not able to resist a joke that is typically delivered by an old man who farts when you pull his finger. Mercifully, the group laughed. "But could we separate the two for the ceremony since they're so, um, how do I put this?"

"Ready to fuck each other?" Faidra said, laughing. She pointed to a fold-up chair where Confucius was tied by his leash. I was grateful that she seemed so easygoing about the issue, but felt oddly compelled to correct that J.Lo most certainly did not return Confucius's feelings. Thankfully, I controlled the urge to set her straight. Let her harbor delusions about her dirty Schnauzer's sex appeal.

Alfie rang a crystal bell from our deck which was the cue for the ushers to start seating guests for the wedding. Until that moment, I hadn't seen Nick, nor did it occur to me to wonder where he was. After two weddings where Kimmy's grooms were obsolete, I'd forgotten all about my soon-to-be cousin-in-law. But there he was, sporting white paint on his entire upper body and long white tuxedo shorts on the bottom. His parents looked as if they were using every ounce of self-restraint they had to refrain from whipping out a notepad and cataloging every detail so they could later regale their anthropologist friends.

"Excuse me. I've got to run upstairs," I told the women. "Faidra, thanks for taking care of Confucius."

"Can they get together later?" she shouted after me. I couldn't tell whether she was kidding or not. "Maybe J.Lo wants to come over and hot tub at our place later?"

# Chapter 36

Chantrell's impromptu quartet began playing the Wedding March as nearly four hundred guests enjoyed the late afternoon sunshine. As rehearsed, the first one down the aisle was J.Lo, who had recovered her hat, a little worse for wear with Confucius's teeth marks around the rim. The guests smiled at the sight of the tiny Chihuahua walking down the aisle keeping pace with the music. Of course, since J.Lo's legs are so short she had to walk double time with the music in order to get down the aisle in a timely fashion. Still, she had good rhythm and her double-time cadence worked well, since she was, after all, of Latin descent. Her little purse bobbed around her neck, weighed down by Kimmy and Nick's rings. As Kimmy promised, J.Lo skillfully turned her head to acknowledge both sides of the aisle. It almost looked like she nodded at faces she recognized, like Alfie and the KAT girls.

I'm not sure why the guests all got up to stand while J.Lo was still walking down the aisle instead of waiting for the bride's descent from the stairs, but they did. It wasn't as if everyone didn't have a perfect view of the Wang-clad Chihuahua. Ever the wise one, Confucius must have sensed that the chair his leash was tied to was lighter now that Faidra was standing. He darted into the aisle, taking the chair with him, and was on top of J.Lo humping her within seconds. The crowd gasped in horror as it watched the Schnauzer completely cover J.Lo. All we saw was a small patch of green silk peeking from under his tail. Still connected to Confucius was the folding chair, now tipped on its side. We all stood paralyzed for a moment. Even the music stopped as everyone's eyes were transfixed on the bizarre prelude to the bizarre wedding. Finally, Anjoli shouted: "Someone get that animal off my baby!" Nick ran from the altar and pulled Confucius off of J.Lo, who was clearly caught off guard by the incident. Anderson III rushed to help Nick, pulling Confucius's leash to bring him back from the aisle. The dog was confused and thought Nick was attacking Anderson. He growled, then barked. Confucius jumped up and bit Nick's tuxedo shorts, tearing most of his right pantleg off.

"Down boy!" Anderson commanded. Turning to the guests, he apologized.

Scooping up a visibly shaken J.Lo, Nick began petting her and assuring her that everything was okay.

"Breathe deeply," Anjoli said, rushing over.

Never one to allow the spotlight to stray far from her, Kimmy scuttled into the dog pile and started carrying on about how grateful she was that Nick had saved J.Lo from "mean old humper."

I caught Jack's eye. His facial expression was clear. *This kind of stuff never happens on my side of the family.* His smirk was irresistible, but retort was part of our game so I shot him a raised eyebrow and tilted my head down to say, *Your family is boring, my dear. We don't do normal in my tribe.*

"Shall we continue?" said Summer, the same minister who had performed Kimmy's wedding to herself.

"Are we ready?" I asked Kimmy.

"I need some water, darling," Anjoli said, wobbling a bit to show how unsteadying the event was for her. A gentle-

man on Nick's side of the family stood up and held my
mother's elbow, showing her to his seat.

"Why, how good of you," Anjoli said sweetly to the
handsome stranger.

"I'll get you some water," Nick offered, his briefs now
peeking out from his shorts.

"Distilled, darling," Anjoli said. "Make sure it's distilled." Turning to the man who had offered his chair, my
mother explained that shock is dehydrating to the system.
He folded a program for Anjoli and asked if she needed
him to fan her a bit to help cool her down. "That would
be delightful, darling. It's so hard to find a true gentleman
these days."

Minutes later, my mother and Nick's uncle were sitting
on the groom's side of the aisle chatting as Kimmy placed
a ring on Nick's finger. "Love, honor, and love is what it's
all about," Kimmy concluded. Just as the two moved in
for their first kiss as husband and wife, everyone's attention was directed to the back of the yard. A booming voice
was heard before we could see to whom it belonged.
"Stop!" he shouted. It sounded like James Earl Jones. "I
want you back. I made a mistake, but I love you." Oh.
My. God. Can Kimmy do anything without major drama?
Now some crazed ex-boyfriend was crashing the wedding
proclaiming his undying devotion. Kimmy and Nick knit
their brows at the sight of the stranger. They had no idea
who he was. As the crowd turned, it appeared no one
knew who this incredibly fat, noisy man was. I couldn't
decide what made him most painful to look at—his barrel
of a belly, his curly outgrown mullet, or his two long,
skinny ratlike buckteeth. "I love you, Renee! We can make
it work this time, I swear."

"Holy shit," escaped from my lips.

"Who the hell is that?" Jack asked.

"Who the hell *is* that?" Kimmy demanded.

Running to find Renee, Dan continued. "Baby, I'm so

sorry for the way I treated you. Give me another chance to make it right." When he reached his wife, Dan grabbed her hands and got down on one knee. "Marry me again and I promise I'll make you happy this time."

Looking uncharacteristically bewildered, Renee said nothing. Faidra rushed to her defense. "Dan, don't be such a selfish oaf. We're in the middle of someone else's wedding here. Talk to Renee about this later."

"I can't wait another minute, Renee," he shouted for all to hear. "I need you to take me back."

"Dan, not now," Renee finally spoke.

There was a moment of uncomfortable silence as everyone's eyes were fixed on the fat man kneeling before the Junior League. Kimmy then burst into tears, claiming her wedding was a disaster. That was enough to bring in the big guns.

Anjoli stood from her chair, holding J.Lo in the crook of her arm. "Well, darlings, I hope everyone has enjoyed the fabulous show my gorgeous daughter and her husband have put on for you today. It would have been enough to come and see the work of these magnificent artists, but never one to settle for fabulousness, our hosts have cleverly injected their own brand of guerilla theatre this afternoon. What delightful social commentary on the state of marriage today when we witness before us two stunningly beautiful people wearing little more than a layer of paint interrupted by not one, but two separate incidents of humping dogs." The crowd laughed. Unbelievably, they were buying it. I knew that when my mother used excessive superlatives, she was grasping for straws, but no one else seemed to catch on. A few heads nodded as if to show that they understood this terribly sophisticated performance piece. "We have staged for you here today both a literal and a figurative humping dog scene to illustrate the challenges that every marriage faces." *What?* Faidra and Anderson held hands and glanced at each other adoringly.

Oddly, so did about a half dozen other couples. "As we see, the first dog tore the pant leg from the groom, symbolizing the emasculation attempts every groom faces by other men out there in the world." Man, was my mother reaching on this one. Walking toward the wedding cake, my mother picked up the cutting knife and held it over her head as if she were going to stab Dan with it. "And now to illustrate the feminine role in extracting evil from loving relationships, I will now chase this fat man from the wedding scene, showing how domestic utensils can be used as instruments of exorcism. If he is smart, he will waddle as fast as he can, or risk being filleted by a very pissed-off aunt of the bride." Dan began to run away and the crowd applauded.

Nick's uncle nodded his head with admiration.

Faidra wiped a tear from her eye as she clapped wildly. "We have *got* to get her for Anderson's next party."

Renee sat with a smile, more than a bit surprised at what she had just witnessed.

When we could no longer see Dan's rotund ass on the grounds, Anjoli turned back to the guests, lowered the knife, and dramatically proclaimed, "You may *now* kiss the bride."

# Chapter 37

The wedding reception was comparatively dull. Kimmy and Nick had their first dance together as the sun set on our first open house. How would we ever top this one?

I made my way to Renee, who was surrounded by our friends. Most of them were genuinely protective of Renee. Others just love being close to the drama. "I have to find Anjoli," Renee said when she saw me approach her table. We walked across the lawn alone together. I couldn't help asking if she was going to get back together with Dan. "Never," she answered immediately.

"So you weren't charmed by him at all?" I asked.

"Charmed? I was humiliated," Renee said, stopping in her tracks. "Lucy, do you know what inspired that?" I shook my head. "His girlfriend probably dumped him the minute she found out Dan and I were through. You know what really charmed me?"

"I know," I said, smiling. "Confucius and J.Lo sure are cute together."

Renee laughed. "Seriously, Lucy. Your mother kicks ass. The way she chased Dan out of here with that knife! My God, I don't think I'll ever forget that."

"Unfortunately, neither will any of the guests," I said.

"You know, when I was watching your mother chase

Dan away with the cake knife over her head, I really couldn't decide who I was rooting for. I think I may be out of love with him."

"Yeah, well, hoping your husband will be stabbed is a good sign that your feelings may be waning, at the very least."

Renee stopped and smiled as if she were taking an emotional photograph of the moment. It was so unlike Renee, I found it jarring. "Thanks for everything."

"Sure," I said. "Any time you need someone chased off with a cake knife, you know who to call."

"No, seriously, Lucy. You've been a good friend," Renee said, placing her hand on my wrist.

"Can I ask you a question?" I hated when people asked permission to ask a question and here I was doing it myself. Renee nodded. "How did a guy like Dan ever wind up with a woman like you?"

She smiled. "You mean the weight?"

"The weight?!" I repeated. "The whole package, Renee! The mullet is a nightmare, and those teeth. I mean, I hate to sound superficial and focus only on his looks. He obviously hasn't got the greatest personality if he cheats on his wife and bursts in to other people's weddings begging forgiveness."

"He was cute once," Renee said, somewhat wistfully.

"When?" I couldn't help asking.

Renee snapped back to her good senses and answered, "Long ago, Lucy. Now he's far from cute, isn't he?" From the corner of my eye, I saw Randy talking to guests in front of his tent. When it got dark, he would whip out his blowtorch and give a glassblowing demonstration for the guests. For now, he seemed to have no problem keeping the heat around him white hot. "He's no Randy, that's for sure," Renee said, also noticing the sculptor. He winked at the two of us, though I may have been flattering myself.

Something about the interaction clearly seemed to exclude me. "Let's go see Anjoli," Renee said as she began to walk again.

My mother was surrounded by Kimmy's Fab Five as well as Robin and Tom. "I've been following your career since Stanford, bro," Tom said to Rafael's boyfriend, Scott, who was a running back for the New York Giants. "I can't believe I'm standing here talkin' to Scott Randall. Can I get a picture?" I wondered at what point Tom would figure out that Scott was gay, and I hoped I could manage to be present for the revelation. I knew there were several doctors in the house to resuscitate him when he passed out. Surely, Anjoli encouraging him to breathe deeply would not do the trick.

When Renee and I made our way to the group, Rafael immediately teased, "Well, if it isn't Little Miss Steal the Spotlight herself. To what do we owe this honor?"

"I wanted to thank Anjoli for chasing off Dan like that," Renee said.

"How on Page Six should *that* be?!" squealed Alfie, clapping his hands. "You were so Norman Bates, love."

Anjoli reveled in the attention. "It was nothing," she said, quickly adding more. "I couldn't stand to watch him abusing you any longer, Renee. You are so much better than that. Why in the world would you ever stay married to a man with a mullet?"

"He had other qualities," she said.

"Like that gorgeous figure?" Scott added.

"Anyway, I absolutely hate the guy not only for what he did to you and Kimmy, but now he's ruined my life as well, darling," Anjoli said. All eyes were on her with inquisition. "Yes, after I met Renee, I couldn't bring myself to date married men any longer. God knows I tried, but I kept seeing this image of Renee in tears and I couldn't go through with it. All I thought about is that each of these married men had a Renee at home who was probably heartbroken by her husband's straying. Who would've guessed it, but I think I may have a conscience after all."

"What a sweet story," Alfie said. "You two are like an Aesop's fable of infidelity," he said tilting his head at Renee and Anjoli.

"When I met Harvey this afternoon, the first thing I did was check for a wedding ring," Anjoli said. "It was like I was possessed by someone good. It was horrid."

"So, is he married?" Robin asked.

"Widowed," Anjoli said.

Kimmy's hairdresser, Felix, chimed in. "I wouldn't go there, honey. Who wants to compete with a dead lady?"

Alfie disagreed. "I think widowers are the way to go. His wife didn't divorce him. Plus there's no chance of her coming back for a reconciliation."

Thinking of Aunt Rita, I smiled. *I wouldn't be too sure of that.*

Renee signaled the waiter to refill our glasses. After we were all replenished, Renee offered a toast. "To new beginnings for all of us," she said.

"To new beginnings," we repeated.

"I want to Samba," said Rafael to Scott when he heard the music begin again.

My eyes shot to Tom. It was all beginning to register with him now. "Don't you want to ask one of the girls?" Tom suggested. Okay, maybe it wasn't registering after all.

Rafael began moving his body to the Latin rhythms. "Ew, girls, yucky," he said in a playful overdone Spanish accent.

"Honey," Robin said to her husband. "Rafael is gay." She sounded as if she was talking to a slow-witted child.

"Yeah, but—" Tom started. No one knows how that sentence would have ended because it was at that moment that Tom realized that this meant Scott was also gay. "Right on," he said. "Right on." After a second, he repeated the sentiment another three times, finally finishing with, "Right the fuck on."

"Okay, stop saying that," Robin whispered.

By nightfall, we were down to our last fifty guests, including unmarried Uncle Harvey and disturbingly chummy Renee and Randy. Jack and I went upstairs to tuck Adam into bed and finally had a chance to catch up. "It's been so great, hasn't it?" I asked Jack.

"Better than I ever thought," he agreed.

"What about Faidra's dog?!" I asked, giggling.

"Nothing compared to your mother chasing Dan away at knifepoint."

"I know this is going to sound weird, but I wish Rita and Arnold were here to enjoy it," I said.

"Honey, if they had stayed, none of this would have happened. Remember what problems they caused?"

"Only Rita," I defended. "Arnold was quite handy around the house."

"I know you miss them," Jack said, kissing my forehead.

"Let's get back to the party," I suggested. "Randy's going to blow some glass in a few minutes."

When we returned, Anjoli came rushing to me. "I have fabulous news, darling. Sit down!" I sat. "As you know, Nick's Uncle Harvey and I have been getting along quite well this afternoon." *Good God, she's going to marry him?* "Would you believe that not only is he handsome and charming, he's a casting director?"

"Casting for what?" I asked, horrified with the thought of my mother starring in elder-porn.

"Commercials, darling! And guess who he wants to cast?"

"What kind of commercial does he want to cast you in?"

"Not me, darling. I would never do commercial work!" she said. "Guess again!"

"Um, Kimmy?" I asked.

"Two strikes, darling. One more!"

"Me?" I asked. I could be the new Weight Watchers girl.

"J.Lo!" Anjoli said.

"Your dog?"

"Don't sound so surprised, darling. Don't I always tell you J.Lo is gorgeous? Harvey was very impressed by how poised J.Lo remained in the face of that filthy Schnauzer attack. Plus, it's not every dog who can walk down the aisle so gracefully. J.Lo has star quality. Anyway, darling, apparently Taco Bell is bringing back their 'Yo quiero Taco Bell' campaign, and they need a mini Chihuahua for the taquito commercials. Naturally, we'll have to find her the right agent. There are so few good roles for Latinas." Mother waved her arms as if to show how very weary she had grown of the business. "Isn't it my luck to find a boyfriend and a career for J.Lo all in one guy?" It was. I was happier that she'd sworn off married men, but J.Lo's new taquitos commercial was what excited my mother at the moment, so I joined her celebration.

"You have the most charmed life, Mother," I said, resting my head on her shoulder as we watched flames shoot from Randy's blowtorch.

"Don't I, darling?"

I didn't have it so bad either. Jack and I stayed up until 2 A.M. giddily going over every detail of our first open house. Jack had sold every one of his paintings and declined several offers for the VW Bug. All of the artists had sold all of their work and ended the evening with orders for more. We were floating with joy.

"You know what, Luce?" Jack asked as we sat facing each other cross-legged in bed.

"What?"

"You're my dream wife," he said.

My eyes welled with tears of joy and fatigue. "I love you so much, Jack. I'm so glad we did this." I leaned in to kiss him. A decidedly different tone had taken over. We had gone from kids at a slumber party to newlyweds in the honeymoon suite. We slipped down beneath the cool sheets and made love until we fell asleep exhausted.

Early the next morning, the phone rang. At first, I thought it had to be Anjoli or J.Lo calling, but realized they were staying in the guest room. Who would call so early on a Sunday morning?

"Hello?" I said, purposefully groggy. I wanted to make sure this inconsiderate caller knew exactly how rude he was being.

"*Mamaleh*! Have I got news for you," Aunt Bernice exclaimed.

"Is everything okay?" I asked.

"Okay? Bettah than okay. This may sound silly to you, but it's got me so excited I had to cawl and share the news."

"Tell me!" I encouraged.

Jack opened his eyes and turned to me quizzically. He knit his brow to ask what was going on.

"You know how you and Jack were such big shots about my needing to get my fawcet fixed?"

"I wouldn't say we were big shots," I returned. "We just thought it would be nice if—"

"You were big shots!" Bernice snapped. "Everyone carried on telling me I had to get the drippy fawcet fixed. 'It won't fix itself' everybody told me. Well, guess what?"

"What?"

"It's awl bettah now," Bernice said.

"What do you mean it's all better?"

"You don't understand what I said? Aren't you supposed to be the big shot who makes a living using words?

What's so hard to understand about the words I'm using? It's awl bettah. The sink. It's fixed!"

"Oh, that's terrific," I said, coaxing Jack to go back to sleep.

"It's bettah than terrific, Lucy. I can't explain it. I woke up this morning with a pain in my leg, a migraine headache, and a case of PMS like I haven't had since before menopause. But when I warked into the bathroom and saw that the fawcet had repaired itself, it made me so happy. And angry at the same time," she said, laughing. "I know it sounds crazy," she said, not realizing the day we had just had before. "I know yawr going to think I'm a kooky old lady, but something about that fawcet working properly again made me feel . . . how can I explain it? I don't know why, but I don't feel so alone anymore."